A New Discovery

Theodora felt a shiver go down her spine. She had almost convinced herself that Wycca and her baby had been a fluke, a hiccup in time. But now, looking at the scale resting on the bed of cotton, she felt a fresh rush of wonder, an electric prickle of mingled disbelief and joy—as though this new scale were a private, magical secret meant for her alone.

ANN DOWNER

The Dragon of Never-Was

ALADDIN PAPERBACKS
New York   London   Toronto   Sydney

This book is a work of fiction. Any references to historical events, real people, or real locales are used fictitiously. Other names, characters, places, and incidents are the product of the author's imagination, and any resemblance to actual events or locales or persons, living or dead, is entirely coincidental.

ALADDIN PAPERBACKS

An imprint of Simon & Schuster Children's Publishing Division

1230 Avenue of the Americas, New York, NY 10020

Text copyright © 2006 by Ann Downer

Illustrations copyright © 2006 by Omar Rayyan

All rights reserved, including the right of reproduction in whole or in part in any form.

ALADDIN PAPERBACKS and related logo are registered trademarks of

Simon & Schuster, Inc.

Also available in an Atheneum hardcover edition.

Designed by Ann Zeak

The text of this book was set in Centaur.

Manufactured in the United States of America

First Aladdin Paperbacks edition February 2008

10 9 8 7 6 5 4 3 2 1

The Library of Congress has cataloged the hardcover edition as follows:

Downer, Ann, 1960–

The dragon of Never-Was / Ann Downer.—1st ed.

p. cm.

Sequel to: Hatching magic.

Summary: With the help of a bottle of blue fire and a magical brooch, Theodora searches for a dragon on an island off the coast of Scotland before it causes any harm.

ISBN-13: 978-0-689-85571-9 (hc.)

ISBN-10: 0-689-85571-0 (hc.)

[1. Wizards—Fiction. 2. Dragons—Fiction. 3. Magic—Fiction. 4. Scotland—Fiction.]

I. Title.

PZ7.D7575Dr 2006

[Fic]—dc22

2005017727

ISBN-13: 978-1-4169-5453-8 (pbk.)

ISBN-10: 1-4169-5453-8 (pbk.)

For the Eggs:
Elissa, Kel, Myra, and Robyn

Contents

The
Dragon
of
Never-Was

Prologue

The Vanishing of Ellic Lailoken

ELLIC LAILOKEN WAS playing hooky. There was an exam today in Snakes and Adders—known more formally at the wizard academy as the Evolution and Natural History of Dragons—but Ellic had not studied for it. He'd spent yesterday on the river, drifting in a canoe and feasting on the wild blackberries that overhung the banks. He'd gotten back to his room late, happily sunburned, to find a note from his roommate, who was majoring in divination.

Pop quiz tomorrow in Snakes and Adders.
Read Chapter 11 in *Walker*.

He'd opened his copy of *Walker's Dragons of the Old World* with a groan and tried to focus on the lesson, "The Wingless Forms," but the blackberries were giving him indigestion, and he worked himself into what his great-grandmother used to call a "high dudgeon." The Lailokens were known for their tempers. In a fit of exasperation, he'd hurled his textbook out the window.

The problem was, Ellic was one slender demerit away from being expelled from the Academy, and he could only imagine what his father back in Edinburgh would say if the last of the Lailokens, a long and distinguished line of wizards, failed to graduate with the Academy's class of 1906 and was sent home in disgrace. Ellic's future was at stake. Graduate with his class, and his father might send him to the Yucatan—one of the family firm's glamour jobs, prospecting for plumed serpents and golden toads. But if he failed to graduate? Ellic didn't want to think about it.

So he couldn't be caught skipping class. But where to hide? The old dragon of a provost, Mr. Sparkstriker, patrolled the obvious hiding places regularly—so that left out the clock tower, the boxwood maze, and the butler's pantry. Only inexperienced first-year students tried to hide among the portraits in the Founders' Gallery. You could never get flat enough to be convincing, and there was the danger you'd pop out of the frame.

But there was the Cage.

And, really, once he thought about it, what better place to hide on a beautiful summer's day than the Cage—the locked room in the Academy's library where the rarest spell books and scrolls were kept? No one ventured into that dusty sanctum if they could help it. And the librarian, Flannery Bellweather, could be counted on to leave her post at the front desk at 10:27 sharp for her 10:30 coffee break. Once she was gone, he would slip inside the Cage and hide, whiling away the hours, perusing the books the stodgy old wizards at the Academy thought best kept out of the hands of the students.

He waited for Miss Bellweather to leave on her coffee break, her bustled skirts swishing away down the hall. Then it was a simple matter of saying a spell over the lock—a very special spell he'd gotten from his ne'er-do-well older brother, Oakie, who had racked up enough demerits to actually get kicked out of the Academy. He'd moved to London and spent his days in the Owl and Moon Club, earning a living as a card sharp and dabbling in séances and leaving Ellic to try and salvage the Lailoken reputation at the Academy. Oakie returned to the family home in Edinburgh only when their father was absent, and he slunk around with a smirk that did not completely hide his shame.

He'd removed the spell from a secret compartment

3

in his flash new cigarette case and handed it to his little brother with a conspiratorial air.

"Don't wear it out," he'd said with a wink.

As he recited the spell, Ellic held his breath, not sure whether Oakie had been pulling a joke. But the words worked their magic, and the elaborate lock on the Cage softly clicked open.

Once he was inside, the charmed books immediately began to cough and mutter, but Ellic silenced them by removing from his pocket and shaking a little box full of bookworms.

Ellic glanced around the shelves of the tiny room. Most of these books were simply too fragile to be handled and so were kept under the extra protection of the Cage— delicate Faerie time maps made of spider's silk and dewdrops and a mermaid's pillowbook: a gossipy court diary written in squid ink on sharkskin. But others were kept under lock and key to keep them out of the hands of students who might use their spells for mischievous ends. So here were kept the Forty-three Heavenly Scrolls of the Jade Emperor (one mispronounced incantation in ancient Chinese could have disastrous consequences) and a shaman's spell book written on leaves of acacia bark— there had been an unfortunate incident a few years earlier in which some students had brewed up a batch of beer made of fermented beetles and roots and turned one of the underclassmen into an anaconda.

There was an Egyptian priest's sarcophagus in the back that some other truant had outfitted on a previous visit with pillows and a stash of mandrake root beer. He settled in for a nap and was soon having a pleasant dream involving Miranda Mothwings-Brown and a late-night tutoring session in Love Philters and Amatory Potions.

He was awakened by voices.

A man spoke in a low, anxious whisper. "Are you sure it will be safe here?"

Another man replied, his words more impatient than reassuring. "The dragonskin box will keep it safe until tomorrow. Besides, you have the only key."

"I don't know," said the anxious voice. "Students have been known to break into the Cage, you know. Take some spell and play an end-of-term sprank." (Spranks were magical pranks the upperclassmen played to leave a mark in Academy lore before they moved on to careers in workaday wizardry.) "Remember the Class of oh-four? They materialized genies inside the bottles of wine for the reunion banquet. All of Reunion Week we had a dozen drunken genies on our hands."

Ellic was wide awake now. He recognized the first speaker as the provost, Nicholas Sparkstriker. Ellic's heart began to pound. Sparkstriker could sniff out a truant at forty paces—any minute now he'd stride over to the sarcophagus and lift the lid with a triumphant cry. But Sparkstriker and the other man kept conversing in low voices.

"Not even the best Academy student can break into a dragonskin box," said the unknown speaker. "Relax. It's as safe as it can be." Now Ellic recognized the second speaker: It was Septimus Silvertongue, the Academy's new headmaster. Ellic rolled his eyes in silent despair. *Oh, great. I'm doomed.*

"I suppose you're right," said Sparkstriker.

Why don't they know I'm here? Ellic wondered, then saw, painted all over the inside of the priest's sarcophagus, powerful charms against magic. He let his head fall back on the pillow in relief.

At last the two men left, and Ellic climbed out of the sarcophagus, damp with nervous sweat. He cautiously crept into the outer room of the Cage and saw, on a shelf, a small box covered in opalescent white leather in a pattern of scales—the dragonskin box.

Ellic had meant to get out of the Cage and escape back to his rooms—no sense in pushing his luck. But the dragonskin box almost seemed to glow in the dimness of the Cage, its surface glistening with a pearly light. It begged to be opened. Ellic felt a strange tingling sensation begin in the soles of his feet and work its way to the tips of his fingers. The ancient Lailoken bloodline has suffered for centuries from a streak of weakness. In Oakie, it was a weakness for gambling. In Ellic, it was a tendency toward impulsiveness, a rash overconfidence paired with an inability to walk away from a dare. The box seemed to taunt him. *Open me.* It did not occur to Ellic that the box's very appeal might be the result of a charm.

What could be so precious it must be locked in a dragonskin box? He had to know. Maybe the spell Oakie had given him still had some juice left in it. But the intricate lock would not yield to Oakie's spell, despite several tries. Ellic ran through all the other lock-picking spells he knew—and he knew rather a lot—and he was not really surprised when none of them worked. But then Ellic thought about the problem another way. What if he gave up the idea of picking the lock? What if there was another way into the box?

On a hunch, Ellic said a simple spell, one of the first spells he'd learned as a boy. It was a spell that would turn something—anything—inside out. No sooner had the words left his lips than there was a strange sound— like a tortoise being threaded through a needle—and Ellic found himself looking at two curious objects.

The first resembled a lumpy cloth bag. That was the box, which had been turned inside out through its key-hole, the crimson velvet lining now outside.

The other object was a small book, its vellum bind-ing testifying to its great antiquity. It looked as if it had been pulled from a fire and doused with water at one point, its pages singed, stained, and curled. Ellic picked it up gingerly and opened it. It was written in an archaic form of Wizard's Latin. Ellic took from his pocket a pair of folding translating specs—one of the many magical cheats banned at the school.

The page was instantly readable, and Ellic nearly dropped the book in shock.

There, on the first page, were the words

Being the True Account of the New Adept.

Every wizard over the age of six knew about *The Book of the New Adept.* It was a collection of spells written by a rogue wizard expelled from the Wizards' Guild back in the 900s. The Guild had its inviolable rules, about what you could and couldn't summon up, magical words best left unuttered. There were certain spells that were simply deemed too dangerous, even for the most skilled Adepts. *The Book of the New Adept* had them all.

The book had been banned at the Constantinople Convocation of 1100. Since then, the Wizards' Guild had tracked down and destroyed all the copies—at least, that was what students at the Academy were taught.

Now Ellic was holding a copy in his hand. One page, badly stained, showed a young wizard, a boy in armor with long hair, riding in a glowing sphere above the waves. On the facing page was a passage, nearly obliterated by bookworms and water stains. Ellic said a spell to restore the faded ink, and for a brief moment the whole passage was legible.

> *From the West you shall come*
> *By the Light and Dark shall you be tested*
> *By Water, and you shall not be Drowned*
> *By Earth, and you shall not be Buried*
> *By Fire, and yet you shall not Perish*
> *I am but a mage of little magic*
> *Yet I listen, and I believe*
> *In the end of everything*
> *Shall be the beginning of thereafter.*

As Ellic turned the fragile pages, looking for banned spells, he found further prophecies, all telling of a wizard of great power.

Ellic furrowed his brow, puzzling. It didn't make any sense. This wasn't a book of dangerous spells at all. As Ellic leafed through it, he realized what it did contain: a different kind of forbidden knowledge, knowledge that went against everything he had been taught, everything the arch-mages of the Guild had spent centuries telling wizards was the truth about good magic and invert magic, about the borderlands between the mundane and magical worlds. But why would the Guild spend so much effort convincing everyone that *The Book of the New Adept* was something dangerous?

Then he found it. Toward the end of the book there was a woodcut showing a wizard holding a stone from which the artist had carved crude zigzags to represent rays of light. From a hole at the wizard's feet emerged squat, misshapen demons and winged men. The stone the wizard held was a key, that could somehow open a gateway to the wizard limbo, the magical underworld of Never-Was.

He heard a sudden sound and turned around, expecting to see Sparkstriker. It wasn't Sparkstriker, and it took Ellic a minute to recognize Headmaster Silvertongue. He was wearing a peculiar outfit, rather like fencing gear with long metal mesh gauntlets, and Ellic recognized it as an ancient dragonmaster's outfit, like the one on display in the great hall.

Idiot, thought Ellic. Of course the moment he'd left the safety of the sarcophagus he'd given himself away. But what was Silvertongue doing dressed up in dragon-handling gear?

"Headmaster." Ellic felt a hot flush creep over him. This was going to be more than one demerit. "I can explain," he stammered.

But the headmaster of G.A.W.A. Academy didn't seem angry or even surprised to find Ellic in the Cage, holding a forbidden book. He was staring at the book in Ellic's hand, his face lit with a fierce triumph. He dragged his gaze away and looked at Ellic—it was a look of strangely impersonal malice that chilled Ellic to the bone. He reached out and took the book from Ellic's hands.

"There's no need. I will do the explaining—about how a dragonskin box with contents unknown was discovered in an old cistern on the Academy grounds by workmen investigating a plumbing problem. How the book was locked in the Cage, how a student playing an end-of-term sprank managed to open the box—with tragic results."

It sank in what the headmaster meant. He was going to steal the book and blame its loss on Ellic. But what did he mean by "tragic results"?

It was then that Ellic noticed something odd was happening to the box, the one he'd turned inside out with a spell.

"What—how—" he stammered in disbelief.

The box was turning itself right side out again, but where before it had been a dragonskin-covered box, the dragonskin now covered flesh and bones. It was a small dragon, white, wingless, blind—and it was alive. It turned toward Ellic, sampling the air with its blue forked tongue. Ellic shrank back from it.

"I won't tell anyone, I swear! Just let me go. I'll leave the Academy, you'll never hear from me. Just take it and let me go. Please."

"I'm afraid it's rather too late for that. Besides, you will prove quite useful to me in another way. When the workmen found the box, they turned it over to Sparkstriker. He's a man of little ambition and less imagination. He insisted we place the book in the Cage for safekeeping and turn it over to the G.A.W.A. in the morning. Imagine my agony. I'd searched for the book for years, and now I couldn't even spend a few minutes alone with it! And if it turned up missing, the evidence would point to me. Then you emerged from the sarcophagus, and I could see a solution to my problems. The dragonskin box itself suggested the plan. Now everyone will believe the box and its contents were destroyed along with you."

The dragon had caught Ellic's scent, and its head bobbed, as if it were gauging the distance of the strike.

Ellic frantically tried to remember what he knew about wingless forms, but before he could remember any of the Charms That Render Harmless the Serpent's Tooth, the thing had reared up and bitten him on the arm, right through his shirtsleeve. Ellic cried out and clutched his arm, which began to tingle and burn as though it were on fire.

"How—how long do I have?"

"Tut-tut," said Silvertongue. "You haven't read your *Walker*, have you? The venom is not fatal. Eventually it has other consequences."

Ellic had begun to feel peculiar. The room was beginning to spin, its colors running together. The room was no longer solid, the walls and shelves seemed to be melting, the books and scrolls forming a multicolored blur. Ellic scanned the shelves, frantically looking for what he didn't know—a handhold, an antidote. His arm was on fire, but his heart was cold as ice.

Septimus stepped forward, *The Book of the New Adept* open in his hands. He read a few words of Wizard's Latin out loud. At Ellic's feet, where there had been a faded oriental carpet, there opened a small circle of nothingness, a small tear in the Here and Now.

A jolt of fear shot through Ellic's spine.

"No! You can't!" He reached out to clutch at Silvertongue.

The headmaster stepped back and bent to pick up the small dragon. He smiled and said, "I'm afraid I must," and lobbed the creature at Ellic. It landed like a cat with its sharp claws digging into Ellic's back, winding its coils around his neck. Then the circle of nothingness yawned, revealing an absolute blackness that fell away to infinity, a bottomless well of emptiness.

Ellic was pulled, struggling, toward the hole. The room pitched and sent both men sliding toward the hole. Silvertongue's suit of armor was anchored with a cable to the stout door of the chamber, but even so his face wore a look of terror as the cable was stretched to its full length. Clutching wildly at Silvertongue, Ellic's hands closed on the fragile book, tearing loose a handful of its pages while the rest fell to pieces. Seized in a magical undertow of great power, Ellic and the dragon vanished from sight, followed by many of the pages of the book. The well of emptiness shrank to nothing, and the spinning room slowed and then stopped. Once again the books sat in silent rows upon the shelves, the Heavenly Scrolls and the shaman's spell book back in their usual places.

Silvertongue scrabbled over the floor on his hands and knees, trying to gather together the remaining pages of the book. It became clear that most of the book had vanished down the well of nothingness with Ellic Lailoken.

The headmaster sat heavily on the floor and let loose an animal snarl of fury. He sat for a long time with his head in his hands, then rose and unclipped the cable from the chamber door. He said a few words in Wizard's Latin, a spell sent some of the contents of the Cage toppling from their shelves, and another incantation burned a large, sooty hole in the carpet where the yawning chasm had been. Finally he said a spell that changed his dragonmaster's gear back into his academic robes.

With the scene convincingly set, Silvertongue left the Cage and called to Flannery Bellweather, who came running.

"Miss Bellweather, fetch the provost. I am afraid there has been a terrible accident."

I

A Rude Awakening

THE WYVERN WAS dreaming.

Stretched out on the end of the bed, her eyelids fluttering and her beak agape, the small dragon named Vyrna twitched and grunted. In her dream, she was chasing a wild pig through the dappled sunlight and shadow of a Costa Rican forest, leaping over a living stream of army ants on the move, flushing squawking parrots from the fig trees, and making the howler monkeys whoop in alarm.

Then a sudden metallic clang and a loud curse woke her, and the dragon snorted with surprise and confusion. Her feline yellow eyes surveyed the unfamil-iar room, and her tongue tasted the air for unfamiliar smells.

Where was she? This was not her wicker bed on the screened veranda where she sat out at night, listening to the chorus of geckos. This place smelled strange: damp and musty, a smell of yellowed newspapers and wet ashes and mice. And it was *cold.* Vyrna shivered, opened her beak, and gave a long, low warble of displeasure.

Now she remembered: the tight quarters of the dog kennel in which Merlin had confined her for the jour-ney, the dull roar of the jet's engines, the uncomfortable skintight coat that, together with Merlin's magic, gave her the appearance of a small German shepherd. They had come by airplane and then by boat to this distant house on a hill, a comfortless, cold place of stone. No wild pigs here, and no geckos. There were sheep, but she wasn't allowed to chase them.

Her master appeared in the doorway. Iain Merlin O'Shea had retired from his position at Harvard, where he had for some years been professor emeritus of medieval history and folklore. He was still a practicing wizard and a card-carrying member of the Guild of Adepts in the Wizardly Arts, known to its members as G.A.W.A.

This morning Merlin wore an apron around his con-siderable girth and an expression of exasperation upon his face. But behind his spectacles, his blue eyes were apologetic.

"Vyrna, can you come into the kitchen? I can't seem to light the stove."

Reluctantly, the dragon clambered to her knees and hopped down from the bed. She was a young wyvern, still only half-grown, with the awkward proportions and ungainly movements of an adolescent puppy. She was a sleek blue-black, covered in scales except for the batlike wings she kept folded across her back. Her talons clicked on the old flagstones as she followed Merlin down the hall and into the large, echoing kitchen, where the wizard opened the oven door of the ancient stove.

"The pilot light is out, the matches are hopelessly wet, and you know how it is with magical fire . . . the coffee never tastes quite right."

Vyrna snorted, took a breath, and obligingly shot a thin stream of flame into the oven. The pilot light whooshed back to life, and with a mixture of embarrassment and relief Merlin set a battered enamel coffee pot on the burner. Then he reached down to scratch Vyrna under her chin.

"I'm sorry for the rude awakening," he said. "I'll have your breakfast in a minute."

Vyrna looked at her master with a reproachful expression that seemed to say, *Can we go back to Costa Rica now?* She retreated under the kitchen table and lay her head between her front two feet. Her eyes followed the wizard as he went to the equally ancient icebox and took out some bacon. Bacon was not nearly so fussy as coffee, so he was able to set it cooking by means of a simple command. Hearing the wizard say "Fry," the bacon obediently laid itself out in the skillet in rows and began to sizzle.

As far as he knew, Merlin was the only wizard in the world with his own wyvern. Vyrna was something of an accident: Dragons were extinct, or nearly so, in the twenty-first century, but Vyrna's mother, Wycca, had come through a bolt-hole, a kind of tunnel through time from the 1200s, and laid her egg at the top of the Customs Tower in Boston. Wycca was back in her own time now, but Vyrna hadn't been able to return with her. She was addicted to chocolate, and there was no chocolate back in the thirteenth century. Wycca had been able to shake her dependence on chocolate and return to a century where the delicacy was unknown, but without her daily dose, Vyrna would sicken and die. So Merlin divided his year between Costa Rica, where Vyrna could pass, if necessary and at a distance, for a particularly large fruit bat, and the Orkney Islands, where Merlin had rented a tiny speck that went unvisited by the tourists who came to gawk at Viking barrows and circles of standing stones. There was nothing on this island but a ramshackle castle, the gatehouse where they lived, and some sheep.

But Vyrna would not be with Merlin forever. Someday, Merlin hoped, Vyrna would be ready to join her mistress, Theodora. Theodora Oglethorpe was the human girl who had found Vyrna as a hatchling and rescued her. Theodora was by all outward appearances an average twelve-year-old girl, but she had an extraordinary family tree—her lineage could be traced back to a sorcerer's daughter in the 1200s. But for now she knew nothing of her heritage and suspected nothing about her magical powers. She was still coming to terms with the Events of Last Summer.

For Wycca the wyvern had not come through the bolt-hole from her distant century alone. She had been followed by two wizards. The first was Gideon, a king's wizard and her own master. Gideon had in turn been pursued by his archrival and half brother, Kobold. Kobold had tried to capture Wycca and use banned magic to turn her against Gideon. It had been an unusually untidy business, and one that had threatened to expose the secretive wizards who lived among ordinary humans. By the time it was all sorted out, it had involved a book of banned spells, the accidental summoning of a Chinese dragon, and a case of demonic possession.

It also had meant no end of paperwork for Merlin, reporting it all to his wizard superiors at the Boston chapter of the Guild of Adepts in the Wizardly Arts.

But in the midst of the untidy business, Theodora had been revealed to be an extraordinary girl. In time she would be told about her magical heritage, and if the higher-ups at G.A.W.A. thought she was a suitable candidate, Theodora would begin training as a wizard and would take over Vyrna's care.

Right now that care consisted of keeping the growing wyvern in chocolate. Merlin filled a large mixing bowl with Choc-o-Blox cereal and set the bowl on the floor for Vyrna. Next to the bowl he set a dog's water dish filled with hot chocolate, made Mexican style with cinnamon and chili powder.

Vyrna appeared from under the table and began to work her way through the Choc-o-Blox with great snaps of her beak, purring between bites and lashing her long, barbed tail over the tiled floor.

Merlin watched the wyvern and wondered how his friend back in Boston, Dr. Madhavi Naga, was coming along with the care and feeding of Theodora.

"Tickets, please. Tickets."

The conductor paused in the aisle and examined Theodora's twelve-ride pass, handed it back, and went on to the next passenger.

Theodora put the pass away in her wallet and went back to her journal, tapping her pen against her front teeth, looking at the sentence on the page but unable to think of what to write next. She looked at the three words she had already written, as though if she looked at them long enough they might make more sense, or seem more real.

Mikko is leaving.

Mikko had been Theodora's nanny since her mom died when she was seven, and after Theodora had gotten too old for a nanny, Mikko had stayed on as the Oglethorpes' housekeeper. Last night her father had sat her down and told her that Mikko would be leaving.

"Is she coming back?"

"I don't know. She and I agreed she could take a leave, to see what it felt like for you and me. You're twelve now, and you don't really need a nanny."

"But Mikko's more than a nanny."

To her surprise, her dad had blushed and said, "Well, I think that's why Mikko decided she should take this new job."

"This new job" was a round-the-world cruise as the companion to two old ladies.

In the seats across the aisle, a high-school couple who had gotten on at Chelsea were tangled up in a long, involved kiss. They hadn't bothered to take off or turn down their iPods, and you could hear the static fizz of music spilling out of the headphones. As the conductor came back down the aisle, he had to shake the boy's shoulder to get his attention. Romeo broke away from his Juliet long enough to dig their tickets from his pants pocket, and the conductor said something sarcastic to them about keeping their feet on the floor.

"Revere," he said in a singsong voice, making his way to the other end of the car. "Revere next."

Theodora turned back to her journal, outlining the words "Mikko is leaving" until the letters all ran into one another, and then she filled up the page in her journal with

Mikko is leaving

over and over and faster and faster until it turned into one long frantic scrawl, as though all the sad, angry, confused hurt inside her was flowing out through her arm, down the pen, and onto the page. Theodora looked out the window at the bare trees and brown grass of the February landscape, the glimpses of backyards and houses and brick buildings as the train meandered along the coastline, her pounding heart slowing, the surge of unhappiness subsiding into a dull ache.

She'd first realized something was wrong three months ago. She had walked into the kitchen the day after the Oglethorpes' Halloween party and found

Mikko and her dad having a serious conversation. They hadn't been kissing or anything—in fact, they had been standing at opposite corners of the room—but they had both seemed embarrassed when she walked in, and things had just been *different* around the house since then.

Inside the front cover of her journal were taped two photographs. One was old and faded. It showed Theodora and her mom looking at a starfish in a beach pail when Theodora was little, before her mom got sick. It wasn't really a good picture of her mom—her face was half in shadow—but for some reason it was the picture Theodora liked best. When she closed her eyes, she could almost convince herself that she remembered that day, that moment, sand on her skin, her mom's voice.

The other photo was from last Halloween. It showed her dad in a kind of Indiana Jones outfit, with a pith helmet and a Hawaiian shirt with a joke-shop arrow sticking out of his back, and Theodora in a sari. Mikko stood on the other side of Theodora, dressed as a mermaid in a sequined green costume, gill frills stuck to her neck with eyelash glue.

In Theodora's opinion, the whole mess was the fault of that slinky mermaid costume and the Russian professor, Boris, who had started calling Mikko all the time and taking her to the movies. (Theodora *had* walked in on *them* kissing.) Her theory was that seeing Mikko in the mermaid dress had made Theodora's dad look at

Mikko in a new way. But instead of taking her to the movies himself, he had started spending evenings in his study with the door closed or working late at the university, avoiding Mikko as much as he could and speaking to her in a formal way he hadn't used since she first came to work for them.

The trip would take seven months, Mikko said, and when she got back in the fall they would all see. Theodora knew what that meant: They would either start living together as a real family or Mikko would go away for good. And there would be another gaping hole in the family. Not that Mikko had filled the hole left by Mrs. Oglethorpe's death, but she had made the hole easier to step around, and not so scary. If Mikko really left, Theodora was going to have to learn to live without her mom all over again.

Romeo and Juliet got off at Revere, and when the conductor called "Salem," Theodora put her journal away in her backpack. As she rezipped the outer pocket, the insignia of the Guild of Adepts in the Wizardly Arts—an owl clutching a crystal ball in its talons— swayed on its clip.

The train pulled into the station at Salem, and Theodora got off and walked to Dr. Naga's house. Theodora made the trip to Salem twice a month for her art lesson. Whether or not any painting got done, the lessons were a chance to say anything she needed to about the Events of Last Summer without anyone telling her she was losing her mind. Dr. Naga had been there, and she knew it was all true: the wyverns, the wizards, the demon—everything.

Dr. Naga was an old friend of Mikko's and, Theodora had learned last summer, no stranger to magic herself. She wasn't a wizard, at least not in the sense that Gideon and Merlin were. One of her hobbies was caving, and she was good, as she put it, at "wriggling out of tight spaces in the dark." But she had stood by Theodora during the worst of the dark stuff, and she was still the only person from Theodora's non-magical normal life who knew about Gideon and the wyverns and everything that had happened.

Some days Theodora didn't say a word and just drew or painted. She had discovered she could paint about what had happened, even if she couldn't put it into words. She could get it all out without having to think or to give her feelings a name.

And the problem was, it wasn't one feeling, or the same feelings, but a great mixed-up bundle of them that was always changing. The wizard Merlin had taught her to do this really scary thing called Delving, which was hard to explain but was sort of like bungee jumping into a canyon with your mind. She and Merlin had joined their minds and managed to hold off the powerful dark magic that was trying to destroy Gideon and threatened to destroy them all. And when it was over, being back in her body had felt weird . . . her own hands and feet and arms and legs seemed awkward and unfamiliar and heavy, and while there was one part of her that longed to Delve again, the other part of her was terrified to.

The Delving had been strange and even frightening, and some of the other things that had happened had been absolutely terrifying, but at the same time she'd held a hatchling wyvern, and met a real wizard, and experienced something—well, something *magical.* Even at the worst of times, she didn't wish it hadn't happened. Not really. But she did wish Merlin and the other wizards at G.A.W.A. would hurry up and tell her how to get on with her ordinary life while knowing something so extraordinary.

When she got to the narrow townhouse with the green door and the brass knocker in the shape of a dolphin, Dr. Naga's two papillon dogs, Rudy and Kip, met her at the door, and on the counter she found a note from Dr. Naga.

"Come on up," it read.

Theodora left her jacket on the back of a kitchen chair and made her way up to the sunny studio at the top of the house, with its view of the seaport. Dr. Naga was standing on a stool, hanging a bat skeleton from the ceiling. Perched nearby on a stand was a taxidermy bird of prey, small, sleek, and gray.

Theodora reached out a finger to touch the soft feathers. "Wow—where did these come from?"

"They're on loan from a friend of mine who works at the Museum of Science."

"What kind of bird is this?" Theodora asked, cautiously touching the hooked tip of the fierce beak.

"A kind of small falcon called a merlin. A favorite familiar of wizards. I want you to spend the afternoon drawing the bones in the bat's wings and trying to get the falcon's eye and beak and talons right."

Theodora stifled a groan. It was wyvern wings and beaks that had been giving her so much trouble. It was hard to draw wings that were both transparent and strong, or the curious wyvern beak that seemed to have a Cheshire cat smile built into it.

"Gee, is that all?" she muttered. She sat down on the high stool pulled up to the drafting table, on which a fresh sheet of heavy paper had been pinned. She chose a pencil from the cup set into a hole in the table and began to draw. Meanwhile, Dr. Naga sat on the floor and paged through Theodora's journal. It was full of drawings of a wyvern—a bat-winged, four-legged dragon—shown over and over in different poses: launching itself into the air to catch a Frisbee, curled on a nest, taking a cat bath, flying, arching its back and spitting flame. The drawings in the front of the book were unsure and clumsy, but as you got to the back they were the work of an artist who still had a lot to learn, but who now possessed considerable confidence and skill.

In among the many sketches of the wyvern were drawings of a young man with a kind, wise face and loose, curly dark hair—hair that seemed beyond Theodora's skill to capture. Once, in frustration, she had turned a failed effort at depicting his curls into a clown wig and then added clown makeup to the face, scrawling "I give up. . . . This is too hard" across the bottom. On the very next page she had gotten the curls right, and that drawing had underneath it, written in clumsy Gothic lettering, "Gideon." The face she had drawn showed a young man smiling faintly. His expression was friendly, but there was something about his eyes that seemed sad somehow. Wise and sad.

And toward the back of the journal there was a single drawing of Theodora's mother, copied from one of her favorite family snapshots. Around the portrait Theodora had drawn a leafy border, its branches filled with birds and flowers—the kind of green heaven she imagined her mom had gone to.

While Theodora studied the bat's wing and how its bones fit together, Dr. Naga came to the page of the journal that was filled with "Mikko is leaving" and the angry scrawl at the bottom.

"I see Mikko has told you her news."

Theodora stopped drawing.

"You knew?"

Dr. Naga nodded. "She made me promise not to tell you. She wasn't sure about taking the job until late last week."

"Well, I don't get it," said Theodora, picking a pencil that was too soft for the delicate bone she was trying to draw and then getting mad when it made a thick, fuzzy line instead of the thin, sharp one she wanted. "I can't believe she's leaving, and I can't believe my dad is just letting her go," she continued in exasperation. "Why can't they see the simplest thing would be for them to just get married? It would solve everything."

"Would it?" said Dr. Naga. She came over to the drafting table, selected a pencil of a different hardness from the cup, and showed Theodora how with a little pressure it made a completely different line.

"Of course it would," said Theodora, a little crossly. She picked up the kneaded eraser and rapidly scrubbed out half of the drawing she had completed, blowing a shower of eraser crumbs onto the floor with more force than was necessary.

"Theodora, I wonder whether your father is as ready to marry again as you think. I think Mikko is wise to go away right now, as hard as it will be on everyone."

Rudy and Kip had appeared at the top of the stairs. Each dog carried a bright pink tennis ball in its mouth and wagged its tail impatiently.

"But there," said Dr. Naga, "I am going to leave you to your sketching while I throw balls to Kip and Rudy."

With a swirl of pink and silver sari skirts, Dr. Naga disappeared down the stairs with the dogs, leaving Theodora alone in the studio at the top of the house. She worked for about twenty minutes, finally getting the shape of the wing the way she wanted it. Then she tried to draw the wyvern hatchling from memory and found the drawing taking shape with more skill than she knew she possessed. The wing was like a bat's wing, and it wasn't. The beak was like the merlin's beak, and it wasn't. Somehow, on the page, they came together and made something new, made a dragon.

Will my parts ever come together again? Theodora wondered. Somehow last summer had left her feeling pulled apart, disconnected, a puzzle with pieces missing. And she knew it was more than just being twelve going on thirteen and being motherless. The whole wizard business had changed her; it was as though she'd been given wings but not taught how to fly.

She was starting to get a little stiff from sitting so long, so she got up from the drafting table and gave the hanging bat skeleton a gentle spin.

But not gentle enough. The pin holding the skeleton suspended from a string in the ceiling gave way, and the skeleton fell to the floor and broke into pieces.

Theodora looked at it with horror, unable to move. It

belonged to a museum, and she had broken it. In a panic, she dropped to her knees and gathered the fragile bones together. She could see there was no way to put the skeleton back together, not without special tools and wire and glue and skill and knowledge. None of which she had.

And in her panic, Theodora did something. It wasn't exactly Delving, because she didn't join her mind to someone else's, but it had that sudden stretchy-weightless-disembodied feeling to it, as though she were rapidly falling, then jerked to a stop, then flung upward. It was as though she could throw her mind, the way a ventriloquist can thrown his or her voice.

There was a strange backward clattering noise, like a recording of a hundred dropped chopsticks being rewound. Theodora uncovered her face and saw that the bat skeleton was swaying from its string once more, apparently unharmed.

Theodora sat staring up at the bat and then down at the floor, where a moment ago the skeleton had lain, hopelessly shattered. There wasn't the teeniest, tiniest speck or shard or splinter of bone anywhere on the floor, and standing up, she looked at the bat and could see that none of the bones had been broken and mended.

I did that, she thought. *I really did that.*

Her heart was pounding, and she felt a little dizzy. Out the window she could see Dr. Naga in the walled garden out back, throwing tennis balls for the black-and-white blurs that were Rudy and Kip. Suddenly Theodora found she didn't want to be alone with herself. She went downstairs and out into the garden.

She meant to tell Dr. Naga about the bat skeleton, but when she opened her mouth to speak she was suddenly afraid. Some part of her thought that if she didn't talk about it, it might never have happened, and she could just close the door on that part of her mind that knew how to Delve. It felt too risky, like being at the open door of an airplane, about to jump. She wanted to slam that door closed. She thought of her dad and thought there was just too much to lose.

Dr. Naga looked at her curiously.

"Do you want to tell me about it?"

"Tell you about what?"

Dr. Naga gave Theodora a skeptical look.

Theodora squatted down to rub Kip's tummy. "I don't know what you're talking about."

"I see. Well, let's go in," Dr. Naga said kindly. "I think you could do with a cup of tea."

Dr. Naga made Indian spice tea, not the stuff sold in supermarkets and coffeehouses, but the real thing. There was something soothing about watching her measure the milk and tea into a saucepan and add the furled sticks of cinnamon bark, star-shaped anise, and papery green cardamom pods. The smell of milk and sweet spices filled the kitchen. When the tea was ready, Dr. Naga poured it into bowls and stirred in the honey.

The tea was too hot to drink, so Theodora closed her eyes and breathed in the fragrant steam.

Dr. Naga blew on her own tea and took a scalding sip. "When you helped save Gideon last summer, you Delved."

"Believe me, I haven't forgotten."

"Delving uses just one muscle in the mind. Once you start using that part of your mind, you might discover other muscles. Tricycle, bicycle, unicycle. But if you don't know what you're doing, your new skills can be unsettling. Especially if you discover them when you're alone, without warning."

Theodora blushed and felt a hot, prickly surge of anger. "I didn't Delve, or Schmelve, or anything else, okay? Nothing happened."

"Theodora," Dr. Naga said gently. She reached across the table to take Theodora's hand. But Theodora got up from her stool and pushed her tea away so that it sloshed onto the counter.

Suddenly she was angry at everyone: at Dr. Naga, at Mikko, at Gideon and Merlin. At her dad. And even at her mom. But most of all, Theodora was mad at herself. When the anger faded, as it always did, she would just be scared and alone.

She grabbed her coat and backpack.

"I have to go. I'll miss my train."

2

The Greenwood Legacy

MERLIN WAS TRYING to get Vyrna to take her worm medicine and allow her talons to be trimmed. As young wyverns are particularly stubborn and ticklish, even by dragon standards, he wasn't having much luck.

Outside, the new lambs braced themselves against a wind off the sea that still seemed to think it was February. After he had trimmed her talons, Merlin noted, under "May" on her growth chart, Vyrna's increased wingspan and the fact that the wyvern's fire appeared to be maturing far more quickly than her common sense.

From the hall came the boom of a resounding knock on the front door, and Vyrna was off like a shot, with the portly wizard in hot pursuit, trying to intercept her before she reached the front door, which already bore evidence of her talons and incendiary breath. At this rate, the gatehouse was going to need a new door.

"No, Vyrna, *heel!* Oh, you miserable sack of scales and cinders, that used to be my great-grandmother's best flying carpet! And no, no, *no fire in the house!*"

As the wyvern neared the door, there was a muffled shout from the other side, something in Wizard's Latin that sounded like "Pachinko, pachyderm, pennywhistle!" The spell came zinging through the keyhole and hit the dragon smartly on her nose. Vyrna came to a skittering halt on the hall tiles and abruptly began chasing her tail.

"Nice work," Merlin muttered admiringly as he slid aside the iron bolt.

Before him stood a woman of striking appearance. She was dressed in black, over which she wore an open coat of gold kimono silk patterned with gingko leaves. Her short silver hair stood up in peaks on her head, like a well-made meringue. She seemed familiar—there was something about that mouth, with its wry curve outlined in Chinese red lipstick. Her black eyes glittered with intelligence and perhaps suppressed laughter. Merlin had the unsettling feeling that he had met her before.

"Hullo, Iain," she said, holding out a hand.

He took her hand and winced faintly at the strength of her handshake. "I'm very sorry, but do we know one another?"

"That's all right," she said. "I wouldn't expect you to remember me." Her eyes glittered a little dangerously and she still held on to his hand. "Margery MacVanish. Evander MacVanish's baby sister. I believe you and the rest of the boys used to call me 'Maggot' behind my back."

Merlin sputtered. "Good heavens! Maggot! Where—when—how have you been? I haven't seen you since . . . since . . ."

"Since the spring of 1906. The Wizards' Walk. You took Esmeralda Quincup and I had to go with Fergis Fowler, who stepped on my toes and gave me a corsage with a wasp in it. I spent the dance in the infirmary holding ice to my nose." Margery's mouth curved downward in a mock pout. "You broke my heart, Iain."

Merlin blushed to the roots of his receding hair. He and Margery had been young in 1906, but they did not seem ancient now. The practice of magic has a remarkable preservative effect, and as a result wizards have a long middle age. They don't start to really wrinkle until they reach the age of 170 or so.

Margery laughed and patted his hand comfortingly. "Don't fret—I forgave you somewhere between husbands three and four. You're looking well," she added, looking him up and down fondly, "even if you have gotten a little thin on top, and more than a little thick around the middle. Now, do ask me in so we can talk properly. I have a great deal to tell you."

As he held the door wide to let her enter, Merlin noticed the insignia that hung around Margery MacVanish's neck. It was not the usual wizard's emblem of an owl clutching a crystal ball, worn by all members of the Guild of Adepts in the Wizardly Arts. The insignia Margery wore was a raven perched on a human skull—the symbol of the Office of the Intercessor General.

The O.I.G. was the branch of the wizards' guild that dealt with mortal affairs when they threatened to collide with the world of wizards in ways dangerous to both. Getting an unannounced visit from an agent of the O.I.G. was something no wizard looked forward to, even if that agent was someone you had called Maggot when she was still in pigtails.

"Now, what brings you, and the O.I.G., to my distant doorstep on this fine morning in May?" Merlin said as they settled into chairs by the fire in the library. "Are you checking up on Vyrna's progress? Or did I leave something out of my report about the Events of Last Summer?"

"Yes, I do want to talk to you about the interesting young Miss Oglethorpe. But not only about her."

"I certainly don't have anything to say that I didn't put in my report. I filed all my paperwork in triplicate last fall with the guild's North American office."

Gideon had gone back to his own When at the end of last summer and left Merlin to fill out the endless G.A.W.A. forms: form 99-BH, to report a new bolt-hole; form 37-AS, to report an accidental summoning; not to mention the forty-nine pages of Supporting Narrative explaining it all. Surely Margery MacVanish wasn't going to ask him to go through all that again?

"I'm in charge of loose ends," Margery explained. "And there are a lot of loose ends in this case. It seems to me much too great a coincidence that two wizards from the thirteenth century should have ended up battling in the living room of a girl with such an extraordinary magical pedigree, as you so aptly put it in your report. In fact," said Margery, "it makes me wonder whether Gideon was really the target after all. Kobold was working for a mysterious wizard, a master who managed to remain in the shadows. We never found out who he was."

"Go on," said Merlin. "I'm listening."

Margery got up from her chair and wandered over to the bookcase. She ran her finger along the spines of the books, newer volumes bound in cloth and thick leather-bound tomes cracked with age. "Do you know why

G.A.W.A. fought so hard to ban *The Book of the New Adept* nine hundred years ago?"

"It was written by a heretical wizard and was full of banned spells. It was the work of centuries to find and destroy the copies."

"There's a theory that the Guild wasn't worried about the banned spells as much as a prophecy in the book. A prophecy that foretold how a powerful wizard would appear and open the gate between this world and Never-Was."

Merlin shuddered at the mention of the magical underworld. Never-Was was a place outside time, a magical tar pit peopled with outcasts, madmen, and various chimeras and monsters. Or so the legends said, retold only in whispers.

"Wizards could be banished to Never-Was, but according to the Guild there was no way back. Now a rogue wizard was threatening to open the passageway and allow everything in Never-Was into this When and Where. *That* was the heresy. That was why the books had to be destroyed. The Guild could never allow the gate to Never-Was to be opened. But more importantly, they didn't want their authority challenged. What if this New Adept came along and started a rival Guild with all the wizards he'd freed from Never-Was? It could ignite a long, terrible civil war among rival guilds."

"So you think Kobold's master was this wizard?

The New Adept whose coming was foretold in the prophecy?"

"Who knows? It's certainly one possibility. He's covered his tracks well."

"Or her tracks."

Margery's dark eyes glittered, and her raven insignia, carved of black volcanic glass, winked in the firelight. "Or her tracks. Kobold thought his master was a man, but he might have been deceived."

"So what does this have to do with Theodora?"

Now Margery was standing in front of a tapestry, one of several Merlin had brought with him from his old apartment in Cambridge, Massachusetts. The tapestry showed a young boy in blue armor, fighting a white dragon.

"I believe she is in danger," said Margery. "She was able to Delve untaught, which places her among a minuscule percentage of ordinary mortals."

"Yes," said Merlin. "She's the great-great-to-the-umpteenth granddaughter of a sorceress named Gwynlyn."

"So you said in your report," said Margery. "We've found out a bit more about Gwynlyn and her descendants. She came through a bolt-hole to Manhattan at the turn of the twentieth century and started a long line of women who had a marvelous way with dragons. Only their dragons were painted on Chinese vases and fossilized into cliffs as pterodactyls. So far Gwynlyn's talent, the full-blooded Greenwood legacy, if you will, has not come out in any of her descendants in full flower."

"The Greenwood legacy?" said Merlin.

"Oh, yes," said Margery. "We have quite a file on the Greenwood women, up to about 1970, when Theodora's mother was born. Then records get a little patchy. The Oglethorpe side is a big washout, incidentally. Brainy lot, but not a speck of magical ability."

"So far you haven't explained to me why you think Theodora is in danger," said Merlin.

Margery had finished her tea and was frowning into her cup at the pattern of the tea leaves floating in the milky dregs.

"I think there is a very real possibility that this wizard unknown, whoever he is, will try to recruit her."

Merlin's own tea had gone cold. He was studying the tapestry. To him, the young face of the boy might have been a girl. A young Joan of Arc—or a young Theodora.

"Let me guess. The O.I.G. thinks Theodora has won the genetic lottery. She has 100 percent of Gwynlyn's gift. And they have decided they will get to her first, spirit her off from her ordinary mortal home and family, and initiate her into the Guild as a wizard in training."

"If she's lucky," said Margery. "There are some at the O.I.G. who feel her powers should be stripped from her before they have a chance to develop. Better one less Greenwood than a Greenwood gone bad."

Wizards who had so transgressed that G.A.W.A. felt they could not be rehabilitated underwent a process called a Great Demotion—something like disbarring a lawyer, something like declawing a cat. It was not a benign procedure. It could go wrong and leave even a powerful wizard a gibbering shell. What it might do to a young girl, Merlin could only imagine.

Looking pale and grim, he rose to his feet. "I will not let that happen. I'll spirit her off through a bolt-hole myself before I let you—"

Margery held up a hand. "Iain. Please. If that was what I had in mind, would I really have come here to tell you all this?"

Merlin slowly lowered himself back into his chair. A log rolled forward in the grate with a shower of sparks. Vyrna raised her head from her napping spot and sent a few sparks back in reply.

"Then what?" said Merlin. "Why have you come?"

"Since last Halloween I have been posted to a small island down in the Hebrides. G.A.W.A. monitors picked up a huge surge of magical energy, and I was sent to try and find out what had produced it. So far I have found no trace of a bolt-hole or anything else that could explain the phenomenon. At the same time, something odd has been happening to the island. The fish catch is way down, and last week a schoolboy found a strange scale."

Merlin sat up. "A scale? From a wyvern?" It was one of Wycca's scales that Theodora's father had described in a scientific journal, and that paper, more than anything else, had helped win him a position as a full professor.

"No, too large for a wyvern. The director of Scornsay's tiny museum has written to Professor Oglethorpe, asking him to come and examine the scale in person and try to identify it. When I checked up on the professor, I found the file with your report about the Events of Last Summer. I've read the O.I.G.'s file on the Greenwoods and I've formed my own theory about Theodora—who she is, what she is. But I think you can tell me more than I've been able to learn on my own."

"Me? Why me?"

"You Delved with her, Iain. You know the mind that is inside that child's head. When she joined her mind with yours, did you sense anything?"

Merlin looked at the tapestry, the face of the boy so young, yet fierce and brave.

"We were helping Gideon battle against Kobold. It was a jumble of impressions. You know what Delving is like."

"Iain, it's important."

Merlin looked at Margery for a long moment. "Yes,"

he said at last. "I sensed that I was in the company of a more gifted Delver than I could ever be. She's 100 percent Greenwood. Maybe even 101."

The look that spread over Margery's face at his words was remarkable. In a fraction of a second she lit up with triumph and delight, but almost instantly something in her, probably her O.I.G. training, clamped down on the joy and she was composed again. "As I thought," was all she said.

"You're going to bring her to the island, aren't you?" Merlin asked.

"Events are in motion," said Margery. "Theodora and her father will go to Scornsay without any help from me. And I think Theodora *needs* to go there, to discover who and what she truly is."

"If anything happens to Theodora, the O.I.G. will have a lot to answer for," said Merlin.

"I know," the other wizard said quietly. "I know. It could be a risky proposition, bringing a young girl with her bloodline to a place where the forces of magic have registered a seismic jolt. But—"

"But what?" said Merlin. "It's a time of great peril for Theodora. She is coming into her powers, but she doesn't know what they are. It seems to me to be the worst possible time to spirit her off to someplace like Scornsay."

"But the danger may be greater if she does *not* go,"

said Margery. "If Kobold's master gets to her while her powers are still half-formed. Her father coming to the island and bringing her along offers the perfect chance to observe her, evaluate her, and if necessary, protect her."

Merlin looked at her closely. "I seem to remember we all used to play hide-and-seek with Evander and his little sister Maggot. We could never find you, Margery. You were so good at hiding, even for a MacVanish. It makes me wonder what you're hiding now."

For the first time in their whole conversation, Margery's dark eyes seemed to have a tender gleam.

"Iain, I myself was once a motherless girl discovering her wizardly powers. I know a little of what Theodora is going through. This isn't just a job for me. It's personal. It *matters* to me what happens to this girl."

"Good," said Merlin. "It had better."

3

The Scale

COLIN FLETCHER LET his bike coast to a stop and stowed it behind a rack of newspapers outside the whitewashed building. Over the low doorway was a brightly painted shingle that declared this to be the Scornsay Heritage Museum, and in the window a notice gave the hours and informed the public that the museum was curated by J. A. M. Grayling, DPhil.

Colin shaded his eyes and peered in the window, scanning the room. He saw low glass cases of mineral specimens and tall cabinets full of taxidermied seabirds and the old ship's figurehead looming in the corner. But there was no sign of Jamie.

"He's gone down to Perley's," said a voice behind him.

Colin turned and saw Mrs. Minchin, who ran the newsagents' next door. She was Mr. Perley's chief competitor selling sundries, newspapers, and lottery tickets in the village, and she pronounced the word "Perley's" with a disdainful curl to her lip. It sat ill with Mrs. Minchin that Jamie Grayling walked to Perley's for coffee and a prawn roll once a week, instead of availing himself of her assortment of perfectly fresh sandwiches.

"Thanks, Miz Minchin. Ta." Colin seized his bike, pivoted it sharply on its front wheel, and sprang aboard.

Perley's was at the end of the village, just where the road turned sharply inland and climbed up the hill away from the sea. As Colin arrived, one of the village ladies was leaving with her weekly lottery ticket and film magazine, and someone from the town council was putting up a poster announcing yet another meeting about the island's fish crisis.

Mr. Perley was at the counter of his tiny shop, making prawn rolls and ham-and-pickle sandwiches for customers brave enough to buy their lunch from the cooler where the bait was kept. Colin took two candy bars from the Nutto-Caro-Crema-Latté display and set them on the counter. Mr. Perley put down his knife and came over to ring the purchase up on his new electronic cash register, of which he was enormously proud.

Colin fished money from his pocket. "Is Jamie about? Miz Minchin told me he'd come this way."

"Just missed him, Col," said Mr. Perley. "He had me wrap his sandwich and put the coffee in a Thermos bottle for him. He said he was headed up to the Stane Folk, where you found the scale."

A few villagers, retired fishermen, were browsing through the newest DVDs in the small rental section. Hearing Mr. Perley say "the scale," they chuckled, and Colin blushed.

"Aye, Colin, now you've got poor Jamie believing in your monster," one of them said.

"Well, what is it, then?" Colin retorted. "You said yourselves it was too large to be from a fish."

One of the fishermen shrugged. "Some genetically engineered salmon, I'd wager, escaped from a lab somewhere."

Colin didn't stay to hear the rest. He put the chocolate bars in his jacket pocket and left the store, retrieving his bike again and heading for the island's highest point, where the Stane Folk were.

He spotted Jamie instantly. The tall, gangly curator had flame red hair, and he was wearing a bright yellow anorak and an electric blue sweater. He stood out against the muted colors of the hillside like some exotic bird.

The hillside was covered with stone pillars, each the size of a small child. From a distance, the group of stones gave the appearance of a gathering of dwarves. Jamie was standing with one hand on his hip; in the other he held the cup from a Thermos bottle.

"Hullo," said Colin, coming up a little out of breath.

"Col," said Jamie absently.

"Find anything new?"

"Nothing." Jamie rubbed his chin, which was covered in a hopeful growth of fuzz masquerading as a beard. He stared out to sea, and then turned to look down the hill in another direction, where the road lay.

"Forget for a moment the question of what it is," he said. "And think, how did it get here?"

Colin thought about that. "Otter?"

Jamie shook his head. "No, not wet enough, and there's no sign of a track."

"Skua?" The large gulls called skuas patrolled the island's cliffs, robbing other birds of their meals and picking puffins from their burrows.

"Maybe," said Jamie. "Or someone could have hiked from that road and left it here by accident—it could have clung to their clothing, like a burr. But what is it?"

Jamie took from his pocket a small, clear plastic box. There, on a nest of cotton, lay the scale. It was larger than a postage stamp, slightly curved, and pale. In the sunlight it gave off flashes of opal fire.

Jamie and Colin stared at it for a long moment, wonderingly.

"Any word from the professor?" asked Colin at last.

Jamie laughed. "I only sent the letter yesterday. He couldn't possibly have gotten it yet."

"You should have e-mailed," Colin chided. Since he'd discovered the scale, he'd found it hard to do his school-work, hard to sleep. He kept thinking about it and the way it flashed with an almost hypnotic hidden fire.

"I wanted to write on the museum stationery. More impressive that way. He gets a lot of e-mail, I'm sure. An airmail letter with foreign stamps is much more inter-esting."

The wind kicked up and scoured the hilltop, whistling in their ears and making the fabric of their jackets flutter furiously. A cloud passed overhead, cast-ing the hillside of stones into shadow, making them briefly appear slightly sinister. Colin shivered.

"I don't much like it here," he said.

"No," said Jamie. "It somehow makes you think that the legend could be true."

"What, that the stones come to life at night?"

Jamie looked at Colin. "That's the schoolyard ver-sion. There's a much older tale about the Stane Folk. You don't know that one?"

Colin shook his head.

Jamie looked at the boy, as if weighing whether he

was old enough to hear the tale. He must have decided the answer was yes, because he looked out across the squat stone pillars that covered the hillside, cleared his throat, and started to speak.

"Back before the castle was built, this island was ruled by a clan chief who had his own sorcerer. A wizard, you'd call him. The chief cheated the wizard, and in revenge the wizard turned all the children of the clan to stone."

The cloud passed away, and the sun shone down once more on the stone shapes, casting stark shadows. Now Colin could see vague necks and shoulders and hips in the twisted shapes. He shuddered.

The boy looked so pale the curator took pity on him.

"Ach, lad! It's just a story, isn't it? Come on, my Rover's down the other side. I'll run you back home."

From the briar bush where he had crouched, concealed, a man watched them go. He saw Grayling and the Fletcher boy load the bicycle into the back of the Range Rover and drive away. Then he climbed the hill and stood among the Stane Folk, with the wind whipping his hair back from his lean, intent features.

He was small and wiry, with dark hair and a tautness about him, the contained energy of an acrobat. His clothing was a bit strange, not worn-looking but old-fashioned somehow. He had appeared on the island the previous October, seemingly out of nowhere, and seemed to live on the moors in a kind of camp. He roamed the island, searching for something, his eyes on the ground. He walked along the banks of the burns, stopping to pull stones from the streambeds. He walked the fields among the lowing cattle, stepping among the cowpats and bending now and again to turn over a rock. He sat for hours in the ruins of the old abbey and wandered among the old gravestones. Always, his eyes swept the ground, searching, searching.

The islanders called him Mad John.

Now he wandered among the Stane Folk, his hands straying across the stones' tops almost affectionately, as though he'd known the stones long ago, when they were children.

Then he paused at the central pillar, taller than the rest, covered in carvings obscured by lichen. Mad John ran his fingers over the carvings, as though he were a blind man reading Braille, his lips moving without making a sound. He looked around the wind-scoured hillside and turned in a slow circle, his eyes searching the landscape. Then he flung back his head and let loose a cry, half shout, half snarl, banging the stone pillar with his fist. His knuckles bled, but he seemed not to notice. He withdrew from his pocket a tattered piece of paper that appeared to be a map and ran his fingers over it searchingly, the way he'd felt the pillar.

Mad John was hungry. He would have to eat soon to

feed the Seeker. The creature that had led him out of his captivity was no longer a small, white, blind thing. It was growing, and he wondered how long he could continue to satisfy its hunger.

In the meantime, he could only search.

4

A Tug on the Mind

O N AN AFTERNOON in late May, Theodora let herself into the house with her own key, set down her
backpack, and retrieved the mail where it had fallen onto
the mat. On her way into the kitchen, she helped herself
to an orange from the bowl on the hall table that Mikko
had always kept full of oranges. Since Mikko had left,
the bowl of oranges was one small thing that hadn't
changed.

It was still weird to walk into the kitchen after school
and not see Mikko busy chopping vegetables and listening to reggae on the radio. But at the same time,

Theodora and her dad had settled into a new routine of their own. Theodora took a brick of chicken breasts out of the freezer and put it on the kitchen counter. Closing the door, she kissed her fingertips and touched them to a picture of her mom stuck to the door in a magnetic frame. "Hi, Mom," she murmured.

She sat at the kitchen table to go through the mail. There were the usual bills, catalogs, and junk mail, but her heart leaped when she saw a postcard from Mikko, postmarked from the Azores. Previous letters had described bouts of seasickness and sunburn and included funny accounts of her employers, Miss Ida and Miss Irene, "the kind of women who could shoot the middle out of the ace of hearts at twenty paces and clean out the fuel line on an airplane with a hairpin."

> *I am learning to dance the tango from an old gentleman from Argentina, but I am afraid I will never learn to beat my employers at bridge. They skunk me every time.*
>
> *The ocean is beyond words: amazing stars, flying fish, dolphins, the sea itself always a different color, silk or metal. I want to grow gills and stay forever. But I miss you fiercely, child.*
>
> *Love,*
> *Mikko*

When she had read it over twice, Theodora placed it in the basket on top of the microwave. If her dad read the letters and postcards, he never mentioned it to Theodora, but sometimes when she put a new one in she'd notice the last one was no longer on top.

She went back into the pantry and began to assemble ingredients for a stir-fry. Then she gave the chicken an experimental poke, put it in the microwave on low to thaw faster, and went into her dad's office to check the answering machine.

There was a message from the dentist's office reminding her dad about his appointment and a message from Brenda about going to the movies.

Brenda was the latest in a string of not-quite-girlfriends. Her dad had started dating. The first woman he brought home to dinner was Mircea, who was Brazilian, petite, and very pretty.

"Did you like Mircea?" her dad asked the next day.

"Do I have to?" Theodora asked back. "She's nice enough and everything, but I wouldn't want her to be my stepmom. And I definitely don't want Gilberto to be my stepbrother." Gilberto was twelve going on ten, and he only wanted to talk about Brazilian soccer and PlayStation.

"Okay," said her dad. "I get the message."

But Brenda sounded okay. Theodora hadn't really spent much time with her, just seen her twice when she'd stopped by to fetch her dad when they were going out. Theodora had a little mental file on Brenda, full of facts she'd stored away. She was a nurse-anesthesiologist who did stand-up comedy when she wasn't on duty. She was a little on the plump side, with wavy auburn hair, hazel eyes, and freckles. Theodora had talked to her once, on the phone, and she seemed nice and funny, and it was hard to dislike her. But Theodora had discovered that you could like someone and still resent them.

Next Theodora logged on to the computer and sent her friends Valerie and Milo instant messages but got no reply. No surprise there. Val was busy with Tae Kwon Do, getting ready for a charity Kick-a-Thon. And Milo was spending his afternoons training his new dog, Yoda, for weekend agility trials, where dogs competed against the clock, racing through obstacle courses of seesaws and tunnels. The three had been best friends for years, but now it felt as though they were all moving on. Theodora couldn't blame them: It seemed whenever they had a rare free day she was either at Dr. Naga's for a lesson or running errands with her dad.

But it was mostly that she couldn't tell them about Wycca and Gideon and everything that had happened. Val especially seemed to suspect that there was something Theodora wasn't sharing with them, and after trying to coax it out of her, she'd given up.

"Gee, Do," she finally said in exasperation. "Even

when your mom died, you didn't freeze me out like this."

Theodora retrieved her backpack, headed to the living room, and flipped on a movie while she decided whether to tackle her math first or her Spanish. She looked up at the screen and they were showing the second *Wizards & Wyverns* movie for the umpteenth time. It was collecting *Wizards & Wyverns* cards that had led to the mix-up that brought her into the whole real wizard business, and now the movies seemed hopelessly fake and hokey to her. Theodora surfed past a dozen channels and finally stopped at a nature documentary.

It was going to take her a couple of hours to craft a five-hundred-word essay in Spanish about the ancient Aztecs, so she got out her math assignment—she liked geometry, and she was good at it.

". . . an entire community of plants and animals in a cubic meter of peat," droned the narrator in a British accent. On the screen a soggy-looking scientist in rain gear was using a trowel to cut out a block of black earth, full of dangling roots.

The first geometry proof was easy, and Theodora went on to the second.

". . . worms, beetles, mosses, ferns, and a great number of microscopic animals and fungi, all forming a complex food web . . ."

Theodora looked up just in time to see a close-up of a beetle eating some kind of whitish larva. She made a face and looked away. In a few minutes a show she liked would be on and she would change the channel. But she had time to do one more math problem.

Suddenly a bird's eerie call made her glance up again, and on the television screen was a view of a golden-green moor broken by shimmering, mirrorlike fingers of water. The sky was a changeable pale gray, as though a storm were just on the way out. A marsh bird swooped low over the water, making the same mournful call. In the distance was a ruined building, perhaps a fort or castle. The narrator was saying something, but the words just washed over Theodora. She felt as though she were being drawn into the picture, as though she could dive right into that silvery water and disappear. The landscape on the TV screen was ancient, beautiful, dreamlike—and again the image seemed to tug at Theodora, as though it would pull her in through the screen, and she pulled her mind away abruptly. The magical mood was broken.

She grabbed the remote and turned the TV off, and she sat there for a moment, her heart beating fast in her chest, trying to figure out what had just happened. Then she turned the TV back on and pressed the info button on the remote to see what the program was.

3:00 p.m.–4:00 p.m. "Tales from the Bog." The flora and fauna of a Scottish peat bog are explored. (Nature)

Theodora decided to finish her geometry assignment at the kitchen table. She had finished it and was patting dry the thawed chicken when her dad came in. He dropped his keys on the kitchen counter and shuffled through the pile of mail.

"Hi, Do," he said, dropping a kiss on the top of her head and reaching into the fridge for the seltzer.

Theodora had peeled some ginger and was slicing it into matchsticks. She was still thinking about the strange thing that had happened with the nature program on TV, but she didn't feel she could tell her dad about it. Instead, she heard herself say, "Are you serious about Brenda?"

Her father had been pouring a glass of seltzer, and now his hand jerked and the seltzer fizzed over onto the counter. He grabbed a towel and mopped it up, then turned and looked at her. He had never worn glasses, but recently he had gone to the eye doctor and come back with a prescription for bifocals. He was always taking them off, looking at them in a mildly annoyed way, and then polishing the lenses with his shirttail. He did so now, stalling.

"No, not yet."

"But you like her."

"Yes. I like her a lot. In fact, Theodora, she'd like to meet you."

"She has met me."

"Well, just to say hello. She'd like to spend some time with you. She and I thought some Sunday we could go to the river and just hang out. Bring the Frisbee and the paper and some bread for the ducks."

Theodora felt a quick stab of resentment. Lazy Sundays on the riverbank had been something they'd done with Mom. But she heard herself say, "Okay. Sure."

She went back to making ginger matchsticks. Without a word her dad went to the pantry and came back with bottles of sesame oil and soy sauce and a jar of hot chili paste. Working in a silence that started out awkward but ended up comfortable, they moved around the kitchen, around each other, making dinner.

Later, while Theodora was finishing her homework at the kitchen table, her father said, "I got a letter at work today."

"Uhmmm?" Theodora was looking up "observatory" in her Spanish dictionary.

"It was from a museum in Scotland. They've found a scale. They want me to come over and see it."

Theodora let the dictionary fall shut. She didn't have to ask which kind of scale he meant. Her dad was the scientist who had written the article announcing the discovery of a mysterious scale and some fragments of eggshell in an abandoned nest in the Custom House tower on Boston's waterfront. It was Wycca's scale and a fragment of Vyrna's egg, but only Theodora and Dr. Naga and the wizards knew that. Everyone else thought Professor Andrew Oglethorpe had identified a mysterious new kind of animal. The article he'd written about it had ended up on the front cover of *Science*, and the cover was framed and hanging in Andy Oglethorpe's office. Thanks to the scale, her dad was now a real professor with a job at the university as long as he wanted it.

Oh, great, Theodora said to herself. *Here it comes.* Just like last summer . . . her dad was going to go off somewhere interesting and leave her behind. Except this time Mikko wouldn't be around to look after her, and he would have to ship her off to a relative for safekeeping: her Aunt Jane, if she was lucky; if she wasn't, her Great-Uncle Hosmer and Great-Aunt Prue.

"Isn't there anyone in Scotland who can look at it for them?"

"Yes, at the University of Edinburgh. But the herpetologist and ichthyologist there both recommended me. I'm as much of an expert as the world has right now on mystery scales."

"Why do you have to go all the way to Scotland? Why can't they just mail it to you?"

"Well, there would be a lot of red tape in customs, sending a biological specimen of an unknown animal out of the country. The museum people want to keep this quiet—they don't want their little island overrun with curiosity seekers. There are some people who think Nessie hasn't been good for Loch Ness."

"Well, if you have to go, you have to go," Theodora said.

"I was thinking we could both go. Mr. Grayling, the curator of the museum, says he can offer us lodging for a short visit. A week or two. Long enough for me to make a useful study of the scale and the site where it was found."

Theodora was staring at her father.

"Do you mean it? You mean, go with you?" She had a brand-new passport, and her father had been promising to take her on his next trip, so long as she didn't miss any school. But somehow she hadn't allowed herself to believe he really would.

Her dad was grinning. "Yes, that's what I mean." He handed her the letter from the Scornsay Heritage Museum. Enclosed with the letter on museum stationery from J. A. M. Grayling, DPhil, was a color pamphlet with the words "Surprising Scornsay" on it. Theodora opened it and almost fell out of her chair.

The color photograph inside showed a golden-green moor broken by slender fingers of silver water. A marsh bird was curving through the changeable gray sky. In the distance was a ruined building, a castle, or a fort. It looked almost exactly like the image on the TV screen that had tugged so hard on her mind. Only now it just looked beautiful, not creepy at all. There was even a rainbow over the castle.

"Are you okay?" her dad asked.

"Yeah," said Theodora. "Just excited." She handed the letter back to him but kept the pamphlet. The tug was not as strong as when she had seen the image on TV, but it was there, as if the silver fingers of water were reaching out.

The final weeks of school dragged on forever. Theodora packed and repacked her carry-on three times: a paperback guide book to Scotland (she'd had it a week and read it cover to cover more than once), the digital camera Aunt Jane had given her last Christmas and that she was still figuring out how to use, her journal, and a new tin of ninety-six colored pencils.

She was pawing through the tangle of chains and bangles in her jewelry box when she came across the old brooch that had been her mother's. It was an abstract swirl of metal that formed a crouching dragon, set with a red stone. She'd last worn the brooch during her magic summer, when she'd cast the clumsy spell that had sent Gideon's wyvern tumbling from the sky and landed

Vyrna in the Oglethorpes' backyard. Theodora blushed at the memory. But something made her pick up the brooch, and as she held it in her hand it grew warm and the red stone in the center glowed. Theodora had a sudden vision of her mother standing in front of the mirror in the hall, dressed to go out somewhere special. Mrs. Oglethorpe put on one earring, then its mate, and finally she pinned the brooch with the red stone to the neckline of her dress. Then the memory faded.

Theodora carefully added the brooch to the zippered case that held the hair clips and bracelets she was taking on the trip. After she had zipped the case shut, she sat on her bed, thinking about the events of last summer, the spell she'd cast with the brooch, and the mended bat skeleton.

She wondered which Theodora had decided to bring the brooch along. Was it the old Theodora, the part of her that remembered her mother and was desperate to keep her memory bright and new? Or was it the new Theodora, the one that could Delve and mend a broken skeleton with her mind? She felt as though the two selves, the old and the new, were like those toy magnets Santa once left in her Christmas stocking. Little plastic Scottish terriers, one white and one black. The more you tried to push them together, the more they seemed to force each other away.

The "Surprising Scornsay" brochure was lying on the floor. Theodora bent down and picked it up, opening it to the picture of the castle on the moor. She traced the rainbow with her finger thoughtfully. Maybe she would get some answers in Scotland, among the green-gold moor and silver water.

5

Glued Together with Ghosts

IT SEEMED TO THEODORA that they landed in a gale. As they stepped off the ferry onto the dock on Scornsay, a young man came forward, smiling, and shook Andy Oglethorpe's hand vigorously, shouting to be heard above the wind.

"Jamie Grayling from the Scornsay Heritage Museum. Did you have a bumpy crossing? You look a wee bit green. The car's along here. We'll get you in out of this weather."

He didn't look much older than some of her dad's students—Jamie Grayling was very tall and skinny with carrot-red hair and had the kind of beard young men grow in the hope it will make them look older, when it somehow manages to make them look even younger instead.

As he led them to a battered Range Rover, Theodora stifled a yawn. Their plane had landed the day before in Glasgow; then they'd caught a train north to Ullapool, where they had stayed the night in a bed-and-breakfast before boarding the ferry to Scornsay. Theodora's body was still on Boston time, and her eyelids felt as though they had sand underneath them.

"I imagine you're both a wee bit weary, so I'll run you over to the cottage straightaway," said Jamie.

Jamie had arranged for them to stay in an "authentic Victorian cottage" in the shadow of Castle Scornsay. Theodora was looking forward to seeing her first real castle.

"Can we stop and see the castle first?" she asked.

"Aye," said Jamie. "Not that there's much to see."

"What do you mean?"

"Didn't I mention? Castle Scornsay is a ruin." Jamie said it *rune*, with a rolled *R*. "There is one surviving wing, but it was an eighteenth-century addition anyway, and the rest is pretty much glued together with ghosts."

Theodora's shoulders sagged. In her imagination, old Dr. Grayling (this was when she was imagining him as a little gray man, bent with age) had handed her a ring of ancient iron keys to the castle and said with a wink, "I shouldn't really do this—it's against the rules—but I know you'll be careful. Have a good time exploring!"

She looked out the window at the passing countryside—green hills dotted with sheep on one side of the road, and cow pastures dotted with the funny, shaggy red highland cattle on the other. Then they left the farmland and drove through a stretch of moorland. Theodora's heart did a funny flip-flop when she saw it. There was the green-gold moor, and the silver-blue fingers of the deep-sea loch—only now it wasn't a picture on TV, it was real.

Next, Jamie took a turn and they were following the sea road again, with a dizzying drop-off to the right. They turned a corner, and there was the castle.

"And here we are," said their guide brightly as he brought the Range Rover to a bone-rattling stop in the graveled space in front.

Castle Scornsay was indeed a magnificent ruin. From the pile of rubble, among which sheep were placidly grazing, there rose a single, nearly intact tower.

"When was it destroyed?" Theodora asked, expecting Jamie to name some battle centuries past.

"In the early seventies. Some picnickers fell through a damaged floor. It was decided to renovate the castle, and the unsafe portions were all pulled down, with the aim of reconstructing them. Of course they ran out of money before they got very far, so a rubble is all we have. And the ghosts, of course."

Castle Scornsay didn't look haunted at all—just fallen down, as though its ghosts had decided they could find a better castle to haunt. But just as Theodora was turning away, she caught a glimpse of something white, flitting between some big blocks of stone that had fallen from the ruined ramparts. When she turned back to see what it was, it was gone. Small, like an animal, but not solid, like a lamb. Theodora stared at the blocks of stone, waiting to see if the white figure would reappear.

"Earth to Theodora . . . are you coming?"

She realized that Jamie and her dad were standing in the doorway of the cottage. How long had she been standing there, looking at the castle?

"Coming."

It hardly seemed possible, but the cottage was even better than it had looked in the photos he had e-mailed them—so storybook-perfect that Theodora half-expected Mrs. Tiggy-Winkle, the hedgehog washer-woman from the Beatrix Potter books, to open the door. The door was painted bright blue and flowers bloomed in the windowboxes. A curl of peat smoke rose from the chimney.

"Oh, good, someone's lit the fire. Theresa must have been by," said Jamie, opening the door, which was unlocked.

"Who is Theresa?" asked Andy, as they went in.

"Mrs. Fletcher, over the hill," said Jamie.

In the little kitchen, a fire was burning, and on the table were a bouquet of bluebells and a plate of fresh scones covered with a napkin. Through a doorway was a tiny sitting room, with another fire and cozy chairs and a window seat. Up the staircase were a bathroom and two bedrooms, all tiny. Mr. Oglethorpe complained only half-jokingly that he would have to sleep with his feet hanging out the window, but Theodora didn't hear him: It was a perfect miniature dollhouse. She felt considerably more cheerful.

Jamie had plugged in an electric kettle, which was just coming to a boil, and he got busy making tea while Theodora's dad wrestled their large American suitcases up the narrow Scottish staircase. Theodora stood and looked out the window over the kitchen sink. Barely visible on the next hill, so that it looked no larger than a Monopoly house, was a large farm house. On the kitchen windowsill was a pair of binoculars, and Theodora raised them to her eyes and trained them on the tiny house. The speck suddenly sprang into sharp focus, transformed into a big, rambling stone farmhouse that seemed to have sprouted additions in every direction. A large, shaggy gray dog lay asleep on the front stoop. It raised its head briefly, as if it felt Theodora's gaze.

"What's that?" asked Theodora, pointing toward the house.

"That's the Lodge, the Fletchers' place. I suppose they're your landlords while you're here. This is their cottage."

Over tea Jamie explained how he had come to be curator of the museum.

"I finished my degree at university two years ago and just wasn't having luck getting a job anywhere, and six months ago I got a letter from the Scornsay Tourism Bureau that the former curator, Ranald Ransay, had finally expired at the age of ninety-eight, leaving the museum in disarray. So I decided to come home to Scornsay and straighten things out. I'm still discovering the things old Ranald had stowed away in drawers! I'm hoping to clear away the antiquarian cobwebs and make it a real museum run on modern museum principles."

Jamie set down his empty tea mug and took the car keys from his pocket.

"You'll be wanting to relax after your flight. Why don't I fetch you in the morning and take you round to the museum? About nine?"

Theodora and her dad soon found themselves alone in the cottage, staring at each other across the table. Theodora gasped and clapped a hand to her mouth.

"What?" asked her father.

"We let him get away without telling us about the

ghosts! If the castle is glued together with them, there have to be good stories." She couldn't bring herself to tell her dad about the white shape she'd seen flitting among the castle ruins.

Andy Oglethorpe smiled and took a swig of tea. "Is that how you plan to spend your time here? Ghost-busting?"

"Well, I certainly can't spend it exploring the castle," she pointed out.

"When we were first married," said her dad, "your mom was convinced we had a poltergeist."

"You mean the kind that likes to throw dishes and move the furniture?"

Andy Oglethorpe nodded. Theodora waited to see if he would say more. Lately he had begun telling stories about the years just before Theodora was born, and she loved those rare, precious glimpses into the secret room of her parents' life together.

"Except this poltergeist liked to make drawings in the steam on the mirror and rearrange things on the dresser. And her poltergeist was responsible for lost socks and things like that. She began leaving things out for it—safety pins, empty matchboxes, stray buttons, cough drops—so it would leave her car keys alone."

Theodora had a good picture in her mind of her mom with her hands on her hips, talking back to the poltergeist. "What happened to the ghost?"

"Well, you were born," said her dad. "We used to

joke that the ghost moved to a family where it could have undivided attention."

It was a long evening, and they were so far north that it took forever for night to fall. At last the Highland twilight began to gather into darkness, and it was time for bed. She climbed the stairs, leaving her dad fussing over the coals so they would burn all night.

She loved her room, with its old-fashioned blue and white wallpaper and its low bookcase under the window crammed with books. From the window she could see the castle, its outlines softening in the weird, long, Highland twilight.

There! And there! A small white shape darted among the castle's ruined walls and tumbled stones. It was just a wisp of a thing, not solid.

She shook her head and turned away.

Jet lag, Theodora told herself firmly. She got into her sleep things, an old T-shirt and leggings, then pulled on heavy socks and climbed into bed. In the little bookcase there was a slim volume by a Miss Fiona MacDonald, titled *Ghosts and Other Legends of Scornsay,* published by the Scornsay Heritage Museum in 1909. Theodora picked it up to see what it said about Castle Scornsay, but it didn't have an index, and she had to turn each page, tediously scanning the text for a mention of the castle. Before she had gotten very far, her head sank onto the pillow and the book fell from her hands.

6

Faerie Tears, Dragon Teeth

J AMIE GRAYLING CAME to fetch them early the following morning. The island's fishermen and farmers had long been up, but most of the dozen little shops along Scornsay's main street were still shuttered as the Range Rover slowed to a stop outside a narrow storefront with a freshly painted sign that read SCORNSAY HERITAGE MUSEUM.

As he fumbled with the lock, Jamie seemed as nervous as an explorer about to open a long-sealed Egyptian tomb. Mr. Oglethorpe seemed just as impatient for the door to open. Theodora hung back, suddenly apprehensive about what they might find inside. If it *was* another wyvern scale, what did that mean? Had another wizard come through a bolt-hole from some other century? Would he be a Gideon or a Kobold, and what sort of creature, if it *wasn't* a wyvern, might he have brought with him?

"There we are," said Jamie, as the door opened at last.

Theodora gazed around, trying to sort out the jumble of items assembled by the previous curator. It seemed that Jamie Grayling would have his work cut out for him to bring "modern museum principles" to the Scornsay Heritage Museum.

The first thing Theodora noticed was a tall cabinet that held an assortment of stuffed owls and foxes with startlingly lifelike gazes. Long, low display cases held nineteenth-century lace and needlework, farm implements, and faded brown photographs of islanders cutting peat, spinning wool, hauling in fishing nets, and engaged in a strange ritual hunt on a nearby island inhabited only by nesting seabirds. Theodora read the description of the smoked, salted seabirds and made a gagging face. In the photograph, the men and boys stood beside a towering heap of dead birds. The seabird hunters looked sullen and cold.

Theodora noticed one boy in the front row, standing in front of a man who might have been his father. The label on the case said that hunters were lowered in rope harnesses to raid the birds' nests that covered the cliff face. It sounded incredibly difficult and dangerous, but the boy looked proud to be here with the men, taking part in the important annual ritual. Like the others, he looked cold, but unlike them, he did not look sullen. He wore a crooked half smile.

Her attention was next drawn to one long case of fossils and minerals. She had spent many Sundays with Mikko at the Museum of Natural History at Harvard University and had especially liked the fossil room and the mineral collection, the stones in all their amazing colors and fantastic formations. She read the old, faded label in the case.

> **Faerie Tears and Dragon Teeth**. *Like the Picts before them, Scornsay's latter-day inhabitants often sought supernatural explanations for the fossils and mineral formations they discovered on the island. Deposits of volcanic zeolite were dubbed faerie tears and deposits of red oxide ore, dragon's blood. The island is unusually rich in magnetite, and the magnetic lodestones, as they were called, were probably used in early Pictish rituals. Fossil ammonites were explained as dragons' tails. Fragments of meteorites that fell to the ground were often preserved as faerie relics, and faerie folk and dragons also lend their names to locations on the island, including the waterfall known as the Faerie's Veil and the rock formation called the Dragon's Teeth.*

In the case itself were some fossils, and Theodora could see how you could look at them as parts of a dragon. There was also a clear gemstone, shaped like a long teardrop, in an elaborate gold setting. A label underneath said it was a faerie tear discovered on the site of Castle Scornsay and thought to have been a clan chief's kilt pin.

Jamie hung up their jackets and began to fuss over the museum's balky heating system, which was giving off loud metallic clangs. While he waited for Jamie, Andy Oglethorpe was reading a brass plaque mounted prominently on the wall, listing the museum's founders and its corporate sponsor. "I see one of your benefactors is Murdoch Single-Malt Whiskey. I thought I knew all the obscure little whiskies. Does the island have its own distillery?"

"No, I'm afraid it's a large, charmless factory in Glasgow. But MacKenzie Murdoch does keep a house here on the island. He is Scornsay's biggest benefactor. You have Murdoch Single-Malt to thank for your tickets. He has been very supportive of my mission to get the museum modernized." The heater began to produce heat, and Jamie began to clear papers off two chairs so they could sit down. "Murdoch has signed on to sponsor a little exhibit called 'The Old and New Religion,' about the intertwined histories of the Christian and pagan religions on the island. It's really quite fascinating."

On Jamie's tiny desk were laid out pictures of the island's *kirk*, or church, and resin castings of the strange carvings left behind by the island's earliest inhabitants, the mysterious Picts. There was a newspaper clipping about a clash between islanders and visiting Cosmic-Pagans, and a colorful poster announcing the Sacred Samhain Fire Festival. MUSIC! CRAFTS! FOOD AND DRINK! it read, and showed silhouettes of strange, antlered men dancing and leaping beside a bonfire. Looking at the antlered figures, Theodora pulled her sweater closer around her and looked down to discover she was wearing her mother's brooch. When had she put it on? Unconsciously she had formed a habit of rubbing it with her thumb, feeling the smooth red stone and the whorls of metal that formed a crouching dragon.

"What's Samhain?" Theodora asked. She pronounced it "Sam-hane."

"Sow-un," Jamie corrected her. "It's All Hallows' Eve—the Celtic Halloween," said Jamie. "But enough about that! I know you're eager to see the scale."

He went to a locked cabinet and removed a small, clear plastic box lined with first-aid cotton. With an air of ceremony, he handed the box to Mr. Oglethorpe.

Theodora craned her neck to see. Wycca's scale had been a deep, iridescent purple-black, like a large sequin. But this scale was different. The Scornsay scale (if that was what it was) was duller, rougher, almost like sharkskin. By the light of the lamp it gave off faint flashes of opal fire, but nothing like the rainbow dazzle of the wyvern scale.

Theodora felt a little shiver go down her spine. She had almost convinced herself that Wycca and her baby had been a fluke, a hiccup in time. But now, looking at the scale resting on the bed of cotton, she felt a fresh rush of wonder, an electric prickle of mingled disbelief and joy—as though this new scale were a private, magical secret meant for her alone.

But then the dark memories came roaring back—what her brush with magic last summer had really been like, with Mikko's body taken over by the demon Febrys, Gideon and Kobold battling in the Oglethorpes' living room, and the hideous, many-eyed creature that was a shadow-wraith. How Kobold had threatened to trap her in her most painful memory, the hour of her mother's death. It was almost as though everything was happening all over again, and she could feel the unbearable sadness and pain beginning to well up inside her. With all the force of her mind, she shoved the memories away. As they faded she saw something else: Gideon's face.

That was how it always happened. Just when she was thinking that she could live without magic, even if it meant never Delving again, she would remember Gideon. But this time it was different. This time she realized that the sadness she always saw in his eyes when she tried to draw him had been sadness for her, because he knew it wasn't going to be easy being the new Theodora. And the memory of Gideon, of his kindness and the wisdom in his eyes, helped her push the dark memories back. Because she did have to hold on to the magic. Letting go would mean letting go of Gideon.

Andy Oglethorpe had taken a special eyepiece from his pocket and was using it to get a better look at the scale. Back at the university, he had access to an electron microscope, mass spectrometers, and one of the best libraries on the planet. Here he had a laptop, all the research he had been able to copy onto a thumb drive, and a jeweler's loupe. He set the loupe down and sat there, looking at the scale lying in the box, seemingly unaware of where he was or who was with him. Then he looked up and spoke to Jamie Grayling.

"Can you show me exactly where this was found?"

A slight tremor of eagerness in his voice made Theodora look up. Her father's eyes had the same smoldering fire as the mystery scale. It was a look she had seen before.

"Aye, I can take you there in the Rover."

But as they left, fat raindrops began to spatter the pavement, and they had to dash back inside the museum for cover.

"It will be too wet to climb the hill today, I'm afraid," said Jamie. "Unless you'd care to hire some scuba gear."

"That's all right," said Mr. Oglethorpe. "We could use another day to rest up after the flight and get our bearings."

Out the window Theodora could see a girl who had taken shelter in the doorway of the shop across the street. She was a year or two older than Theodora, tall, with a head of loose, dark curls. She was wearing a skirt and a dark sweater under a light blue anorak. Her legs were bare, and between the hem of her skirt and the tops of her green mud boots, her knees were pink with cold. As she stood under the awning, a truck full of sheep slowed to a stop, and the driver, a boy of about seventeen, shouted something to her. It was clear from the girl's expression that she was turning down the offer of a lift in a confident, cheeky way, her body language clearly saying, *As if.* The driver dished something right back at her. They both laughed, and he drove off.

Theodora turned around to see what her dad was doing and found him engrossed with Jamie in a map that, unfolded, covered most of the curator's desk. She turned back to the window.

Now an unusual figure was making its way down the narrow street of the village: a woman with short silver hair, dressed all in black, over which she wore a long, vaguely Asian coat. She carried a large black umbrella with a blue lining in a pattern of clouds. Mikko had one like it back home, but this one was curious. The cloud lining seemed odd somehow, as though it were made out of a piece of real sky, or as though a movie of a blue sky with puffy clouds were being projected inside the umbrella.

As the woman passed in front of the museum, she glanced in the window, and her dark eyes met Theodora's. There was the faintest flash of recognition, although Theodora was certain she had never seen the woman before. Now that Theodora could see the umbrella up close, it seemed completely unremarkable. Then the woman with the curious umbrella crossed the street and went into the post office.

When she got back to her weaver's studio at the Curlew's Nest, Margery shook the rain from her umbrella with its lining of blue sky and hung it by the door, then eagerly undid the parcel she had claimed at the post office. It was wrapped in brown paper and addressed to Margery MacVanish, Curlew's Nest Artists' Colony, Scornsay, Scotland. It was a cherished piece of furniture from her rooms in the old Elphinstone Hotel in Edinburgh—her wizard's pocket-desk of black lacquer, gilded with scenes from an imagined Japan. She now removed the desk from its leather traveling case and set it on the floor; pressing the secret catch, she stood back to watch the desk unfold.

Nothing happened.

She pressed a different catch, and now the desk

rapidly began to fold itself up smaller and smaller like a piece of origami until it was the size of a postage stamp, and then a piece of confetti, and then it was gone altogether.

Margery said a Very Bad Word in Wizard's Latin and got down on her hands and knees, like someone looking for a contact lens on speckled linoleum. She was muttering under her breath, still in Wizard's Latin, but no longer in curses: She was rapidly reciting a spell of Finding, and with a cry of triumph she wet a finger and touched it to a tiny black speck, like a flake of ground pepper. With the flake sticking to her finger, Margery peered at it through a special magnifying glass and used some tweezers to press a little catch only she could see.

Rapidly the desk unfolded to the size of a handkerchief, and Margery set it on the floor just in time. Now the desk began to unfold the way it was meant to. This it did like a camel getting to its feet: with an unsteady lurch, accompanied by a series of well-oiled clicks as various brass joints locked themselves in place. In a minute there it stood, a mid-eighteenth-century lady's spell-casting desk, with inkwells for regular and disappearing ink and a number of hidden compartments that had yet to yield their previous owner's secrets to Margery's prying.

"There!" Margery pulled up a chair and fondly caressed the wood, checking all the desk's pigeonholes and dovetailed drawers. She did her best thinking at her spell-casting desk, and since her arrival on the island, she had collected a lot to think about.

What had generated the jolt of magical power picked up by the O.I.G. sensors? The sensors suggested it was something far more powerful than an ordinary bolt-hole. Was it a portal to the limbo known as Never-Was? If a portal had opened, had anyone come through it, and if so, had they brought anything—animal, vegetable, or mineral—with them?

Local lore held that the hill of the Stane Folk was a place of Faerie, but lore was sometimes wrong. Her inspection of the hill, and of the islands' bogs and moors, had not turned up any traces of a magical portal. So she had turned her attention to the islanders themselves, and the question of whether any of them were not what they pretended to be. She had quickly come to focus her attention on the mysterious Mad John.

He had appeared out of nowhere, moved into a shepherd's hut on the moor, and promptly established himself as an eccentric hermit, if that term could be applied to someone who compulsively walked the island with his eyes on the ground.

Margery dipped her pen in the well of invisible ink, put on a pair of tinted spectacles so she could read what she was writing, and began to make out a report on Mad John. Gathering wild plants to make dyes for her weaving had given her an excuse to wander the moor close to the hermit's hut when Mad John was away on one of his prowls. There had not been much to see at the camp. There were signs that his diet consisted of birds' eggs and fish. A lot of fish. Along with a battered tin plate and a knife and fork, she had found a fragment of mirror, apparently used to shave with, though any wizard could use a mirror for spellwork. She'd said a spell over the mirror so it would send Mad John's reflection to a mirror in her studio at the Curlew's Nest. She'd then transferred the reflection from that mirror to a piece of paper using a simple spell, and now had a sketch of the mystery man that she could show to Merlin. Looking at Mad John's face, she couldn't escape a feeling that she knew him, had seen him somewhere, somewhen.

Now she wrote down what she had learned about him. There wasn't much.

- Jealous of his privacy, dislikes people, or has something to hide. Maybe all three.
- No sign of equipment, magical or otherwise (except possibly the mirror).
- Is his madness a cover? Could he be a wizard? Ex- O.I.G.? G.A.W.A.? (Can Merlin check the academy yearbooks?)
- What is he looking for?
- Why can't he find it?

Margery took off her spectacles and rubbed the bridge of her nose. The last point was the most puzzling. If Mad John was a wizard of any skill, it would be a simple matter for him to find and retrieve the object he sought. That meant one of two things: He was a wizard, but had been stripped of his powers; or the object itself was powerful enough to keep itself from being found.

The first step was to try and determine who Mad John really was.

Margery blotted her invisible report, folded it, and hid it for good measure in one of the desk's secret compartments. Then she got a fresh piece of paper, dipped her pen in regular ink, and wrote a short letter to Merlin. When she had finished, she folded the letter and put it in an envelope, to which she added the mirror sketch of the hermit's face. Then she addressed the envelope to Merlin and slid the letter into one of the spell-casting's desk's pigeonholes, the one marked with a label that said OUT. There was a muffled sound like a tiny bell, and the letter vanished, on its way to Merlin.

Then Margery sat at her desk and thought about the young girl she had seen in the window of the museum, the girl she knew to be Theodora. A girl half-grown into her looks in that awkward, twelve-year-old way, not quite comfortable in her skin. But her face—her face had the most remarkable expression, a window on an inner life in which a powerful storm had just passed. The face of a young girl who had just made an important decision.

A face bright with a brand-new determination that was not yet, not completely, courage.

7

The Field of Stones

THAT NIGHT THEODORA dreamed of the wizards,
the wyverns, and everything.

Usually when she had this dream, it was about finding the baby wyvern in the tree in her backyard, or
watching the wizards battle in the Oglethorpes' living
room, or watching Mikko, possessed by a demon, make
an anchovy omelet with chocolate sprinkles.

But this time the dream was different. She was in her
bedroom, dressed in a pink sari. She had a large book
open in front of her, which looked like a textbook but
seemed to be about dragons. She was chanting something

in a funny language while she molded a creature out of clay. Once it had the shape of a dragon, the Theodora of the dream set it on the floor and it uncurled into a tiny, living creature that began to grow, rapidly doubling in size every few seconds until it ran out of room, its reptilian head scraping the ceiling and its scaly sides pressing against the walls. When it lashed its tail, it knocked the lamp over, and Theodora could hear Mikko's rapid, I-mean-business footsteps coming down the hall.

The door opened and Mikko stuck her head into the room and started to say "Theodora," but all that came out was a "Th." She did not seem at all surprised by the enormous dragon. She was staring at Theodora as if she had seen a ghost. Stammering and looking confused, Mikko backed out of the room, murmuring as she closed the door, "I'm *so* sorry, Mrs. Oglethorpe. We all thought you were dead."

And in the dream Theodora looked in the mirror and saw she was no longer herself in a pink sari, but a girl she recognized from old pictures as her twelve-year-old mother, wearing a faded YMCA camp T-shirt and denim cutoffs.

Theodora woke up, her heart beating rapidly, confused at first to find herself in a strange room. For a minute she lay remembering where she was and why; then she sat up, thinking back over her dream. *It must have been that scale,* she thought. Jamie Grayling's mysterious scale had awakened enough memories of the whole wizard business to plant the dream in her mind. Or maybe her dad, telling that story about her mom and the poltergeist.

That was it: Her brain had scrambled those two things, the scale and the ghost story, the way your brain does when you're dreaming. It didn't mean anything.

She got out of bed and went over to the chair, where she had left her backpack. The brooch with the red stone was still pinned to her sweater. Theodora unpinned it and ran her fingers over the abstract swirl that formed a crouching dragon, trying to remember other times she'd seen her mom wear the pin. Was she just imagining that she remembered her mother putting it on? Was it just some junk that had gotten pushed to the back of her jewelry box?

The dream was fading, but the memory of the girl in the mirror stayed with her: a face familiar and yet unfamiliar, her mother as Theodora had never known her, looking out at her daughter across the gulf of time. As though she had a secret to share, but a secret it was too soon to tell.

Her dream had put Theodora in a funny mood, and she decided a walk would help clear her head. She quickly put on a heavy fleece hoodie, jeans, and two pairs of socks—her feet hadn't really been warm since they had arrived in Scotland. Even when it seemed warm enough for a T-shirt, the wind could come suddenly, without warning, bringing in a sudden chill from the sea. On her way downstairs she paused to peek in at her dad's room; his bed was empty. So was the bathroom. On the kitchen table was a note: "Gone to see the site. Back soon. Dad."

Besides the signs of a hasty breakfast, there was evidence that her father had stayed up late researching the scale mystery. His laptop was plugged in to a European current adapter to recharge, a detailed map of Scornsay was still spread out on the table, and there was a mug with a quarter inch of cold coffee in the bottom. She peeked at his scribbled notes but couldn't make sense of them—something to do with beta-keratin, whatever that was.

In the cupboard she found a box of cereal that looked suspiciously like shredded cardboard with petrified raisins. She couldn't bring herself to try it and ended up taking down a loaf of bread and a jar of jam. She made herself a jam sandwich and a cup of instant coffee, thinking it might help with her jet lag. The bread and jam were delicious; the coffee was bitter, but she drank it anyway. Then she put on her jacket, put her journal and an apple into her backpack, left her dad a note, and went out. A minute later she was back: She picked up the binoculars from the kitchen windowsill and slipped them around her neck, then went out again.

All around the cottage in every direction stretched a landscape of silent gold-green moor probed here and there by fingers of silver-blue loch. Standing in front of the castle, she could see the Fletchers' farmhouse way away on top of the next hill, and some white dots near it that must be sheep. The single paved lane—what Jamie had called "the wee, mad road"—twisted away out of sight. That was all. It was like being on the moon.

She meant to head out onto the moor to see if she could find the exact view of the castle shown in the brochure, the image that had tugged so hard on her mind. But she found her footsteps taking her to the ruins of the castle instead. There was a sign cautioning visitors to explore at their own risk. Here and there fragments of sheep fencing remained from a halfhearted attempt to shore up the crumbling foundation. As she approached, a sheep and her half-grown lambs looked up from their grazing spot, in a ruined castle hall now carpeted with grass. The same tug she'd felt from the image of Scornsay on TV tugged at her now, and she stepped past another cautionary sign showing a stick man recoiling from falling boulders.

Theodora wandered from room to room through the skeleton of the castle, peering through doorways, climbing over the fallen chimney of a giant fireplace. She closed her eyes and imagined the hall as it must have been seven hundred years before: a fire burning, a long table set for a feast with gleaming goblets and a roast boar with an apple in its mouth, a jester juggling, and presiding over it all, the king and queen. Then she caught herself thinking, *And a wizard,* and stopped herself. The wind kicked up and whistled through the gaps in the stone, sounding uncannily like a human whisper. Theodora pulled up her hood and walked out of the shadow of the ruined wall back into the sun.

All of a sudden she heard a sharp bark, and a small dog with enormous ears bounded up to her, its eyes almost hidden in its dense black fur, its bright white teeth and pink tongue flashing in a canine smile. It wasn't a Scottie, but some other kind of terrier whose name she didn't know. The dog's whole hindquarters wiggled with joy, and it leaped up to lick Theodora's face. Then it bounded back, head down, tail in the air, in the universal dog invitation, *Let's play!* It spun and raced away, bounding over the enormous stone blocks and barreling through tiny openings in the walls.

Theodora laughed and followed at a run, doing her best to keep the dog in sight. She climbed over a tumbled stone staircase in time to see the dog on the wall above her, its tongue hanging out as it panted. It seemed to be laughing.

She was standing there, catching her breath, when she heard people approaching: young voices, and with them a low, deep bark. The terrier heard them too: It pricked up its ears and then, as Theodora watched, it rapidly faded to dark gray and then light gray and then a gauzy shadow, and suddenly it wasn't there at all.

It had disappeared, right before her eyes.

Theodora didn't do any of the things people do in movies when something disappears. She didn't rub her eyes and stare or cry out. She felt as though her legs had turned to jelly, and she sat down hard on the ground, covering her eyes, afraid to look at where the dog had been. Then she peered out cautiously through her fingers. The spot where the dog had stood was still empty, but as she watched, something fell from the wall where the terrier had been perched. It landed at Theodora's feet. Her heart began to pound, and she scrambled forward on her hands and knees and picked it up.

It was a dog's collar of leather, cracked and worn with age. Set into it was a tarnished metal plate with letters engraved on it. Theodora removed some encrusted dirt with her fingernail and made out the word UILLEA and either an N or an M at the end.

She was still looking at the collar when the deeper bark sounded again, much closer. Theodora put the collar in her pocket just as a large gray dog bounded up, ahead of a boy and girl.

It was one of those huge dogs the size of a pony—a wolfhound or deerhound or one of those hounds, anyway—and Theodora jumped back against the wall before it could knock her down. But at a whistle from the girl, it sat down meekly and began to pant, its head on one side and one ear turned inside out. Sitting down, it was nearly as tall as Theodora.

"Odin, stay," said the girl.

"Sorry," said the boy.

She recognized the girl as the one she had seen taking shelter from the cloudburst. The newcomers were obviously brother and sister. They were both tall, with dark, wavy brown hair. It made Theodora aware that the fine Scottish mist was turning her own hair into rusty brown Brillo. The boy's face was open and friendly, the girl's face more closed, not offering anything. She seemed older, and not just because she was taller.

"What were you doing, running away from a bee? We could see you from up in the tower, running around in circles."

"I was chasing a dog," Theodora said. *And then he just disappeared.* She looked up at the castle's one intact tower, puzzled. If they had been able to see her, why hadn't they spotted the dog?

"You're Theodora, aren't you?" said the girl. "You're staying in our parents' cottage. I'm Catriona. That's my brother, Colin."

"Hi," the boy said. "Jamie asked us to swing by and check on you, and if you wanted, to bring you to the Stane Folk." Seeing Theodora's blank look, he added, "The spot where the scale was found."

"You mean where *you* found it," said Catriona, teasingly.

Colin ignored her. "There are some cool Pictish carvings there too."

Theodora remembered reading something about Picts in the guidebook. She was still thinking about the vanishing dog, and she realized that for some reason, Colin and Catriona hadn't been able to see the little black terrier. Theodora felt her face grow hot with confusion.

They couldn't see him—but she could. How was that possible?

"Do you want us to take you?"

"I'm sorry, what?"

"To the Stane Folk." Colin's look seemed to say, *You're either really jet lagged or really slow.* "It's a hike, if you're up to it." He seemed doubtful.

Suddenly Theodora wanted to go, to get away from the castle and push the disappearing dog incident to the back of her mind for the time being.

"Sure. Let's go."

"Odin!" Catriona said sharply. "Come here."

The hound had been digging at the base of the wall where the terrier had disappeared.

"He smells something," said Colin. "A rabbit, probably."

Odin came over and pressed his wet, muddy nose to the pocket where Theodora had the old dog collar. He whined and pawed at the pocket.

"Odin, down," said Catriona.

Theodora slipped a hand into her pocket and felt the old leather, the smooth, cool metal of the plate, the pattern of the letters. U-I-L-L-E-A . . .

Catriona had distracted Odin with a dog treat, and now they were lagging behind, dog and girl racing in wide circles.

"Come on," said Colin. "No use waiting for them. Catriona's incapable of walking in a straight line, and so is Odin."

It was a long hike. On the way, Theodora learned a little about the Picts and quite a lot more about the Fletchers. Catriona was almost fourteen and would be starting her third year of secondary school, which was like ninth grade. Colin was two months younger than Theodora and would be moving up from primary school to his first year at the island's secondary school.

"Have you lived here all your lives?"

"Just since I was seven," said Colin. "Our mother's people have lived here for generations, and we're cousins of one sort or another to about a third of the folk on Scornsay."

"Where were you born?"

"Edinburgh. But we moved to London when we were still babies. Mother was studying art and working at a gallery."

"What does she do now?"

"Paints. Sells a few, shows a few, but mostly just paints. My dad has a job in Glasgow. You'd call him a fund-raiser. Basically he guilt-trips old, rich people so they'll leave their money to charities."

Theodora made a face. "Does he like it?"

Colin shrugged. "He's good at it, though—he's never home except on the weekend, and sometimes not even then. How is it having your dad be a professor?"

"He's working a lot even when he isn't traveling."

"What about your mum?" Colin asked.

Catriona and Odin had caught up with them, and suddenly Theodora found herself not wanting to explain that her mother had died of cancer. It always made other people act funny.

"My mom's not around anymore," she said. As she said it, she had a clear image of her twelve-year-old mom in the camp T-shirt, looking back at her from the mirror.

"Oh. Sorry," said Colin. Theodora could see the Fletchers run through all the possibilities in their minds. Catriona seemed to look at Theodora with new interest.

The question of what had happened to Theodora's

mother hung in the air for a moment, and then Odin suddenly darted after some unseen quarry, and Catriona dashed after him. Colin started talking about how, if archaeology didn't work out, he might study to be some kind of biologist, he wasn't sure what kind yet but maybe a marine biologist, and he had a lot of questions about Theodora's father's work, and Theodora was careful to steer the conversation away from the issue of mothers.

"We're almost there," Colin said. Up ahead Catriona was sitting on a stone wall, swinging her legs, waiting for them to catch up. Odin was at her feet, gnawing an enormous branch as though it were a mere stick. As Theodora and Colin came up, Catriona hopped down, whistled to Odin, and fell in beside them. She seemed content to leave the social stuff to her younger brother.

They came upon a road, and on the other side of it a glimpse of cliff and sea. Overlooking the sea was a scattered group of low concrete buildings that had been brightened with paint and a garden of cheery wooden whirligigs, fanciful carved people and animals, arms and wings wildly spinning in the wind. A carved sign proclaimed it THE CURLEW'S NEST.

"It's an early warning station left over from World War II. Now it's an artists' colony—just a bunch of old hippies. The stones are just on the other side."

They passed one large whirligig that seemed to be a kind of scarecrow, dressed in cast-off clothes faded by the sun and worried by the wind into rags. The irises of his painted eyes were bits of mirror that gleamed uncannily, and his mouth was set with teeth made from fragments of broken china saucer. When the wind blew, he flailed his arms and pumped his legs, as though pedaling a bicycle, and he made a rapid, wooden *th-th-th-th-thut* as a wooden clapper rattled in the wind.

They left the artists' colony behind and climbed another hill. Theodora's exhausted leg muscles would barely obey her. At last they reached the top, a windswept meadow dotted with stones and sheep. The only sign of Jamie and her dad was some equipment spread out among the stones.

"Eerie, isn't it?" said Catriona. "They call them the Stane Folk."

Each stone in the meadow was roughly the size and shape of a small child, and the effect was of a bunch of children—or dwarves—turned to stone. As you got closer, you could see they were carved with zigzags and spirals, shields and animals: a wolf, a goose with its neck craned backward, and something like an aquatic elephant or a dolphin with a strange, long snout.

Theodora wasn't spooked by graveyards—she spent a lot of time walking in Mount Auburn, the Victorian cemetery back home that was kind of like Cambridge's own Central Park—and she didn't get creeped out by mummies at the Museum of Fine Arts. But even in the bright sunlight, with the Fletchers and Odin there with her, there was something unsettling about the Stane Folk.

"I found the scale over here," said Colin.

He led them to one stone that stood out from all the rest—it was taller and square sided, like a pillar from a building. Theodora saw that it, too, was covered in carvings, its designs obscured with clinging scarlet lichen. At the base of the stone was a black-and-white marker, the same kind her dad used to indicate scale when he took pictures of things in the field. There were a lot of baby pictures of Theodora back home with a black-and-white marker to show the scale.

"Can we pull this stuff off and look at the designs?" Theodora asked.

Colin shook his head. "There isn't much to see. Someone's gone at the carvings with a hammer, and they're almost completely unreadable. Jamie thinks the old priests believed the carvings were the devil's work and had them removed. But it's funny they only did it to this pillar and not the other stones." Colin's accent was much softer than Jamie's, but he pronounced the word "stones" as "stanes."

All of a sudden Odin began to bark, and over the

hill came Jamie Grayling and her dad, carrying some battered aluminum sampling cases and a camera bag. Mr. Oglethorpe was wearing his faded Red Sox cap and a happy grin. He greeted his daughter and shook hands with Colin and Catriona and patted Odin on the head, then stood looking around at the Stane Folk.

"We've had a good look around already, but Colin, I'd love to hear from you how you found the scale. Exactly where at the pillar was it?"

Colin led him to the broken pillar stone, the base of which was much trampled by grazing sheep.

"Right there. It was lying on the dirt, and when it flashed in the sun, I noticed it. I thought it was a bit of zeolite. You know, a faerie tear. The rock shop in the village pays me for them, so I'm always looking."

Mr. Oglethorpe squatted beside the pillar, peering at the ground. "Was it by itself or stuck to something? Was there skin or flesh or anything else clinging to it? Was there any sign a bird or animal had eaten a meal there? Or a person, for that matter?"

"No. I would have noticed, too. It was just lying there."

Mr. Oglethorpe turned and looked back down the hill at the artists' colony below with its whirligig garden, and beyond that the cliff road and the sea.

Theodora could imagine what was going through his mind: If she were a large animal, the last place she would pick for a meal was an exposed hilltop that offered no cover. It was an unlikely spot to find a scale.

Down below in the whirligig garden the wooden scarecrow man pumped his legs in a sudden gust off the sea, the sun casting rainbows off his mirrored eyes.

8

On the Moor

THEODORA DIDN'T HAVE a chance the rest of that day to get back to the castle alone and try to find the ghost dog again. When she woke up the next morning, it was raining.

"What's Uilleam?"

Theodora and her father were sitting at the cottage's kitchen table. Mr. Oglethorpe looked up from the notes he'd taken at the site and some photocopied journal articles.

"Say that again?"

"You-ee-lee-um?" She said it slowly, to rhyme with "helium."

"How do you spell it?"

Theodora thought a moment, picturing the leather dog collar in her mind. "U-I-L-L-E-A-M, I think."

Mr. Oglethorpe buttered a second piece of toast and brushed some crumbs off the page of his journal. "Sounds like Latin. Maybe the Latin version of William?"

"Oh." Theodora sipped her coffee cautiously. It was from the pot her dad had brewed. Her dad hadn't said anything as she poured herself a mug and doctored it with milk. Real coffee was better than instant, but she was still surprised coffee didn't taste the way it smelled. She still wasn't sure she liked it, but now that she had poured it she was going to finish it.

"Where did you see it?"

Theodora froze for a moment, thinking he meant the ghost dog. Then she realized that her father was only asking where she had seen the word "Uilleam."

"In a book, in the bookcase next to my bed. About an old king."

As she said it, it occurred to Theodora that she had never finished Fiona MacDonald's book, the one about the legends of Scornsay. It was still up in the little bookcase underneath the window.

After breakfast it was still too wet to go out, so she went up to her room and found *Ghosts and Other Legends of Scornsay.*

There was the one about the Stane Folk, and one about the Faerie Tears—Fiona MacDonald didn't have much more to say about those legends than the labels on the case in Jamie's museum. But she finally found the part of the book that talked about Castle Scornsay. She was just settling in to read when she felt something jabbing her painfully in her hip. It was the dog collar. She must have taken it out of her pocket last night. Funny, she didn't remember leaving it on the bed. She tossed the collar onto the chair by the window and kept reading.

Fiona MacDonald had a lot more to say about the legends of Castle Scornsay.

Once long ago a clan chief sought to build his fortress on a hill that commanded the sea, but the spot was sacred to a great dragon. He consulted his sorcerer, who advised him to make the dragon an offering. So the chief offered the dragon gold, but the dragon said, "My scales are more precious than your gold." The chief then offered his finest battle sword, but the dragon said, "My talons are sharper than your sword." The chief said to his sorcerer, "The dragon will not take my gold or my sword," and the sorcerer advised him to offer the dragon something more precious still. The chief then offered the dragon his daughter, and the dragon said, "Your daughter is as beautiful as the mote in my eye. Your daughter I will have."

And so the clan chief's daughter was promised to the dragon to be his wife, and her father built the castle upon the dragon's hill. On the night of her wedding feast, the chief said to his daughter, "When the creature sleeps, stab it in the left eye, and take the carbuncle you find there. That is the Mote in the Dragon's Eye, more precious than gold." So the daughter hid a dirk in the bodice of her dress and was married to the dragon. After the wedding feast, the dragon took his wife away beneath the hill, to a chamber filled with gold and riches. When the dragon was sleeping she drew the dirk and stabbed her husband in the eye and cut out the carbuncle she found there. But the creature awoke with a cry and said, "Wife, wife, would you betray me?" and as its life's blood flowed away, it was transformed into a prince, sweet of face, passing fair of form. The dragon's wife returned to the home of her father, but in the single night she had spent under the dragon's hill, a hundred years had passed in the world above, and she was an old woman, and her father long dead.

What the heck is a carbuncle? Theodora wondered. She was just about to get up and go ask her dad when she noticed it had stopped raining. There was a rainbow. She was reaching for her camera when she saw something on the chair, something shaggy and gray.

The ghost dog was napping on the chair. It was not quite solid, and not quite misty, but some state halfway in between, and it seemed to get more solid when it breathed in and fainter when it breathed out.

Theodora stood rooted to the spot, afraid to move in case it would vanish. As she stood staring at the dog, it opened one eye and looked at her. It yawned, grew dark and solid, and jumped down on the floor, tail wagging.

At that moment Theodora heard her father come upstairs, and she panicked, picking up her bathrobe and throwing it over the dog just as her dad knocked and came in.

Theodora hoped she didn't look as guilty as she felt. Behind her back she could feel the thump of the ghost dog's tail against her leg, through the fabric of the bathrobe.

"You okay?" her dad asked. "You look as though you've seen a ghost."

Theodora was still holding Fiona's book. She held it up with a sheepish grin. "Just reading about them. You did kind of spook me."

"Well, it's stopped raining, and I'm going to head to the site. Do you want to come with me?"

Thumpa-thump went the dog's tail. *Thudda-thud* went Theodora's heart. Could her dad see the bathrobe moving?

"Um, no, I promised Dr. Naga I'd make some sketches while I was here. I want to practice drawing the castle."

"All right—just make sure you don't climb any of the unstable parts. No going behind the orange fencing. Jamie's cell number is by the phone if you need me, and so is Mrs. Fletcher's."

The thumping of the dog's tail had stopped, and for a moment, it seemed, so did Theodora's heart. Had the ghost dog escaped from under the bathrobe? Was he still visible? Then, out of the corner of her eye, Theodora saw the bathrobe creeping under the bed.

Fortunately, her dad's mind was clearly already on the scale mystery and getting to the site. He left the room and went down the stairs, whistling.

Theodora let out her breath and dropped to the floor to peer under the bed. There was no sign of the ghostly terrier, just his empty collar.

Once her dad was gone, Theodora made her way back to the castle. She found the spot where she'd first seen the little dog and set the collar on one of the fallen blocks of stone. Immediately the collar rose into the air, and within it a faint mist began to swirl and gather itself into a ghostly, doglike form. Then the mist grew darker, passing through all the shades of gray until it was black. And then the little terrier was there, solid and real.

"Well, hello there, Uilleam," Theodora said softly, holding out her hand. "Can I just call you William?"

William came over to her and pressed his wet, doggy

nose into her hand and sponged her cheek with a pink doggy tongue. His thick black fur was wet from the ground and his muddy paws left prints on her pants.

He felt real. He sounded real. He even smelled like wet dog. But when she tried to take his picture with her digital camera, the whole frame was strangely blurry.

How could it be? She stood there, puzzled, and William sat back on his haunches, panting.

"Whose are you?" Theodora wondered aloud. How long ago had people spelled the name William "Uilleam"? Back when kings and queens and courtiers and jesters had walked within these walls where sheep were now grazing?

"Do you talk?" she said to the little black terrier.

William merely laid his head on one side.

"I guess not." Theodora felt silly. She hadn't *really* thought he was going to open his mouth and speak English, like some Disney dog, but if he could materialize from an old dog collar, it didn't seem so unreasonable to think that he could communicate in *some* way, more than meaningful whines and barks while tugging on her sleeve.

She was just working up the nerve to reach out and pat him when the bright black eyes looked into her own and she felt her mind being—well, *sniffed*.

"Oh!" cried Theodora, falling backward and bumping her head on the broken stone wall. The connection was broken, and William sat there, looking at her with his large, dark eyes, his pink tongue flashing between his sharp white teeth as he panted.

When William's consciousness reached out and touched hers, she had instantly recognized the action for what it was. The dog was Delving. During the brief second her mind struggled against it, it hurt in a dull way, the way your ears hurt from the pressure when an airplane is in its final descent. But when the dog reached out again, Theodora quit struggling, and her mind and William's were joined.

All around her, the long-ago life of the castle had sprung into being. The picture she saw in her mind's eye was fuzzy, and objects were unexpected colors: The apple in the mouth of the roasted suckling pig was tan, not red, and the boughs of fresh greenery strewn on the floor were white. *Dog vision,* Theodora thought. She had teamed up with Milo to do a science-fair project on red-green color blindness in dogs. But if the ghost dog was color-blind, it smelled in Technicolor. Theodora smelled the many hunting dogs wandering the room and begging for scraps, the wood smoke from the fireplace, the roasted game and pies, the sachets the courtiers wore because no one ever took a bath, and the really bad breath of the queen. Under the table a dog just like William accepted a scrap of meat from the hand of a man. A short man with shoulder-length hair, a short beard, and a long, clever face. His slender, nimble hands reminded Theodora of Gideon's. Was he a wizard, like Gideon?

She felt a calm, peaceful feeling, a wordless assurance that William meant her no harm. He was there to protect her. She could have done without the Delving, but she trusted the little ghost dog, the way she had instantly trusted Gideon, even the way she had recognized the goodness in the demon Febrys.

Then abruptly the connection was broken, and with a rush the present came flooding back, in a thousand human-vision colors. Her vision was back to normal, and she had her human sense of smell back too.

A change had come over William. The ghost dog had lifted his little black nose to the wind and was quivering with excitement. A low tremor began deep inside him that rolled up and out of his throat as a growl. He exploded into action and sped away from the castle, kicking up clods of earth in his haste, tearing off across the wide green expanse. Theodora scrambled to her feet and followed.

The green-gold moor was much rougher than it looked, pocked with holes and boggy places and stones. She had a hard time keeping up, because she had to spend a lot of energy trying not to twist an ankle. But up ahead she could hear William's bark, and Theodora followed it toward a curious low structure that, as she came closer, appeared to be an abandoned hut. It was a small house of earthen walls half-sunk into the ground, so it seemed to be gazing out at the moor like the eye of a buried giant. It had a stout wooden door, which was barred, and a piece of metal stovepipe sticking out through its roof, but no windows.

As Theodora got closer, she changed her mind about the abandoned part. On one side of the door was a large blue water barrel, and beside it a red can with a spout. Theodora's dad had one like it to put gas in the lawn mower. Theodora bet this one held kerosene, for lamps and cooking. There was a strong smell of fish and what looked like a fresh garbage heap not too far from the house.

William was busily running his nose over every inch of the site. Then he suddenly looked up and barked.

Theodora suddenly felt herself being watched. But when she whirled around and scanned the moor, no one was there.

Then she turned to find a man standing in the open door of the hut.

He was about her dad's age, or maybe older. He was dark haired, with a face that was too thin and cold and lined to be handsome. His eyes were hollow with sleeplessness, and his cheeks and jaw were covered with a growth of stubble. Theodora couldn't see past him into the hut. But then, she didn't want to.

"I'm sorry," she stammered. "My dog ran up here. I

just came to get him back. I didn't realize anyone lived here."

"Dog? What dog?"

Of course William had chosen that moment to disappear. The man stepped forward, and Theodora could see there was something really odd about his eyes. They were old, much older than the rest of his face. Theodora was suddenly hot, then cold, then dizzy. Her mouth was dry, and she couldn't make any words come out.

The man stepped forward, locking his eerie eyes with hers.

"Are you looking for it too? Have you found it?" he demanded in a hoarse whisper. "You must give it to me. It's mine, you see." He lifted a hand to scratch the stubble on his chin. Something stuck to the back of his hand flashed oddly in the sunlight.

Then behind her there was a deep bark, and a familiar female voice shouted cheerfully, "There you are."

Catriona Fletcher came up with Odin and linked her arm in Theodora's, drawing her away from the door. The strange man shrank back from the enormous dog, but Odin was much more interested in sniffing all the spots where William had been applying his own nose minutes before.

"Sorry for the intrusion. We'll just be going now," said Catriona in a firm voice.

The odd man wasn't listening. He took a look at

Odin, disappeared into his hut, and shut the door.

"Thanks," said Theodora, as she and Catriona walked back to the cottage.

"Oh, Mad John is pretty harmless. He mostly just mumbles and wanders and smells of fish. But I wouldn't want to go near his place alone. I'm surprised you did."

Theodora decided to tell the truth, or part of it, anyway. "I made friends with a little dog at the castle yesterday. He seems to be a stray. He ran off this way and I tried to catch him and ended up at the hut." Theodora described William, minus the disappearing act.

"Oh?" Catriona looked at Theodora. "I don't remember seeing a dog like that. Well, he must belong to Mad John."

"How did you know I was out there, anyway?" Theodora asked.

Catriona laughed. "Colin has him under surveillance. He's convinced Mad John is really some kind of antiquities poacher, selling Pictish artifacts on eBay or something. He saw you run off this way. We split up to look for you."

They could see Colin now, headed toward them, something like a long-lens camera around his neck. When he got closer, Theodora could see it was a scope, the kind really serious birdwatchers used. She and Mikko had seen birders using them to count songbirds in Mount Auburn Cemetery.

As he approached, Theodora thought that if they didn't look so much alike, you could almost forget the Fletchers were related. Colin was so open and enthusiastic, and Catriona so closed-up-in-cool, a walking "whatever." But now Catriona was helping her. Theodora couldn't figure her out. Maybe it was just that she was used to getting her little brother out of jams, and rescuing came naturally.

Colin came up to them, brimming with excitement.

"Did you see inside?" he asked.

"No. I wasn't trying to," said Theodora.

Colin was clearly disappointed. "Drat. I'm sure if I could only see inside—"

"—you'd see he sleeps on a nasty old mouse-eaten mattress and doesn't sweep up the crumbs," said Catriona. "Honestly, Col! You think that loony bird has the wits to sell artifacts on the Internet? He doesn't even have electric out here."

"Not here," said Colin darkly. "This is just the front. The Mad John thing, it's all an act."

"I don't think so," said Theodora quietly.

"Why not?" said Colin.

"Because," said Theodora, "I saw his eyes. Who is he, anyway?"

"No one knows his real name," said Catriona. "Everyone just calls him Mad John. He showed up last fall and started living out on the moor."

117

"But he's not mad," said Colin. "He's always out with one of his funny old maps. Patched things, old tattered paper, all torn and stained. They look like they're torn out of an old book."

"Well, even if he's not crazy, he's too odd for me," said Catriona, with a shuddery shrug of her shoulders. "And he smells of fish."

"A lot of men on Scornsay smell of fish," her brother pointed out.

Theodora pictured the man with the strange eyes out with one of his old, patched maps. They were back at the castle now, and she was glad of even its ruined walls, glad to be off the moor.

"What do you think he's looking for, exactly?" Theodora said.

Colin's eyes lit up, while Catriona rolled hers in a way that seemed to say, *Here we go again.*

"Lots of people lived on Scornsay. The Picts, the Celts, the Vikings. It could be anything, really. An artifact, a golden brooch. A ring."

Theodora remembered the legend she'd read about in the book and started to ask Colin if he knew what a carbuncle was, when the church bells in the distance began to peal ten o'clock.

Catriona groaned. "Gotta go to work," she said. "Ta." She ran off through one of the ruined archways, down the hill in the direction of the village.

"Where does she work?"

"Some days she makes beds at the B and B, some days she helps serve lunch at the nursing home. She's saving up for a school trip to London. She'd love to be discovered."

"Discovered as what?"

Colin laughed. "I don't think it matters. Actress, model, singer. So long as she can leave Scornsay and be rich and famous."

Theodora was suddenly self-conscious of her Brillo hair blowing in her face and her muddied cargo pants. Catriona could somehow look glamorous in mud boots with red, chapped knees showing and her hair blowing in her face. Theodora could imagine her being famous some day.

"What about you?" said Colin. "Are you going to be a scientist, like your dad?"

Theodora shrugged. "I don't know. I like math. I'm pretty good at drawing. Maybe an engineer, like my Aunt Jane. I haven't figured it out yet."

Colin hopped back up on a low wall and began to walk along it, higher and higher, his back to Theodora as he talked more about his own plans to be a marine biologist. "I'm trying to get into an advanced science program in a school on the mainland. But I haven't told my dad yet. He never says anything, but I can tell he hopes I'll go into something to do with charities and money, like he did."

Theodora suddenly wondered whether Colin was

being nice because his mother had asked him to, or because Theodora's father was a scientist and getting close to Theodora was his way of getting to know a scientist who worked at Harvard. Could his friendliness genuinely be because he liked her?

Colin turned around and jumped down to the ground. "Cat and I were headed to the Veil tomorrow. You could come along, if you like."

"Veil? Like the thing you wear over your face?"

Colin nodded. "It's a waterfall. It's supposed to be the veil of the faerie queen. Newlyweds used to walk through it, for luck. There are some good Pictish carvings on the rocks behind the falls."

"Oh, cool. Sure."

"If it's not raining tomorrow, we'll stop by for you around nine, okay?"

"All right."

On her way back to the cottage, Theodora actually forgot about William. She just let her mind wander, and her thoughts had circled around to Catriona and Colin when she caught herself. She had a sudden mental image of Mad John's weird and empty eyes and the strange way the light had glanced off the back of his hand.

9

The Owl and Moon Club

IN ALMOST EVERY city of a certain antiquity and size, in a quarter where buildings stand unchanged by the passage of centuries, you might be lucky enough to spy a strange, crooked building with an owl weathervane. It's just a glimpse seen across the other rooftops, but you're intrigued by its air of quaint mystery and gargoyle downspouts. You decide to get a closer look, but you search for it in vain in your guidebook or on your map. Finally you decide to set out in its general direction through the maze of narrow streets, doing your best to keep the weathervane in sight.

But it never seems any closer. Around every corner, you find your way blocked by a snarl of delivery trucks, or you discover a dead end. You may finally think you see the strange, crooked building at the end of the block, only to discover it is a different address, a building with a rooster weathervane and cherub downspouts. At last, tired and discouraged, you give up. Across the rooftops the owl weathervane winks in the sun, and the gargoyles seem to be laughing at you.

You have just run afoul of the Owl and Moon Club and its famous way-losing cobblestones.

Iain Merlin O'Shea knew all about the cobblestones, and before setting out on his errand for Margery MacVanish, he had put on his special Featherweather Way-finders ("Why wear ordinary galoshes when you can have a pair of Way-finders?"). At eleven o'clock he arrived on the doorstep of the Edinburgh chapter of the Owl and Moon Club with Vyrna in her dog-coat disguise and a leash, which she tolerated with evident disgust.

"Good to see you, Professor," said the doorman, handing back Merlin's membership card. "May I take your familiar for you?"

Merlin helped Vyrna slip out of the magical dog coat and she shook out her wings vigorously, sneezing a shower of sparks. The doorman looked a little uneasy—dragons were a decided rarity in the twenty-first century, rumored to persist only in some remote locales away from human habitation.

"Shall I take her along to the Familiars Parlor for you, sir?"

"No, I'm afraid she might view some of the smaller familiars as snacks. Could she have the run of the Aerial Room, if no one's using it?"

The Aerial Room was a vaulted gymnasium for the use of wizards who wanted to practice their flying skills safely away from the gape of mortals.

Merlin made his way down the carpeted corridor, past the shop where cloaks of invisibility might be left for mending and crystal balls checked for astigmatism. He passed the bar that served Twelve Elves ale and Dragon's Blood stout and a very special old sherry that made you weightless for six hours.

Merlin came at last to the library. He went past the sign reading PLEASE CHECK ALL FAMILIARS and entered the main reading room. To one side, a staircase led to the mezzanine, and above that a ladder led up into the dome that housed the club's excellent telescope. Thaqib was perched, as usual, at a curved desk at the back of the reading room, poring over an ancient celestial atlas, a Moorish text with paintings of comets in the margins. At his elbow was a brass beaker covered with mysterious signs, from which Thaqib drank a minty tea.

The librarian of the Edinburgh chapter of the Owl

and Moon Club was an expatriate *sahir*, or Arabic court wizard. Thaqib had come through a bolt-hole many years ago, fleeing the Crusades. Nominated many times to be the head of G.A.W.A., he always demurred, saying he wanted to be left alone with his books and his telescope.

"*Salaam*, Thaqib," Merlin said.

Thaqib was as tall and gaunt as Merlin was short and stout. He glanced at the other wizard over his spectacles and got to his feet.

"Arch-Mage," he said, using the polite but old-fashioned form of address that had passed from common use among wizards. "What can I do for you?"

Merlin glanced around quickly to see how crowded it was in the reading room. Just a few wizards, consulting the latest issue of *Rune & Ruminator* or attempting the crossword in the *Warlockian*. One particularly elderly patron was napping beneath the pages of the *Spell-Intelligencer*.

"I need to consult the Academy yearbooks from the early 1900s," he said. "Say, from oh-three to oh-six."

Thaqib went to a nearby bay of shelves. The room was lined floor to ceiling with shelves, which were crammed with scrolls and leather-bound books of all sizes. There was a ladder, but Thaqib clapped his hands and called out a word in a language that was a pidgin of Wizard's Latin and a smattering of Djinn, the Arabic dialect spoken by genies. Three blue-leather albums on a higher shelf wriggled their way free of their shelf-mates and floated down into the *sahir*'s arms.

Thaqib handed the heavy books to Merlin. "These are the yearbooks for oh-three, oh-four, and oh-five."

"Wait," said Merlin, "what about the yearbook for oh-six?"

"Not on the shelf," Thaqib said with a shrug.

Merlin took the heavy blue books to a private corner and soon surrendered himself to memories of his schooldays. He said a charm over the portraits, so he could study his old classmates without their winking or wincing or crossing their eyes. Then he turned to the beginning and began to page through the pictures of his junior-year classmates from G.A.W.A. Academy.

There was Oberon "Obie" Adams-Apple, the class clown.

Juan-Esteban Estrella y Luna, who used to employ Obie as a taster at meals in order to elude female class-mates desperate enough to slip a love powder into his soup. Someone had told Merlin that Juan-Esteban had stayed on as the Academy's master of fencing and fire-work, and the girls were still swooning over him.

Here were the Charmways boys—Caspian, Cuthbert, Cedric, and Cyril—quadruplets who used to animate their shirt collars and then set them singing as a barber-shop quartet.

Cordelia Crumplewing, clumsy and shy and forever scorching the cuffs of her sweaters on the Bunsen burner in Alchemy II. When extremely embarrassed, she used to take on the pattern of the wallpaper and disappear.

Oh, and here was the great beauty, Miranda Mothwings-Brown, president of the Incantations Society and the Chinese Sorcery Club. Brainy, too, with a double major in languages and levitation theory. She had been his old Geology lab partner, married a Charmways—he'd forgotten which one—and had a large brood of rambunctious children—and grand-children, now.

He took out the image of Mad John that Margery had sent—it had appeared magically with her letter in the pigeonhole of his own spell-casting desk—and compared it with every face in the yearbook. He could not find a match.

He did linger over three faces where there seemed to be a faint resemblance. There was something about the sweeping eyebrows of Mercurio Marchbank, the long, clever chin of Tommy Oddbody, and the high cheek-bones of Arlo Glimmerglass. But none of the eyes were exactly right.

Odd eyes, the ones in the mirror sketch Margery had sent. Very odd eyes.

Merlin was about to close the book when his gaze

fell on a blacked-out face among the portraits. Right between Viola Ladyslipper and Thelonius Lake, there was a black rectangle and the words "Ellic Lailoken: Portrait Not Supplied" underneath.

Merlin let his gaze wander to the framed portraits of famous wizards that lined the room. He had forgotten all about Ellic Lailoken. He came from a long line of wizards, talented but high-strung and perhaps even a little unbalanced. He had left the Academy near the end of their senior year. A scandal of some kind, it had been whispered—but whatever had happened, it was hushed up. Suddenly Lailoken was gone, and none of the masters at the Academy had much to say about it. There had been rumors that he'd broken into the Cage, the locked inner sanctum of the Rarer Book Room of the Academy library, and gotten into one of the banned books—perhaps even *The Book of the New Adept*, the book that maybe did, maybe didn't, exist. Of course, all the students were dying to see *those* spells (well, maybe old Crumplewing wasn't, she was terrified of her own familiar). But to break into the Cage—that took someone who was either very smart or very, very foolish.

Merlin stared at the black square and murmured a couple of words of Wizard's Latin. Across the room, Thaqib coughed and, without looking up from his comets, gestured toward the large sign that said NO SPELL CASTING. It might be all right for the librarian himself to summon a book from a high shelf with a spell, but visitors to his library had better not try it.

Merlin's surreptitious spell casting hadn't done any good anyway. The square remained black.

Margery's note had been vague.

> I'm not sure what to tell you to look for—
> just anything unusual. Anything that
> strikes you as odd or out of place. And any-
> one who even slightly resembles the man
> in this mirror sketch. Thaqib is an old
> friend—feel free to ask him for help.

He approached Thaqib's high perch.

"Thank you," he said, handing back the yearbooks.

"Did you find what you were seeking?" As he sipped his tea, the *sahir* regarded Merlin frankly above the rim of his brass beaker.

"Perhaps. Does the name Ellic Lailoken mean anything to you?"

"Lailoken? Let me see his picture."

Merlin opened the yearbook and showed the librarian the black square.

"Ah," said Thaqib. He took a key from about his neck, unlocked a door in his desk, and took out a small brown bottle with a faded label in Arabic. Thaqib unscrewed the top, which had an eyedropper built into it, and carefully drew out a few drops of the liquid. Merlin wrinkled his nose. There was a smell of moth-balls and caraway seeds.

Thaqib let a single aromatic drop fall on the black square in the yearbook. For a second, the black faded to gray and a face began to form, but then the ink on the page began to blister and smoke, and Thaqib had to put out the smoldering fire with Merlin's handkerchief.

The wizards exchanged a look. Someone was determined indeed to keep the likeness of Ellic Lailoken a secret.

Seeps were making Margery's head ache.

She had sent Merlin off to Thaqib to research Mad John, but back on Scornsay she'd been pursuing her own research on seeps, the kind of disturbance in time that could explain the readings G.A.W.A.'s monitors had picked up on the island.

Margery had written to her old roommate and lab partner, the person largely responsible for her passing Alchemy II. Despite the fact that she was always setting her sweaters alight in the Bunsen burner, Cordelia Crumplewing had gone on to a distinguished career in seepology. It turned out that old Cordelia had gone into Whither-When Theory in a big way and spent a lot of her time writing about it in the more obscure wizardry journals.

That morning Margery had received a reply to her letter, a fat envelope that appeared tightly wedged into the in-pigeonhole of the spell-casting desk. Spread out on the desk were the journal articles and clippings that Cordelia had sent, along with photos of her garden and her cats. In seventeen pages of her peculiar wandery handwriting, Cordelia told Margery everything about seeps.

Every wizard you asked could tell you about seeps, but it turned out most of it was wrong—lore that had been handed down, embellished and embroidered with each new telling. There were the Wizzenby Diaries, of course, but no one seemed to be able to agree on whether Waldo Horatio Wizzenby had really sent diaries back from Never-Was in 1802, or whether they were a hoax. In any case, even old Waldo didn't have much to say, whether you believed him or not.

What everyone seemed to agree on was this: A seep was like a bolt-hole gone bad. Instead of depositing you in the blink of an eye in another When and Where, it spat you out in Never-Was, a land outside of time, teeming with banished wizards from centuries past and a number of unpleasant creatures.

If there were few facts, there were plenty of theories. G.A.W.A. had its share of old codgers and codgerettes who spent their time (and yours, if you weren't careful) arguing Whither-When Theory.

The "Good Magic Out" theory held that seeps were black holes of invert magic, sucking in all the magic from this Here and Now and making the world dangerously unstable. As Margery understood it, if seeps sucked in too much magic, the whole world might suddenly go *pop* like a giant soap bubble.

The "Bad Magic In" theory argued that seeps let invert magic leach in from Never-Was, and it was corroding the good magic in this Here and Now. No one really knew what would happen when all the good magic was corroded away, but one model showed the world collapsing in on itself like an overtoasted marshmallow.

Neither was a very cheerful scenario.

Cordelia Crumplewing, of course, had her own theory, that seeps were good. Bad for people and magic and wizards in the short run, but seeps were the way magic kept itself in balance. Wizards had done what they could to contain and bottle up invert magic, but that had actually been bad. The world needed both kinds of magic, and with all the bad stuff banished to Never-Was, the world had gotten out of balance. It was overdue for a big hiccup that would balance out the regular and invert magic and set everything on an even keel again.

Of course, no one wanted to be around when that happened.

Margery scanned the clippings that Cordelia had

enclosed. The Whither-When Theory journals were full of letters from proponents of the Good Magic Out and Bad Magic In theories, saying that, with all due respect, good Dr. Crumplewing was crazy as a loon, and citing lots of reasons why, with copious footnotes.

And then there were the real nutters writing in to relate the true significance of seeps—some incomprehensible bunk about the next coming of the New Adept.

Margery frowned to herself and thought, *Of course it isn't bunk. Not if I'm right about Theodora.*

If she was right about Theodora, the young girl would need protection—from whatever shadowy figure had been behind the whole Kobold affair, and perhaps from the O.I.G. itself. Theodora might even need protection from her own considerable powers, if they began to express themselves before she was ready to deal with them. Theodora would need all her talent and all her courage if she was to deal with the denizens of Never-Was.

Her head was still hurting, and she was thinking that a brisk walk along the sea path must be just the thing for it, when the studio bell pealed, and some tourists came in to examine her wares and ask if she had any of those little knitted hats for golf clubs. As she smiled and showed them the display of tea cozies and baby blankets, Margery's thoughts were on Theodora.

—☩—

Merlin stopped by the Aerials Room to retrieve Vyrna, but the young wyvern wasn't there. The attendant (he manned the long bamboo pole with a hook, for retrieving wizards who got stuck up among the ornate light fixtures) told Merlin he had not seen any wizards or familiars all morning.

The portly wizard hurried out of the Aerials Room and cast a worried glance along the corridor. Down by the cloakroom he could see a small but growing knot of wizards, jostling each other to get a closer look and murmuring.

Now what? thought Merlin, breaking into a trot.

But when he elbowed his way through the gathered club members, Vyrna was just standing at attention, stretched to her full length, the tip of her beak almost touching the ornate brass grate that closed off the club's Lost and Found.

The Lost and Found did not have many articles in it. Most wizards could say a simple Finding spell and retrieve an item that had gone astray. But some of the more elderly wizards were too absentminded even for that, so behind the brass grate there was a forlorn assortment of items: a raincoat, a very overdue library book, and the inevitable assortment of umbrellas.

It was one of the umbrellas that had attracted Vyrna's attention. Tightly furled, it was large and black and otherwise unremarkable, just an ordinary gentle-man's bumbershoot with a bamboo handle. Yet the wyvern was stretching every fiber of her dragon being toward it, as though it were an imp fresh from the gates of Never-Was.

"What is it, my girl?" Merlin said, placing a hand on the dragon's withers. He could feel the creature tremble with the effort of containing her spring. If she could have burst through the brass grate, there was no ques-tion in Merlin's mind what she would have done with the umbrella.

Vyrna was young for Delving, and Delving with a young wyvern was a little like trying to climb on the back of a wild mustang. But Merlin decided that it was the only way to learn what Vyrna sensed in the umbrella. Merlin cautiously offered the young dragon his mind, the way one would offer a hand, palm up, to a strange dog. Vyrna's mind leaped up and almost knocked him over with its force. *Dark! Dark! Dark and cold.*

He instantly yanked his mind away from the con-nection. What the dragon saw in the umbrella was the soul-print of its owner's nature: a mixture of intelli-gence, concentrated malice, and pitiless cunning.

Evil.

Merlin turned to the doorman, who had come hurry-ing to see what the commotion was about.

"Have you got the key to this grate?"

The doorman shook his head.

"Then I hope you won't mind if I . . ."

As a body, the gathered wizards took a step back. Merlin said a spell in Wizard's Latin that sounded something like "sassafras, salamander, syllabub," and the grate cracked down the middle and curled away to either side.

"Fetch it," he said to the wyvern.

But as the wyvern's beak was about to close on the umbrella, it suddenly opened with a click and a whoosh, and when it just as suddenly snapped itself shut again, it was gone, leaving nothing but a faint smell of brimstone in the air.

10

Faerie Fire

Mr. Oglethorpe reappeared briefly at lunch but Theodora had the afternoon to herself, sketching and writing a letter to Dr. Naga that left out Mad John. Her father got back late, caked in mud, with a deep scratch on one arm. His face was glowing with an excitement that made Theodora sit up straight.

"Did you find another scale?"

"No, but I got some excellent plaster casts. They should be dry by morning." Mr. Oglethorpe rubbed his hands together gleefully, his eyes focused on something only he could see. "And I set up a camera trap. A good day's work. What time is it?"

"Six o'clock."

"Well, you'd better get cleaned up. Jamie's taking us to dinner at the Veil."

Theodora was surprised. "The Veil?" She was picturing a picnic at the waterfall Colin had told her about.

"It's the local pub."

She ran up to change, grabbing a shirt and turning it right side out only to realize it was still inside out. She and Mikko were always mixing up their near-identical orange hoodies. They were almost the same color, except that Mikko's top had exposed seams, and she always complained she could never tell if she had it on the right way. Folded up in her suitcase she hadn't been able to tell the difference, but unfolded she could see the spot where Mikko's cat had snagged it and Mikko had fixed the snag. Theodora felt in the pockets and found a tiny tin of strawberry lip gloss, a ponytail holder with a few strands of Mikko's blond hair, and a stick of the Japanese gum she liked to chew. There was a folded scrap of paper, too.

Theodora unfolded it and found a grocery list in Mikko's handwriting. She could picture Mikko writing the list at the kitchen table, wearing the ponytail holder on her wrist, twisting the ends of her hair around her finger while she thought about what she would make for dinner the day after tomorrow. She looked at the list a long time, until the writing grew fuzzy and she realized her eyes were full of tears.

William sensed her distress and hopped into her lap, whimpering.

Theodora looked deep into the little terrier's eyes. "Where did you come from?" she murmured.

William panted and tilted his head to one side.

Theodora remembered something Milo had once said when she'd asked him how he'd picked Yoda out from all the other dogs at the animal shelter. He'd said it had been the other way around: Yoda had picked him.

She ran her thumb over the worn letters on William's tag. Maybe that was what had happened to her and William. Had the ancient dog collar lain forgotten in the castle ruins all those centuries, waiting? Had her presence somehow released William, like a genie from a bottle?

I'll probably never know, thought Theodora, as William gave her a wet dog-kiss on the chin.

This time of year, so far north, the long Highland days seemed to stretch on forever. When they arrived at the Veil, Theodora had a hard time believing it wasn't still late afternoon, it was still so light out. She had been picturing the pub with a thatched roof and old-fashioned crisscross glass in the windows, but the Faerie Veil was a low, unassuming building without much outward charm. The exception was the handsome pub sign that swung over the door. Lovingly painted by a skilled hand, it showed a cascading waterfall with a white-gowned woman kneeling to bathe in the mist. The pub windows were fogged over, and through the glass came the muffled din of conversation, laughter, and music.

Theodora felt funny walking into a bar, but as they came through the door, she saw there were a lot of families, eating fish-and-chips dinners and watching soccer on TV, or cheering on the darts players. There was a sleek new jukebox that played CDs. While her father got their drinks, Theodora scanned the titles of the songs. She recognized a lot of bands from her father's CD collection and newer ones. Suddenly she remembered a sleepover with Val and a bunch of other girls; they were all trying on clothes and lip gloss and posing like divas while VH1 played, and Theodora had just wanted to go home. Val had started sneaking her mother's mascara after that.

Theodora's father came back with Jamie in tow, carrying two pint glasses of something darker than cider and a smaller glass with her soda.

A dark-haired teenage boy in an apron came up to their table and, with a silent nod, placed a plate of sizzling fried rings in front of them, and beside it a bowl of something that looked like mayonnaise.

"Compliments of the house," he said.

"Wow," said Mr. Oglethorpe. "Back home the free bar food is pretzels."

"Oh, we don't usually rate free pub grub," said Jamie. "This is in honor of the great professor from Harvard."

Andy Oglethorpe dipped a ring in the mayonnaise, ate it, and quickly took a swig from his glass. "I didn't think you Scots believed in garlic."

"We don't. Lucky for us, the old owner sold the pub to a family from Sardinia. Cheers." He raised his glass and took a swallow.

Theodora picked up a ring and bit into it. It was calamari, and really yummy. She tried the mayonnaise and immediately had to take a big gulp of her soda.

While her father filled Jamie in about the plaster casts of footprints and the camera trap, Theodora let her gaze wander around the pub. The conversations that washed over her were in such a strong Scottish accent she couldn't make out a word, but she was tired, and she enjoyed the music of the nonsense words and the laughter and music, even if it was her dad's old music. From the jukebox some guy was warbling and mumbling about a brown-eyed girl. Theodora leaned her head on her dad's shoulder and yawned.

The teenage waiter came back and took away the calamari and placed bowls of fish stew in front of them, hot pepper flakes floating on top. The conversation at their table came to a stop as Jamie and Mr. Oglethorpe tasted the stew.

As she ate her own stew, Theodora noticed a woman seated across the room who stood out from the crowd. It was the silver-haired woman she had seen walking in the village during the cloudburst, the one with the peculiar umbrella. She was sitting at a table with three men in paint-spattered clothes, and one of her companions was telling a story, kneading the air with large, reddened hands as if he were shaping words out of it. Suddenly the woman looked up, right at Theodora, with dark, bright eyes. Theodora quickly looked down at her stew, her heart thudding, though she couldn't have said why.

It was as though the woman with the silver hair had stopped just short of Delving and caught herself at the last minute. It was as though those dark eyes could have reached right into Theodora's mind.

But the connection was broken by a man who walked up to their table and cut off Theodora's view of the umbrella woman.

The newcomer had the look of someone used to frequenting finer establishments than the Veil but doing his best to blend in. He was casually dressed in a blazer and turtleneck and jeans, but even Theodora could tell the clothes were designer brands not hanging in her dad's closet at home. He placed a hand on Jamie's shoulder and said in a joking, scolding way, "Jamie, Jamie, aren't you going to introduce me?" And then, without waiting, he extended his hand to Andy.

"MacKenzie Murdoch. Murdoch Single-Malt. We're so pleased to have you here consulting with Jamie on his little mystery." Murdoch winked, as if to show what he thought about the scale. "Once you find out what sort of beastie left that scale, I want a sketch of it. I want to produce a special edition of the whiskey with your creature on the label. Murdoch's Dreadful Dram." He spread his hands in the air, as though envisioning an ad campaign. *"If you care to . . . if you dare to . . . drink a Dreadful Dram!"*

He noticed Theodora and smiled.

"Well, hello. You must be Theodora."

Suddenly tongue-tied, Theodora could only nod. She felt as though Mr. Murdoch had stepped out of an ad for his own whiskey: he seemed two-dimensional, too bright and slick, not real. And while he was quick to smile, the smile never reached his eyes.

"Well, I trust you are finding enough to amuse you on our splendid little island."

Theodora tried not to squirm, and she managed a reply. "We went to the Curlew's Nest, and I went for a walk on the moor."

Was she imagining it, or did the masklike cheerfulness of Mr. Murdoch's good humor slip a tiny bit?

"Only two of our many attractions. Now that we've opened the new factory in Glasgow, I don't spend as much time here on Scornsay as I'd like. Sometime before you leave, you must be my guests."

Then he turned to Mr. Oglethorpe, bombarding him with questions about Harvard and bourbon and baseball, and Theodora suddenly wanted to get away from the noise and the gusts of laughter and the soccer game on TV. She slipped away from the table and headed to the door at the back of the pub with the silhouette of a woman on it.

In the restroom Theodora ran cold water in the sink and splashed her eyes. The face that looked back from the mirror was small and pale. Theodora did what she could with her hair and was fishing in her pants pocket for lip gloss, when the toilet in the stall behind her flushed and the umbrella woman came out.

She smiled at Theodora, and up close she seemed perfectly normal and nice. Theodora was suddenly embarrassed that she had let her imagination run away with her. *Okay, Dodo,* she said to herself sternly. *You really have to get a grip. You're seeing wizards everywhere. Ordinary people don't Delve—just magical halflings like you.* Feeling herself blushing, she moved aside so the older woman could reach the sink.

Margery MacVanish washed her hands, dried them, and reapplied some Chinese red lipstick from a tiny tarnished tube. She darted a sideways glance at the girl beside her.

"Are you all right, child?" she asked gently, returning the lipstick to the pocket of her kimono coat and running a hand through the silver spikes of her hairdo.

"Yes, ma'am," said Theodora, startled.

The black eyes met hers again, but this time there was no hint of Delving, and she could see that the eyes had a kind twinkle in them.

"You look a little pale," said Margery, and she opened the door to the bathroom, letting in a blast of music and talk and two young women who were cackling over a shared joke. Then she herself was gone, in a swirl of kimono silk.

Margery walked back to her table, silently cursing herself. She had come within a hair's breadth of Delving with Theodora and exposing herself as a wizard. There would be a right time and place for that, but not here, not now. The pull of the girl's mind had been instantaneous and strong—she was a natural Delver, clearly unaware of her power. That was going to be dangerous. But how could Theodora be taught to be cautious with her powers, if she still didn't know she possessed them?

Then Margery remembered something from Merlin's report, the one he had filed with the Boston office of G.A.W.A. Gideon had come through the bolt-hole with a Biddable Fire, an intelligent, obedient flame that burned without consuming fuel and did the wizard's bidding. Biddables were rare nowadays, not because they were hard to get, but most modern wizards were really too lazy to give an intelligent Fire the training it needed to be really useful. A badly trained Fire was more trouble than it was worth.

But a Fire, now. That might be just the thing for Theodora.

Back at the table Theodora was relieved to see that MacKenzie Murdoch was gone. When another old song came on and the whole pub rose up dancing, her father swept her out into the crowd and Theodora let herself do a wild, whirling, stamping dance. *Delving, schmelving,* she thought, and suddenly she found herself dancing beside Jamie, who looked so funny trying to do the Robot that she burst out laughing.

It wasn't much darker when they left the Veil after ten o'clock, a kind of eerie twilight, as though time had stopped. The Oglethorpes said good-bye to Jamie and walked back up the hill to their cottage.

From the doorway of the newsagent next to the pub, Margery MacVanish watched them go. In an hour it would briefly be dark enough for the errand she had to do. She looked down at her high-heeled boots with their silver chains.

"Not quite the thing for a walk in a bog," she said to herself. Fortunately, her boots were Featherweathers ("Cobblers and Harness Makers to the Faerie Queen since 1718"), and at a word from the wizard they changed themselves into a pair of waterproof Bogtreaders.

Bogs can be treacherous places to go walking, even in the gray of a Highland midnight. Margery was sure of foot, thanks to her footwear. As she skirted a particularly dangerous pocket of ooze, she wondered whether she was going to be able to complete her errand. Every faerie girl knew how to summon *teine sithe*, or faerie fire: She could spin it and weave it, for that matter, into a cloak of invisibility, or shoes for walking on the waves. But Margery was a wizard, and even though she had spent her junior year abroad under the Hill, her Faerie was pretty rusty. What if the fire would not come to her? Or, having come, would not do as it was bid? A disobedient Fire would be worse than no Fire at all.

She came at last to the place that lay at the heart of the peat bog, the ground so saturated by water only her Bogtreaders allowed her to stand there. Nearby she heard the cry of an owl as it hunted for voles. The moon shining down from broken clouds picked out the glittering black water, from which there rose a mist.

Margery suddenly hoped there were no faerie folk within earshot to hear her mangle the pronunciation of the Old Tongue. Faerie was a daunting language, and younger Folk, once they had had their fire-summoning ceremonies, usually forgot much of its arcane grammar and fiendishly irregular verbs. But for summoning the *teine sithe*, it was the only language that would do.

Margery cleared her throat and began.

> *"Teine sithe! I summon you,*
> *Teine sithe, silver Otherworld fire,*
> *You are sparks struck by the heels of Angels*
> *As they fell from Heaven.*
> *As you are bound to Earth, now bind to me*
> *And do my bidding."*

As the last of the words faded away, the mist rose from the bog, the surface of the black water was still, and the moon hid its face behind a scudding cloud.

Margery was about to try again when she saw it, blue light bubbling up from under the water, gathering at the surface with an electrical sizzle, slowing forming into a soft mass. It rose from the water, stretching and flowing through the air toward her. Like an amoeba, it reached out to sense what had summoned it, using fingerlike projections to feel Margery's face. It seemed startled to find that a wizard had summoned it, and it dimmed and shrank into itself like a snail retreating into its shell.

"I bid you," she said softly, "if you will come."

The Fire hesitated, then glowed a deep blue in consent.

Margery produced the empty bottle she had brought with her, and the Biddable Fire flowed into it.

In the wee hours, Theodora was awakened by William's whimper and felt a cold, wet nose against her hand.

She sat up and saw the ghost dog sitting by the bed.

"What is it?" she whispered.

William sniffed her mind swiftly and Theodora knew that she should get up and follow the dog without waking her father. She slipped on a sweater and wriggled her feet into her shoes.

Theodora crept after William down the stairs and out of the house. The dog immediately went to the flower bed underneath Theodora's window and began to dig, throwing up a shower of dirt.

"William!" Theodora hissed. "Stop that!" She reached for his collar to pull him away.

But William had already unearthed something. In the strange light of the Highland night the corner of a piece of paper was showing through the dirt. It said,

Theod

A shiver ran down Theodora's spine as she knelt by the hole and brushed the dirt away. The paper was thick, like a gift tag, and it said,

Theodora

On the back was written,

From one who wishes you well.

The tag was tied around the neck of a glass bottle that had been corked and sealed with red wax. In the wax was the impression of an owl holding a crystal ball, the insignia of the wizards' guild.

Theodora looked at William, and he wasn't snarling or growling, and his hair wasn't standing on end. Instead, he was smiling his doggy smile and wagging his tail as if to say, *All right, what are you waiting for?*

Theodora took a deep breath and pulled the bottle from the hole.

It was full of something liquid and electric that glowed with a strange blue fire.

11

The Veil

THEODORA STOOD HOLDING the bottle of blue fire, then hurried into the cottage with it, closing the door so that William was caught with his front half protruding through the solid wood.

"Sorry," she said, as he wriggled free.

She sat at the kitchen table looking at the stuff in the bottle and wondering what to do.

Gideon had a Biddable Fire—Ignus, a tame blue flame that did what he told it to and burned without heat. Was this the same kind of magical fire? Even if it was, how could she be sure it would obey her if she let it out of the bottle? It might not be dangerous—William didn't seem to think it was—but if she let it out and it scattered all over the cottage, how would she explain *that* to her dad in the morning?

Theodora decided she would have to find the right time and place to let the fire out of the bottle. For now, she would have to keep it hidden. She tiptoed back upstairs and crept past her dad's bedroom door. Back in her own room, she found the special bag she used to send her camera through the airport X-ray machine. The bottle didn't fit, so at last she just put it in the dresser drawer with her skin and hair stuff, pushing it way to the back.

The clock said 2:55 a.m.—only a few hours before she would have to get up to meet Colin and Catriona for the walk to the Veil. Her mind raced with questions, mostly to do with the identity of the mysterious well-wisher who had left the bottle in the flower bed. Theodora put her head on the pillow without much expectation of falling asleep, but William hopped up on the bed and wiggled under the covers, burrowing against her, and something about his presence lulled her to sleep and then into dreams.

She was running through a green boxwood maze with high walls. Up ahead she could hear someone else's footfalls, someone at a quick run, and from time to time she thought she caught a glimpse of the other runner—a girl in a faded camp T-shirt and cutoffs.

In the dream, she tried to say, "Mom, stop! It's me!" but the words came out strange and garbled, like a CD skipping.

It was cold. There was snow on the path, and the twigs of the hedge seemed to pluck at her clothes like skinny fingers. She rounded a corner and suddenly the path divided. Her twelve-year-old mom was nowhere to be seen. Theodora shivered, and when she looked down she saw she was wearing a T-shirt and frayed denim cut-offs.

One branch of the path showed no sign that anyone had passed there. The other branch showed the staccato footprints of someone running. Theodora (or was she her mom now?) turned down the path with the footprints.

But as she followed the footprints, they changed from those of a person running to those of a creature— something with talons. As she was about to turn the final corner and come to the heart of the maze, she was knocked back by a blast of white fire and woke up.

Theodora lay in bed as the dream faded. She used to dream a lot when her mother was sick. Dreams about falling, mostly. And when her mom died, bad dreams about getting separated from her father in an airport or lost in some city where no one spoke English.

But this dream had been so real. She could almost smell the evergreens from the maze. Her skin tingled like a mild sunburn, as though it remembered the blast of white fire.

Had something happened to her mom the summer she was twelve? Had she come to a fork in the road? Theodora thought about what her dad had said about the poltergeist. For the first time, she wondered whether her mother had known about wizards too. Had she had her own brush with magic and struggled with that knowledge the way Theodora was struggling now? What path had she taken, and what did it mean?

Beside her William was asleep, and at last Theodora rolled over and turned her pillow until she found a fresh, cool spot and fell back asleep.

"Dodo?"

Sunshine was coming through the window, and squinting her eyes, Theodora could see her dad in the doorway. Her heart skipped a beat, remembering William, but under the covers the only sign of the ghost dog was his collar.

"Humnh?" She had slept with her mouth open, and her tongue seemed glued to the sandpaper on the roof of her mouth.

"Colin came by a little while ago. You were supposed to go for a walk. He left a note."

Theodora sat up with a groan and took the scrap of paper from her dad.

It was one long scrawl without capital letters or punctuation.

> hey sleepyhead did u forget we
> were going to the veil today —
> anyway well be at perleys at
> 10 if youre up by then ☺

Seven minutes later Theodora came downstairs dressed for a hike, her hair damp from her hasty shampoo. She filled a water bottle at the sink and added it to her backpack, which already had her camera and journal and pencils. Her father handed her a cup of coffee, with enough milk in it that she could take a few gulps.

"Thanks," she said as she raced out the door and down the hill.

Colin was waiting outside Perley's. There was no sign of Catriona.

"She decided to work an extra shift at the B and B," Colin explained. "Extra money for her trip to London."

"Aren't you going, too?"

Colin shook his head. "I spent the last summer hols there, a special science camp at the Natural History Museum. I'm saving for an underwater camera."

He was standing next to a moped. Colin put on a helmet and handed Theodora the spare.

"Ever been on a motorbike?" he asked.

"No. At home you have to be older . . . sixteen, I think."

Colin grinned. "So do we, but the constable usually looks the other way. Hold on. The road gets a little bumpy."

He started up the moped, and after following the paved road a short distance, he turned onto a rough track. Theodora would have felt self-conscious holding Colin around the waist, except she was too concerned that every tooth would be shaken out of her head. The bumpy ride made talking impossible, and the countryside was a blur of green and brown dotted with white blurs of sheep and reddish blurs of Highland cattle.

At last Colin brought the moped to a stop. The track had turned from rocks to mud, and he leaned the bike against the sheep fence, which brought some sheep over to see whether the moped was good to eat.

"Hullo, Colin," called a red-haired woman in a field coat and rubber boots. She was dosing a struggling lamb with pale blue medicine from an oversized syringe.

"Hullo, Bridie," said Colin. "We're hiking up to the Veil. How's the road?"

"Gavin cleared away the deadwood after the last

wind . . . you should be able to get through. Hullo," she said, nodding to Theodora.

"Hello."

"This is Theodora. She and her father are staying at our cottage."

"I heard you had Americans." As though having Americans was like having mice. "Well, Theodora, does your father know young Colin is taking you to the falls? When I was young, an unchaperoned trip to the Veil was as good as reading banns in church."

"There, that's enough of that," said Colin.

Theodora started to ask what banns were, but Colin looked embarrassed enough that she stopped herself.

"Bridie's the vet," was all Colin would say, and he walked a little ways ahead.

Eventually they fell into step together, and he seemed to forget Bridie's teasing and was his friendly self again. She started to tell him about Mikko, but then remembered he didn't know her mom had died, so she ended up telling him about the five-minute claymation film she and Milo and Val had made for their project in Media Arts, *Zombie Mice on the Moon*. They talked a lot about school stuff. He liked math too, and like Theodora he found languages hard (he struggled with German), but his favorite courses were science. On his computer at home he'd bookmarked dozens of science cams: remote video cameras at zoos, research stations in

Antarctica, high in the rain-forest canopy, and a small yellow submarine that patrolled deep-sea vents.

"Has your dad ever taken you with him on one of his trips?"

"Just this one," Theodora said.

Colin rolled his eyes. "No, I mean somewhere really exciting."

"No, not yet. He's always saying I have to learn to fix a Jeep axle first."

"Yeah, that's why I want the underwater camera. If you've got a skill like that, they'll put you on a team."

"A team?"

He nodded. "By my second year in university I want to be on a research team somewhere. Doing something real."

Theodora laughed. "That's planning ahead."

Colin grinned sheepishly. "Well, yeah, it is, I guess."

As they neared the falls, Theodora began to hear the sound of rushing water, but she wasn't prepared for the sight of the Veil as they turned the final corner and it came into view. The slender cascade of white water fell 150 feet down a green and rocky gorge and ended in a churning pool of mist. The sun on the mist threw up fractured rainbows, and little dark birds darted and flitted among the spray-drenched rocks.

"Wow," she said.

"We take the trail around and end up on the other side of the spray," Colin said. "There's a shallow cave, and at the back are some Pictish carvings. Have you ever done brass rubbings?"

"I did gravestone rubbings once, in Girl Scouts."

"Same thing. I brought rice paper so we can try and make some copies."

They stopped to drink water from their bottles before beginning the loop that would take them behind the falls.

"Catriona and I used to come here all the time," Colin said. "We used to play games where I was a shaman and she was a Pictish queen."

"I can't picture that at all," said Theodora.

"No, she's snuffed that out, the imagination stuff. Though she's still keen on ordering me around." Colin put the cap back on his water bottle and began to stow it back in his pack. Watching him, Theodora wondered if he felt about Catriona the way she was starting to feel about Val and Milo. That there was some important part of himself his sister didn't understand and no longer wanted to share.

As they started toward the falls, Theodora began to realize that she had never *really* used all the muscles in her legs, at least not judging from the way those muscles were complaining now.

They passed behind the churning curtain of mist, getting pretty wet, and then they were on a stone ledge that extended a short distance back into the hill. There were cigarette ends and some graffiti, the usual fifth-grade-boy taunts and something she couldn't make out: HCSVNT. Those letters were more deeply carved, worn and older.

But none of the graffiti artists had defaced the carvings, and they were magnificent. There were spirals, and antlered men, and crosses, and shapes for which Theodora had no names. Someone, perhaps a New Age pilgrim, had visited, and beneath the Pictish carvings were some burnt-down votive candles and wilted flowers.

"Ugh," said Theodora, holding her nose. "What's that smell?" Inside the rock shelter the roar of the falls wasn't as loud, but she had to raise her voice to be heard over the rush of the water, and it came to her muffled, as though she were wearing earplugs.

"Rotten fish," Colin shouted back, nudging some fragrant remains with his foot. "Probably a meal for a pine marten." But he frowned and looked around the cave as if that answer didn't satisfy him. "Why would—" he started to say and then stopped himself. "Do you want to make those rubbings?"

From his knapsack he took out a metal box that held a roll of masking tape, an old toothbrush, and some extra-large, flat-sided black crayons Theodora recognized as the kind you used to make copies of gravestones. Colin also had a lightweight waterproof tube meant for blueprints, from which he removed two sheets of rice paper.

They set about preparing the carvings for the rubbing technique, using the old toothbrush to gently brush away a thin fuzz of green, and taping sheets of paper to the rock. The tape didn't stick to the rock very well, so they took turns, one holding the paper in place while the other made a rubbing.

Colin was making a rubbing of the antlered man when Theodora suddenly felt the hair on her arms rise in goose pimples, and she gave a violent shudder. The paper jerked, and Colin's hand slipped.

"Sorry," said Theodora. She was looking over her shoulder.

"What?" Colin asked, turning to look too.

"I don't know," said Theodora. She had started to shake.

Colin rolled up his incomplete rubbing. "I was done anyway. Come on, let's go. It's cold in here."

At the entrance of the cave they found themselves face-to-face with Mad John. Colin was clutching the long waterproof plastic tube that the rubbings were in. Theodora saw his grip tighten on it.

Mad John had the look of someone dropped out of the middle of a tornado—his hair had been whipped into a wild disarray and his eyes had a glazed look, as though he'd been roughly yanked out of another time and place and deposited rudely into this one.

And he had those spooky eyes. They seemed to bore

into Theodora's own, and briefly it was like that awful time when the wizard Kobold had her in his grip, rummaging through her memories, pressing on the painful ones. But at the last minute, just as the connection was broken, Theodora realized something. It wasn't her pain. It was Mad John's pain she was feeling, so old it was without beginning or end, a deep, bottomless, hopeless ache.

Then it was over. Mad John turned on his heel and walked away, heedless of the slippery rocks.

Colin let out a long breath.

In the sunlight Theodora stood there shivering. But when she spoke, it wasn't about Mad John.

"Colin—"

He looked at her.

"What does this mean?" She picked up a stick and wrote in the dirt

HCSVNT

He seemed to have decided to be tough and male and pretend the Mad John thing hadn't bothered him. "Dunno," he said carelessly. "Where did you see it?"

"It was part of the graffiti in the cave. It seemed different."

"Probably some kids' initials or something."

Theodora felt warmer. She watched a little bird emerge

from the spray, carrying the wriggling larva of some water insect, and fly off to an unseen nest among the rocks.

She knew it wasn't kids' initials. While she had been holding Colin's paper for him she had sensed something, had felt her mind touched by something Other with a capital O. Not the sniffing William did when he Delved, but something different.

Something cold, but with fire at its heart.

Away from the spray, Colin spread his paper out to look at his rubbing. It was still impressive, even with the antlered man's left foot missing.

"Let's see yours now."

Theodora spread out hers, something she had chosen because she thought it was an unusual spiral pattern. Here in the sunlight she saw it was a coiled snake with wings.

"Some kind of dragon," Colin said. "Cool."

No, thought Theodora to herself. *Cold. Ice-cold.* She could feel it extend its icy reach through her veins, into her bones. The metal tag on William's collar grew so cold that it was painful through the fabric of her pants. Suddenly the fish smell seemed overwhelming.

"Ugh! That smell . . . let's get out of here."

Colin laughed. "The only cure for that is a deep breath in a sheep pen. Come on—if she's not too busy, Bridie will feed us."

As they left, the sunlight glinted on the wet rocks at the base of the Veil, and one of the little dark wading birds landed and gripped the slick surface with sure, clawed toes. It pecked at something bright, drew back, pecked again, and flew off in search of better prey.

What lay on the rock, flashing in the light, was a twin to the scale Colin had found, the one that now lay in a clear plastic box on a bed of cotton in Andy Oglethorpe's pocket.

12

Hic What?

THE NEXT MORNING Theodora was quiet, thinking about everything that had happened on the trip to the waterfall—the ride on Colin's moped, Bridie's smiling teasing, the carvings behind the falls, Colin's intent expression as he'd made his own rubbing, and the little dark birds darting in and out of the mist. The brief moment she'd locked gazes with Mad John and shared the hermit's pain. But mostly she thought of the letters she had seen carved into the rock face.

HCSVNT

That, and how long it had taken her to stop shivering once they'd gotten back into the sun. It was only in Bridie's bright kitchen, drinking tea and eating toast with marmalade and listening to the vet talking to Colin in that soft Scots accent, that she had felt warm again. Then she had been able to forget, for a little while, the look in Mad John's eyes.

The funny thing about HCSVNT was that it was so familiar, as if she had seen it before, if she could just remember where.

Her father put his hand on her shoulder, and she jumped about a mile.

"Sorry, Dodo," he said. "I didn't mean to startle you. I was going to walk into the village to send a fax. Wanna come?"

"Sure."

"Then I thought we could rent a couple of bikes in town and ride them back. We can use them as long as we're here."

It had rained earlier that morning, and now the sun was drying up the puddles. The sky had a fresh, washed look to it. Theodora felt a wildly happy feeling well up inside her. It made her want to skip, except she was too old for skipping.

Halfway to the village they had to stop as a girl, younger than Theodora, herded some Highland cows with long, shaggy red hair across the road into a new pasture. Neither the girl nor the cows were in any great hurry, and at last Mr. Oglethorpe and Theodora sat on the fence beside the road to wait.

All of a sudden one of the cows began to low miserably, and to kick, and this discontent soon spread through the herd. The girl tried to control them, but the cows bolted back across the road and down a slope into a rocky creek bed. Two men in a truck coming the other way were also waiting for the cows to pass, and when they saw the animals begin to panic they jumped out of the truck and ran to help round them up, but not before one calf had slipped down the slope and injured itself.

With the men's help, the girl finally had the cows securely in their pasture, and the men offered to load the injured calf into their truck. Theodora heard one man ask the girl what had happened. She turned around, pointed straight at Andy Oglethorpe, and said, "He gave them the evil eye."

Mr. Oglethorpe looked startled, but Theodora realized the other men were looking past her dad at someone else. Theodora gave a little shiver, and in her pocket, the tag on William's collar went cold.

She turned around and saw Mad John standing just behind them.

"Now, Ellie," said one of the men, sharply. "Mind what you say."

"You'll pardon her, sir," said the other man, putting an arm around Ellie and gently pulling her back behind him. "She's upset about the calf. The creature's fine, no need to call the vet. We'll be going now."

Mad John was looking at Theodora. He stepped toward her and leaned forward so that she could smell his breath. He reeked of fish.

"Watch out for things that crawl and creep . . . they're white and wingless and blind, but they have a nasty bite. I know." Then he cackled.

"You'd better move on," said Andy Oglethorpe, putting an arm around Theodora. "We don't want any trouble here."

"No? Well, trouble wants you," said the hermit. "Yes. Trouble wants you."

Mad John brushed past them roughly and stalked on down the road. As he went, one of the red cattle threw back its head and lowed.

A familiar-looking gentleman, out for a walk on the same road, approached them, and Theodora recognized MacKenzie Murdoch. This time Mr. Murdoch was dressed in clothes that suggested he'd just mucked out a stable: a barn coat, sweater, jeans, and boots, but like the clothes he'd worn before, these were expensive designer copies of work clothes.

"Is everyone all right?" he asked.

The cows were still in a dither, but the girl and men

had managed to move them along down the hill, away from the road.

Mr. Oglethorpe looked after them.

"Those cows were frightened by that old hermit. I wonder why?"

Theodora shivered. "If I were a cow, I'd be scared of him too. He's creepy."

Mr. Murdoch laughed. "Miss Oglethorpe, don't tell me you're superstitious. Do you believe in the evil eye?"

"That girl did. The men did too."

Mr. Oglethorpe looked down the road where Mad John had gone.

"You're right, Dodo," he said thoughtfully. "I think they did."

"Don't put much stock in that, Professor Oglethorpe," said Mr. Murdoch. "They're all hooked up to the Internet and have their satellite TV. They're more in touch with *Buffy the Vampire Slayer* than their own folk tales."

They walked into the village together. In the daylight, Mr. Murdoch didn't seem as slick as he had in the pub. He asked her a lot of questions, and Theodora found herself telling him more than she meant to, about how she used to like the *Wizards & Wyverns* movies and how Dr. Naga was teaching her drawing.

"And at school? Are you good at science, like your father?"

"I'm okay at it, I guess." She told him about a unit they'd done in her science class, solving a mystery by taking each other's fingerprints and looking at hair under a microscope.

"A detective, eh? I can see I will have to watch what I say around you. So, Theodora, what do you think of the mystery scale?" Mr. Murdoch's eyes seemed to glitter. "Do you think it's a hoax, or do we really have a monster walking our glens?"

Theodora shrugged. "Some kind of creature. But a monster? I don't know about that."

Andy Oglethorpe laughed. "Good girl, Dodo. We don't believe in monsters, Mr. Murdoch. Just amazing creatures waiting to be understood."

It was Murdoch's turn to laugh. "Very scientific. I confess I am rather hoping for a monster myself. Imagine the marketing possibilities." And he winked at Theodora.

When they got to the museum, they found Jamie up on a ladder, hanging a banner above the entrance. It said THE OLD AND NEW RELIGION, framed by a Pictish spiral on the left and a Celtic cross on the right.

They all admired the banner, and as Jamie climbed down from the ladder, Mr. Murdoch gave Jamie a hearty clap on the back that nearly made the skinny curator lose his balance.

"I see you're putting my money to good use," said Mr. Murdoch.

"Oh, the exhibit doesn't open for another week yet," said Jamie a little apologetically. "I'll have to take that down. But I did want to see how it looked."

"What's this?" asked Andy, tapping a decoration that was hung on the museum's front door.

It consisted of two leafy branches with faded white blossoms, lashed together in the center to make a cross with arms the same length.

"It's a rowan cross," said Jamie. "'Rowan' comes from an ancient word that means 'charm.' The tree 'belonged' to the faeries—it was placed over doorways to deflect evil and used in Druid ceremonies. But as the new religion spread, the Christians adopted it. They brought rowan into the house on Good Friday to defend against otherworldly trickery and planted it in churchyards. It's a little early, but let's see if I can find a berry for you." He reached up and parted the leaves on one of the branches. "Ah. Here we are." He plucked a red berry and sliced it neatly in two with the tiny penknife on his key chain. He showed the halves to Theodora.

On each cut surface was a faint five-pointed star.

"Cool," said Theodora.

"It's a pentagram, a pagan symbol of protection." Jamie's face was alight with enthusiasm. "I love how the old and the new religions are bound up in this one tree."

Jamie looked up at the rowan cross, then back at his visitors, and smiled. "Shall we go in? I have a lot to do, but I can find time to show what I've set up so far." He opened the door and stood aside to let them in.

Murdoch hung back, looking thoughtfully at the rowan cross. "My work is calling me, too, I'm afraid." He smiled at Theodora. "One of the stills back at the factory in Glasgow has had an expensive hiccup. I'm afraid I must catch the next ferry. Jamie, about the banner—"

"Yes?"

"Let's make the Murdoch logo a wee bit bigger." And he walked away down the street.

Inside, Jamie had indeed cleared away most of the clutter, and half the cases had been emptied to make room for the new display. There was a case of Pictish artifacts, with labels explaining what archaeologists did and didn't know about the Picts and their religion; a diorama of a shaman as he might have looked performing a ritual; and a display showing how old Pictish symbols had been worked into the Celtic crosses as Christianity took hold on the island, contrasting Pictish carvings of dragons with Bible scenes of the Apocalypse. There were also psychedelic posters from the 1960s, when the island had rediscovered its pagan roots and outsiders had begun to flock to a folk festival celebrating Samhain, the Celtic Halloween.

Theodora's eyes were drawn to a photo on Jamie's desk. It was old and fragile, and the people in it wore clothes from the early 1900s. In it a boy of ten or so stood on the hill among the Stane Folk, next to the stone pillar. But in the photo the pillar wasn't broken.

"Dad, look at this!"

Andy Oglethorpe came over to look.

"Hey—it's the spot where the scale was found," he said.

Jamie came over to look too.

"And look," said Theodora, pointing. "You can see all the carvings. This must have been taken before they were damaged." It was true. The photo showed enough detail that you could make out the figure of a man—a king, a warrior, a wizard?—holding something in his hand surrounded by a starburst meant to represent rays of light. At the man's feet a winged creature with open jaws was emerging from a hole in the ground.

"What is he holding?" Mr. Oglethorpe leaned over the photo for a closer look.

Jamie got a magnifying glass and handed it to Theodora. "I haven't been able to figure it out. A gem, perhaps, a sacred object, perhaps a lodestone."

"What's a lodestone?" Theodora asked.

"A kind of naturally magnetic rock," said her father. "Before people understood magnetism, they used to think they were magic."

"Oh!" exclaimed Theodora, nearly dropping the magnifying glass.

"What? What's wrong?" said Jamie.

Theodora had been looking at another photo lying on the desk, which showed a close-up of the back of the pillar, where someone had chiseled the letters

HIC SVNT D

"There's some writing on the back of the pillar," she said. The same writing she'd seen back at the cave, just before they'd run into Mad John. The writing that had made her feel ice-cold. But she didn't tell Jamie any of that.

"Let's have a look," said the curator. "In old carvings a *V* is a *U*. So it's *Hicsunt*, and it should have a space in the middle and be *Hic Sunt*. It's Latin for 'Here are.' So someone added it long after the Picts carved the pillar. Probably a priest."

"Here are what?" said Mr. Oglethorpe.

Jamie ran a hand through his hair so it stood on end. "Well, usually you see it on old maps, right next to where a sea monster is rising out of an uncharted sea. *Hic Sunt Dracones.* 'Here be dragons.'"

Theodora didn't seem to hear him. She was looking at the first photo again, the one of the boy standing next to the pillar. He was the same boy she had seen in the photo in the display of the ritual seabird hunt. There he had worn a crooked smile. But here his expression suggested another emotion.

He looked afraid.

Jamie had turned away and was fiddling with the fax machine while Mr. Oglethorpe asked about places to rent bicycles. Theodora sat down in Jamie's desk chair and struggled to make sense of what she had just learned.

Hic Sunt. Was the HCSVNT in the cave the same as the HIC SVNT D on the stone? It didn't have to be dragons, just because it said 'dragons' next to a sea monster on some old maps.

So *Hic Sunt* what? Theodora looked at the creature coming out of the hole in the ground in the carving on the pillar. She thought about the other case, the one where Jamie had shown a Pictish carving of a dragon beside a Bible open to a passage in Revelations about a dragon. Two different visions of the end of the world. Theodora shuddered and pulled her sweater closer around her.

"Demons" began with *D* too.

"Jamie?" she said suddenly.

The museum curator looked up from where he was standing over the balky fax machine. "Yes?"

"Do you know the boy's name?"

"No. There was no inscription on the photo."

"What about the other photo, the one of the tower of birds?"

"Tower of——? Oh, you mean the seabird hunt. Is he in that one too? You have sharper eyes than mine. Let's see."

Jamie left the fax machine to Mr. Oglethorpe's care, took a key from his desk, and unlocked the glass case with the seabird hunt photo in it. He retrieved the photo, and they gathered around it.

"Here he is," said Theodora, pointing.

It was clearly the same boy. Jamie turned the photo over and read the rows of names written out in ink, names of men and boys now dead.

"Hamish MacRae," he read. Then he turned to Theodora. "Why did you want to know?"

Theodora shrugged. "Just curious. I wonder who he was, what happened to him." She added to herself, *I wonder what he was so afraid of?*

"I think I've got it working," said Andy Oglethorpe.

He had fixed the fax machine, so he sent his fax. Then he and Theodora said good-bye to Jamie and went down to the end of the street to the shop Jamie had recommended, a gas station that repaired bicycles, where the owner took them into the back and showed them some bicycles he was willing to rent to them for a week or two. They were heavy and ancient.

"Where are the speeds? Where's the brake?" said Theodora.

The man laughed, and Theodora's father explained. "It's a one-speed. To brake, you pedal backward."

It took Theodora a few trips up and down the street to master braking with her feet instead of with a hand brake on the handlebars. Then they started back to the cottage. All the way home Theodora tried to think of things that began with *D*, but she kept coming back to dragons.

Margery MacVanish sat at her loom, weaving a piece of cloth with all the colors of the sea in it. She was thinking not about water, but about fire, in particular the Biddable Fire she had left for Theodora.

There were risks—that someone else would find the bottle, or that Theodora would use it recklessly and attract attention. So in the safety of the bog, full of its own volatile magicks, she had cast a small spell, to keep the fire safe from other eyes until Theodora should master it. Any echo of that spell, coming from the bog, would seem to any wizard like the natural magic bubbling up from a faerie spring, and not like another wizard's spellcraft. At least, that was what Margery hoped.

She wished she could have given Theodora some guidance, but Fires didn't come with instruction booklets. Every partnership between a wizard and her Biddable was unique, and had to be negotiated between the adept and her Fire.

Just then the shuttle stopped, snagging on a knot in the thread. Margery gave an exclamation of annoyance and wished, not for the first time, that she could indulge in some spellcraft to help the weaving along.

As she struggled to untangle the knot, she became aware that she was being watched with great interest by a spider up near the ceiling. Now it lowered itself swiftly on a filament of silk, stepped onto the frame of the loom, and made its way over to the knot, where it gently touched the tangled threads with its frontmost pair of legs.

"Be my guest," said Margery, gesturing toward the knot with a flourish of her hand and a slight bow.

The spider grasped the knot and rapidly turned it over and over, plucking at the thread with its legs and occasionally running the thread through its jaws the way a seamstress licks a thread before she threads a needle. Before long, the stubborn tangle of thread gave way.

"Much obliged," Margery said, as the spider returned along its silk to the ceiling.

Margery rubbed her temples, which were throbbing with the beginnings of a headache.

The situation was clear. Theodora had arrived at a crossroads. She could embrace her heritage and her Greenwoodness and develop her powers. Or she could close the door on them forever.

The problem was, it was too late for that. The O.I.G.

wasn't going to let Theodora just walk away, now that she knew about wizards and Delving and shadow-wraiths and demons. She hadn't told Merlin, but Margery had in her pocket an envelope with a warrant for Theodora's Demotion. Until now, she had tried to tell herself there would be no need to use it—she was just here to protect Theodora from her own powers, from Kobold's master, from the other agents of the O.I.G. *But the truth is,* Margery thought, *Theodora might need protection from me.*

Part operation, part incantation, Demotions were used to strip mortals and wizards of their magical powers. The procedure was usually performed in a clinic, with specialists present to prevent complications. Stripping someone of his or her magical powers was a delicate business. A lot could go wrong.

But sometimes it was necessary to perform a Demotion in the field, without any safeguards. If it came to that, Margery would have no choice.

13

Enter Electra

THEY RODE BACK to the cottage, where Theodora's father loaded a backpack with some field gear and said he was going to look at a spot on the other side of the island.

"Do you want to come? It should be a great ride—along the coast but not too tough."

Theodora thought of William and the bottle of blue fire. With her father gone for at least the afternoon, here was her perfect chance to let the fire out of its bottle without risk of discovery. It was an opportunity too good to pass up.

"I dunno," she said. "I kind of want to just hang for a while—write some letters, do some laundry." It was a small fib as fibs go, but Theodora's heart beat a little faster as she told it, and she worried that the lie might be visible on her face.

If it was, her dad didn't seem to notice. "That's fine. By the way, Mrs. Fletcher said she was making lamb stew and would bring some over for dinner—around six."

"Okay."

As soon as he had ridden out of sight, Theodora retrieved the bottle of magic fire from her dresser. She was just about to break the wax and pull out the cork, when she had a sudden vivid mental image of the magical fire slipping out from under the front door and up the chimney, like lava from a lava lamp gone beserk. Theodora got some towels from the bathroom and ran around the house, plugging all the cracks she could find.

That done, she sat down on the couch with the bottle and discovered that her courage was gone. She held the bottle in her hands, suddenly too chicken to open it. She decided it might help if William were beside her, so she went and got his collar from upstairs and waited until the ghostly terrier had materialized. When he saw the bottle, William immediately assumed a serious pose, paws together, ears alert, tail still, as if he somehow sensed that this was work and not play.

Theodora took a deep breath, removed the red wax

that sealed the bottle, and carefully pulled out the cork. She half expected the blue fire to come flying out, like seltzer from a bottle that's been shaken, but the fire just swirled around inside the bottle, pulsing among different shades of silvery blue.

"It's okay," breathed Theodora in a tone just above a whisper. "You can come out."

The fire formed a stubby tentacle and poked the tip of it cautiously out of the bottle, as if sampling the air. But it didn't seem to like what it found, for it drew itself rapidly back in, huddling in a dense mass at the bottom of the bottle. It went so dark, without any of its silver light, that Theodora was afraid for a moment that the fire had gone out.

"Okay, I'll start," she said. "I'm Theodora Oglethorpe, I'm twelve years old, and I live in Cambridge, Massachusetts, with my dad. He's a scientist. My mom died when I was little."

Some of the silver color returned to the fire and it lightened just a little. But it stayed huddled at the bottom of the bottle.

William looked at Theodora, one ear up and one ear down. He whined.

"Well, I'm trying!" Theodora protested. She untied the tag from the neck of the bottle and reread it.

"From one who wishes me well. That's *so* helpful. What the heck am I supposed to do with it?"

William barked and started pawing at his collar, as if he were trying to get it off.

"Now what?" said Theodora.

Another bark, another swipe with his paw at the collar, then there was that sudden sniffing of her mind, and the dog vision with weird colors. She could see the letters UILLEAM on the collar, and the word THEODORA on the tag around the bottle.

"Oh, I get it," said Theodora. "I'm supposed to name it first."

William barked and wagged his tail.

Theodora looked back at the fire in the bottle. All the names that came to her mind sounded like colors for nail polish or house paint or rock bands, but not names for a magical fire.

"Bluey?" she said hopelessly.

William gave her a look, and if dogs could roll their eyes, he would have. Instead he just sneezed, as if he were allergic to that name.

Theodora stared at the blue substance in the bottle, dark cobalt blue shot through with veins of silver light. It was so beautiful. Just like electri—

"Oh! That's it! Electra!"

And as if she'd said "Abracadabra," the fire immediately flowed out of the bottle, getting bigger and bigger until it surrounded Theodora and William in a sizzling blue electric bubble. It tickled a little, and Theodora could see her hair was all static and standing on end, the way it had once in class during a science demonstration. And the air was different—Theodora felt that she'd never breathed real air before, not like this air—and she had a powerful feeling of being at once alert and calm.

Then the bubble got smaller and smaller until the fire was a blob floating in midair about level with Theodora's face, swirling into and around itself in a pattern that made Theodora dizzy to follow.

Theodora smiled. "Hi, Electra," she said softly.

Electra glowed a deep blue.

Next the fire made a complete circuit of the downstairs of the cottage, sliding in and out of crevices and corners, sliding over the pages of Theodora's open magazine, caressing the neck of the faucet on the sink, as though marveling at the temperature and texture of the metal, lingering a long time in puzzlement over Andy Oglethorpe's laptop charger, and peeking up the fireplace so that a shower of soot fell down on her. The Fire shook herself like a dog, and the soot flew off in a shower of sparks.

Seemingly satisfied with her surroundings, Electra returned to Theodora and assumed a pose of neutral buoyancy, about level with Theodora's chest. She appeared to be waiting for Theodora's orders.

"Oh, yeah, right. If you're a Biddable, I guess I should do some bidding, huh? Let's see." Theodora tried to remember what commands Gideon had given his own fire, Ignus. She closed her eyes and did her best to picture the wizard, his face bathed in blue light as he motioned the fire upward with a slight flourish of his hand.

Theodora opened her eyes and tried the same gesture, at the same time intoning as commandingly as she could, "Electra, up!"

She'd put a little too much into the gesture: Electra shot up to the ceiling and splattered against it like a big blue paintball.

Theodora winced. Apparently Gideon had had a lot more practice or a much higher ceiling.

After a few more tries, they both had the hang of it.

Electra floated up, and then at Theodora's commands, down, ahead and back, and back into her bottle. She could also brighten herself into a light good enough to read by, spin herself into a thin, strong rope of light, and make a bubble around William and lift him into the air, which the dog did not like at all. When Electra set him down again, he faded away until only his collar was left.

Then Electra formed a bubble around Theodora that fit her snugly, like a diver's wet suit. Theodora discovered that the bubble was waterproof and cutproof—at least, a table knife wouldn't cut through it; she didn't quite have the nerve to try the sharp knife. She could hold her hand quite close to a match without feeling any heat at all. In fact, Electra made a quite effective suit of armor.

Theodora had just formed Electra into a thin flat sheet and was using her for a trampoline when there was a knock at the door. Electra instantly shrank back into her normal form and deposited Theodora with a bump on the floor.

"Hello?" It was Catriona. "I've brought my mum's stew." She spied the towel that had been stuffed under the door, frowned, and stepped over it, setting a lidded casserole on the counter.

"It's only two o'clock," said Theodora, scrambling awkwardly up from the floor. "My dad said you'd be coming over at six."

"I know. But our oven's gone on the blink, so you'll have to cook it in yours. Mum says gas mark two for four hours."

Theodora's hair was still full of static electricity, and she desperately tried to smooth it into place while she kicked the bottle under the sofa. She picked up the cork and bits of sealing wax and stuck them in her pocket, stealing a furtive glance around the room. Where was Electra?

"Oh!" said Catriona. Her voice was full of an open eagerness Theodora hadn't heard in it before. "Where'd you get this? I've seen them in the magazines, but you can't get them here yet."

Theodora turned around and with horror saw Catriona picking up a transparent blue "jelly" handbag like the plastic ones that were all the fashion. Except that Theodora didn't own a blue plastic jelly bag, and this one was a deep cobalt blue, suspiciously like—

"Ooooh, this is nice," said Catriona, looping Electra over one arm. "It's really light, isn't it? And it doesn't have a plastic smell at all." Catriona put her nose close to the cobalt blue handbag and breathed deeply. "Mmmmm. It smells like rain. And it tickles a little."

Theodora spotted the magazine she'd left on the sofa earlier. It lay open to an ad for jelly handbags. *Very clever, Electra,* she thought with grudging admiration.

Catriona was twisting this way and that, trying to see how the bag looked on her without the benefit of a mirror. "I really want one in the raspberry color, or maybe the lime."

How long can Electra hold that shape? Theodora wondered to herself. *What if it's like holding her breath, and when she can't hold that shape anymore she suddenly just pops back into a floating blob?*

But before that could happen, there was a deep bark from outside and an answering high-pitched bark Theodora recognized as William's. The ghost dog must be teasing the Fletchers' dog again.

"Oh, I forgot about Odin," said Catriona. "Well, ta. Remember, gas mark two, four hours."

"What's a gas mark?" asked Theodora.

Catriona showed Theodora the dial on the oven, with markings that were different than the ones on the stove Theodora and her dad had back at home. Then Catriona paused in the doorway. "I can help you with your hair sometime, if you want." She sounded almost shy as she said it. "Instead of fighting the frizz, you might just try to let it curl more."

Theodora would have been shocked at such a friendly overture, but she was too anxious to get Catriona out of the cottage before Electra resumed her normal form. "Good idea! I'm going to try that. In fact, I'm going to go wash my hair right now. Tell your mom thanks for the stew," she said, practically pushing the older girl through the doorway and leaning against the closed door in relief.

With an audible *pop*, the plastic handbag turned back into Electra. The Biddable Fire flowed back into her bottle on the counter, and Theodora replaced the cork firmly.

"I agree, Electra," she said with a sigh. "That's enough for one day."

By the time her dad got back, Electra's bottle was safely hidden away in the dresser drawer, William's collar was safely in her pocket, and Theodora had finished the laundry and was reading with her iPod on. The cottage was filled with the smell of stew.

Andy Oglethorpe came in, dropped his backpack by the door, and sank into a chair wearily.

Theodora took off her headphones and put down her book. "Any luck?"

"Yes and no. I met some workmen repairing the road who told me something has been taking the fish from all the local lochs—the catch is way down. And they took me to see some tracks they'd found, but when we got there the tracks weren't good enough to cast. But I did find this."

He reached into his pocket and pulled out a tiny plastic vial. Inside, Theodora could see a curved object that flashed with opal fire.

"Another scale!"

"I think so. But it's much larger than the last one. Sometimes the scales on an animal vary in size. But it could also mean the scales are from two different animals."

"Or it could mean the same animal is getting larger," Theodora pointed out.

Andy Oglethorpe shook his head. "I don't think so," he said. "That would be a huge leap in growth in a short period of time. I want to look up some data about reptilian growth rates, but I don't know of any living reptiles that grow that fast."

In Theodora's pocket, the metal tag on William's collar grew cold.

14

The Ceilidh

THE NEXT DAY ANDY Oglethorpe was on the phone, trying to get some scientific articles faxed to the museum and hunting down more plaster of paris, so the next time he found any footprints he would be ready.

Theodora started to write a letter, but after she had written, "Dear Valerie," she just stared at the page, her thoughts in a whirl, and discovered she had written "Hic Sunt Dracones" and under that "Mad John."

Theodora stared at what she had written, tapping her pen against her front teeth absently. Did the *Hic Sunt* carvings mean dragons or something else? And what, if anything, did they have to do with creepy old Mad John and the cows? Or the broken pillar in the field of stones? She tried hard to remember all the times that the metal tag on William's collar had gone cold, but just when she seemed on the verge of putting two and two together, there was a silent whimper, William asking her to let him out.

She got the collar and set it on the floor, and William slowly materialized with a shake and a sneeze. He came over to Theodora, tail wagging, and slipped his head under her hand, begging for a pat. He saw the pen and notepad in her lap and sat down, head to one side.

Theodora flipped to a new page on her notepad and wrote down:

HCSVNT _____ in cave
HIC SVNT D on pillar
Wizard (?) and dragon (?) on pillar
Mad John scaring the cows
Mad John stealing relics (according to
    Colin)
Scale Colin found
Scale Dad found
Footprints Dad found

If the scale was from a dragon, it wasn't from a wyvern like Wycca. It might not even be from a dragon at all. And there was nothing to prove that the pillar had anything to do with the scale, or that Mad John had anything to do with the pillar.

But what was Mad John looking for, and why were the cows so frightened of him? Why did the metal tag on William's collar keep going cold?

Theodora took William's head in her hands and stared into his dark eyes, inviting him to Delve. But for once there was nothing. Maybe William wasn't making the metal tag on the collar go cold; maybe the collar was magic and went cold all on its own.

Theodora sighed. Maybe the Events of Last Summer had given her an overactive imagination. Maybe poor Mad John was just a creepy, sad, and lonely human being, maybe the carvings on the pillar were just from some ancient Pictish legend, and maybe the scale was just from some exotic fish snatched from a fishpond by an eagle. There were just too many maybes.

But even as she tried to convince herself of some unmagical explanation, Theodora remembered the pale rainbows of opal fire glinting off the surface of the scale.

There was a knock at the door, and Theodora went to answer it. She was a little surprised to see a taller, grown-up version of Catriona.

"Hullo," the woman said, with a warm smile. "I'm Mrs. Fletcher, from over at the Lodge."

She was wearing a worn man's cardigan with holes in the elbows, and old shoes, and baggy, paint-stained clothes, but she managed to look quite elegant all the same.

"Colin and Catriona don't think you'll be interested—they rolled their eyes and groaned 'Oh, *Mum*,'—but I've come anyway. I want to invite you and your dad to come to the *ceilidh*," she said.

"What's a kay-lee?" Theodora asked.

"A kind of village dance. They happen once a month at the Veil, more or less, and there's one tonight. Nine o'clock. It's traditional music—pipes and fiddle—and if he's neither too drunk nor too sober, Angus MacMillan on the squeeze box."

"It sounds like fun," Theodora said, thinking that going to the *ceilidh* would torpedo any chance she had to gain respect from Catriona. She could imagine Colin being into traditional Scottish stuff, but not Catriona, who only wanted to leave Scornsay as fast as she could.

But Theodora thought that her dad had been working hard, and it would be good for him to go and relax a little.

Mrs. Fletcher reclaimed the empty casserole dish that had held the lamb stew, and she headed back to the Lodge. Theodora was turning back to her notepad, thinking about the dance and Colin, when her father bellowed her name from upstairs.

Theodora ran up the stairs and stopped in the doorway of the bathroom, frozen in horror. Her dad was leaning out of the shower, dripping wet, wrapped in the shower curtain. His hair was completely covered in a silvery-blue goo. The air of the bathroom was full of little iridescent blue globules, like blue Jell-O floating in zero gravity.

So that's what happens when you mix Electra with hot water, Theodora thought.

"What *is* this stuff?" asked her father. He had his eyes squeezed shut and was trying without success to pull the slippery goo out of his hair.

Theodora looked around desperately for the empty bottle. "Did you take the bottle from my dresser drawer?"

"I don't know!" wailed her dad, groping for a towel on the rack with one hand while he held the shower curtain around his waist with the other. "I just grabbed it. It was blue—it looked like shampoo."

"No, it's—it's a new kind of—um, nail polish remover," she said. "All natural, nontoxic—Mikko gave it to me. It's perfectly safe, but keep your eyes closed just in case."

Her dad squeezed his eyes shut, grumbling under his breath, and Theodora found the bottle where it had rolled under the sink. She held it up and clucked softly under her breath. Electra rose up from Andy Oglethorpe's head, a little unsteadily, and as she did all the little blobs float-ing in the air began to join together into bigger blobs, which began to attach themselves to Electra, until she was once more a single blob of silver-blue light. She slipped into the bottle, and Theodora replaced the cork.

Then she pushed her dad back into the shower.

"I think I got it all off," she said. "But rinse really well. I'll go get you some shampoo."

Fifteen minutes later Mr. Oglethorpe emerged dressed, his hair damp but undamaged, smelling of Theodora's rain-forest shampoo.

He squinted at the label. "Awa-pu-hi? Well, I'm not used to smelling like fruits I can't pronounce. But at least I still have my hair, and it's not blue."

"It looks great, actually," said Theodora, thinking Electra did make a decent conditioner. "No cowlick."

"I'll live with the cowlick, thanks," said her father darkly.

After dinner, as she was getting ready for the *ceilidh*, Theodora paused with a fashion magazine open to an ad for shampoo that showed a model with gorgeous, romantic, shiny tendrils of auburn hair. Theodora thought about the magic Electra had worked copying the jelly bag, but she decided she just couldn't chance it. She was going to have to go to the dance with Brillo hair. But she remembered what Catriona had said about letting it curl more, so she ran a wet comb through it, then her fingers, and let it dry without brushing it.

She had decided to wear cargo pants and a white peasant top that had been Mikko's, but as she was getting dressed she noticed the blouse was missing a button, and she didn't quite have the guts to wear it unbuttoned that low—as if her dad would let her. While she was looking for a safety pin, she remembered the brooch of her mom's, the abstract dragon swirl with the red stone. It looked good with the blouse, which had some folk embroidery on it, and a pair of dangly earrings—little horses made out of straw. Letting her hair air dry had tamed the frizz, and while they weren't tendrils, her hair wasn't Brillo, either.

Her dad looked so shocked when she came downstairs that Theodora instinctively checked for the brooch. It was safely in place, and only about a half inch of midriff peeked out between the hem of her blouse and her waistband.

"What?" she said, a little defensively. "My belly button isn't even showing!"

"Oh, no, you look fine. It's just—for a moment, with your hair like that, you looked like your mom."

"Really?"

Her dad nodded, and Theodora found the expression on his face hard to read—proud and happy and a little sad all at once.

He cleared his throat. "I think it's already started." He went over to the open window, listening. "Isn't that a bagpipe?"

On the way to the Veil they met quite a few villagers, all headed to the *ceilidh*. Theodora didn't see the Fletchers, but she recognized the man who had rented them their bicycles and the silver-haired woman she had met at the Veil before. And there was Bridie the vet, carrying a small black case for a musical instrument.

Music was already wafting from the pub's open door, the sound of bagpipes and accordion. Bridie fell into step with the Oglethorpes and introduced herself to Theodora's dad.

"Is that a violin?" Theodora asked.

"Yes—I guess you can say I'm second fiddle."

"When do you find time to play?" said Mr. Oglethorpe. "I thought vets were too busy for things like music."

"Oh, well, I don't practice so much anymore. But you'd be surprised: A ewe in labor quite likes a little fiddle music."

The *ceilidh* was already in full swing at the Veil. Bridie cast off her denim jacket, put the violin to her chin, and launched right into the middle of the reel that the piper was playing. The music grew more and more lively, and there was stomping and clapping and whoops of approval, and couples whirling around the floor. The tables and chairs and glasses in the pub rattled and shook.

Theodora stood in the corner, drinking a lemonade and scanning the crowd. There was Jamie, there was Mrs. Fletcher, but no sign of Colin or Catriona. Her dad was busy dancing with the island's Jamaican doctor. The pub's cook, a white-haired woman in a black dress and sneakers, was dragged protesting from the kitchen onto the dance floor, where she managed to do a Sardinian folk dance to a rousing Celtic tune.

Theodora slipped outside to breathe the cool air. It was still light out, like twilight, even though it was now well after ten thirty. A young couple was having a lovers' quarrel under the pub's sign, so Theodora walked around to the little garden patio at the back, where wildflowers were taking over the square of flagstones on which the owners had set out three tables with umbrellas.

She sat on a bench under the arbor and sighed, wishing she'd brought William, wondering why she felt so mopey. In the pub, watching the dancing and listening to the music, she couldn't help feeling like an outsider, not because she was an American, but because after what had happened to her with the wizards and wyverns and everything, she had a hard time being Theodora. And it wasn't going to get any better when she got back to

Boston. Val just wanted to go to the movies or the mall with her new Tae Kwon Do friends, and Milo and his dog, Yoda, were spending a lot of time with a girl named Sylvie and her dog, Chewie. And really, who could blame them? She hadn't exactly been a lot of fun to be around. She thought of Gideon, back on the other side of the bolt-hole in his own time, and of Mikko on her cruise, and wondered if she'd ever see either one of them again. She felt a lump forming in her throat.

Beyond the little patio the wildflowers gave way to brush and then woods, and now the light was at last fading and the wind stirred the branches, whispering in the leaves. Theodora sat up, suddenly sure she was being watched by someone, or something, hidden in the trees. She felt her mind seized and probed, but not by the Other she'd encountered at the waterfall—there was no cold fire. This time it was like an eclipse happening inside her head—a shadow creeping across her memory like a dark, sinister tide. It was like the time last summer when her mind had been in Kobold's grip.

Theodora stood up, clutching her head. "Who are you?" she called into the woods. "What do you want?"

The other mind was shielded from her somehow. Like a thief wearing gloves, it expertly rifled through her memories, lingering on the scenes of her Delving with Merlin, her breaking and then mending the bat skeleton, and her finding of William.

Theodora clenched her teeth and squeezed her eyes shut, trying to force the shadow out of her head. "Let me go . . . get out. Get out!"

For a terrifying moment, the shadow completely covered her mind. Then slowly it began to move aside.

The red stone on her mother's brooch was glowing. With shaking hands Theodora unpinned it, but she couldn't bring herself to throw it away. Even as she was looking at it, trying to think what to do, the color faded rapidly from the stone and it lay in her hand, familiar and harmless once more. The sinister shadow that had covered her mind was gone. She stared into the woods, breathing hard, wondering what had just happened.

"Well, hello," someone said. "May I join you?"

Theodora looked up and saw MacKenzie Murdoch. Her shoulders sagged with relief. She gave him a weak smile. "Sure," she said, and slipped the brooch into her pocket.

Murdoch smiled at Theodora and sat beside her on the bench. He looked off into the trees as though he had seen something. Then he looked back at Theodora and smiled again more broadly.

"I hope it doesn't rain," he said, turning up his collar against the sudden chill. "I seem to have misplaced my umbrella. Are you enjoying the *ceilidh*?"

She shrugged. "Oh, it's okay, I guess. It just got a little

crowded. The music was giving me a headache. How is the hiccup?"

Murdoch seemed startled and looked at her sharply. Theodora added, "You know, the one at the factory? You said some machine had an expensive hiccup."

Murdoch's features relaxed in a laugh. "Oh, you mean that little mishap," he said easily. "Everything is up and running once more. But you don't want to talk about whiskey. How is your father's research going? Is he close to finding the creature?"

"I think you have to ask him that." Her fear had faded, but she was left with a conviction that something wasn't right. In her pocket, the red stone in the brooch was glowing again. She could see it through the fabric of her pants. Theodora wondered if Mr. Murdoch could see it too. She slipped her hand in her pocket and hid the glowing stone in the palm of her hand.

The wind had risen again, and in the failing light the trees on the edge of the patio seemed to take the shape of a large, awakening creature. Theodora shivered. She thought about going back inside, but she didn't want to be rude. Mr. Murdoch was in a teasing mood.

"So Detective Theodora, what have you found out about the creature?"

It took her a moment to remember that she'd told him about her science project on forensics and finger-prints.

"Well, it's funny," she said. "We found a photo of the pillar, the one where Colin found the scale, and it says *Hic Sunt D* on it. And then, behind the Veil—you know, the waterfall, not the pub—there was another *Hic Sunt.* Jamie says it might stand for 'Here Be Dragons.' I wonder whether the same creature has been on the island all this time."

"Why hasn't one been found, then?" said Mr. Murdoch. "If a creature, a dragon as you call it, has been prowling Scornsay since the time of the Picts, where are the bones? There would have to be bones, wouldn't there? Or some other trace, more than a scale?"

Theodora felt silly. "I suppose," she said. She didn't tell him that her dad had found another, bigger scale. The stone had stopped glowing, and behind her the wind in the trees had died down. Theodora decided she could risk being rude now.

"I'm getting kind of cold," she said. "I'm going to go back inside. Good luck with your Dreadful Dram."

Once more Mr. Murdoch looked a little startled. Then he remembered about putting the creature on the label of the whiskey bottles. He laughed, then raised both hands, raking the air with imaginary talons, and roared a fake roar.

Theodora gratefully made her escape.

As she went back inside, she spotted Colin's motorbike parked next to some others outside the Veil, but inside she couldn't spot him among the crowd. She got herself a lemonade and found him at the back of the pub by the restrooms, playing an arcade video game.

"Hi," she said.

"Hi."

"Are you the high score?"

"And the low score and all the ones in between. Want to play?"

"No, thanks." She watched him blast a few enemy spacecraft and weave his way through an asteroid belt. "Want to dance?"

He made a face. "It's not my kind of music."

"Mine either," she said.

He looked up, then looked back down, just in time to see his spaceship vanish down a black hole. He slammed the game screen with the palm of his hand.

"Okay. Let's dance."

Theodora was a major dance dropout: she'd quit classes in tap and hip-hop, and one of the most embarrassing moments of her life had been going to a pool party expecting to play Marco Polo and discovering it was a boy-girl party with music and dancing. She and Milo had escaped into the house to watch a horror movie about giant mutant earthworms, but Val had stayed out by the pool with Jake Woo, dancing in a new tankini that showed off her tan-in-a-can.

But Theodora discovered she was good at this kind

of dancing. It was like geometry: It had a pattern. And there was no way to look cool doing it, so you didn't have to worry about that. Theodora disappeared into the pattern gratefully, letting the music flow through her, letting her mind go blank. While she was dancing, it didn't seem to matter which Theodora she was, the old one or the new one. While she was dancing, she was the music.

The fiddling grew faster and faster, and she changed partners and clapped and stamped and spun, and then she was back with Colin briefly, clasping his hands before spinning away again. Then all of a sudden the black shadow had returned, blotting everything out. The music seemed to go sour, the room began to spin, and before she knew what was happening, she fell to her knees on the dance floor, gripping her head.

Her dad got to her first.

"Dodo! Are you all right?"

Theodora looked up at her father. A minute before, her face had been flushed with the effort of dancing, but now it was drained of color. And her hands were cold, ice-cold.

"Daddy, something's wrong."

The island's doctor kneeled next to Theodora and started to feel her pulse, but Theodora snatched her arm away and struggled to her feet.

"I'm fine," she said, shaking off Colin and her dad,

who were trying to help her up. "Don't you under-stand?" Now she was shouting, panic in her voice. In her pocket, the stone on the brooch was glowing bright red.

"*Something—is—wrong.*"

"Listen," said the man who had been playing the bagpipes. "She's right."

There was the *dee-da-dee-da* of a siren. A truck squealed to a stop outside the pub, and Mr. Perley, the shopkeeper, burst into the room.

"Jamie! Where's Jamie Grayling?"

Jamie stepped forward, mute with surprise.

"Your museum's on fire."

15

Hamish's Tale

SHE WAS HAVING THE same dream over and over. Gideon was trying to teach her to spin fire, turning Electra into a sphere and the sphere into a thin rope, but every time she tried, Electra ended up as a blue puddle on the floor. She could not control the blue fire, and the spell kept going wrong. Gideon ran out of patience and chided her, saying, "Didn't you read the assignment?" Theodora frantically paged through a heavy tome titled *The Uses of Magical Fire,* but every page was just covered in HICSVNT HICSVNT HICSVNT, over and over. She tried to perform the spell once more, and now, instead of being a magical blue fire, Electra turned white-hot, and then red, and began to lick up the walls of Gideon's chamber, out of control.

Theodora woke up with her heart hammering and looked around the room in confusion. Her head hurt and she felt groggy. She must be home sick. Any minute now Mikko would come in with a bowl of soup on a tray and some Japanese comics. But there was an anti-septic smell more like the nurse's office at school. So why couldn't she hear the muffled slam of lockers and the babble of voices in the hallway outside?

As the cobwebs cleared and the dream faded, Theodora found herself lying in bed in a strange room. It looked like the nurse's office at school, but it was painted sunny yellow with bright turquoise windowsills. A metal cabinet with glass doors held rolled gauze bandages, jars of cotton balls, and tongue depressors. Charts on the walls warned of the dangers of smoking and unsafe sex. There was a framed travel poster for Jamaica and a small tank of tropical fish. Theodora sat up and saw that she was lying in a small cot with a metal railing to keep her from falling out. On the other side of a flowered cur-tain that divided the room in half she could hear heavy, labored breathing.

There was a knock on the door and a woman came in. Theodora recognized her as Josefina Moody, the doctor who had been dancing with her dad at the Veil the night before.

The night before.

Suddenly everything came flooding back in a rush, and Theodora frantically tried to get out of bed but got tangled up in the sheets, flailing her arms and trying to kick free of the bedclothes.

"Oh, my God—the fire!"

The doctor calmed her down and helped her get resettled against the pillows.

"Jamie's fine," she said in a softly lilting Jamaican accent. "No one was hurt. The fire is out."

"The museum—"

"Jamie had moved a lot of things out to make room for the new exhibit, so the loss wasn't as bad as it might have been."

Theodora pictured the old photograph of Hamish MacRae standing next to the pillar among the Stane Folk. In her mind's eye a hungry edge of flame ate its way across the frame, and Hamish's fearful face blistered and blackened and was gone.

"Why am I here?" she asked. "Is this a hospital?"

"No, it's just my surgery." Seeing Theodora's blank look, she explained. "You'd call it an office, or a clinic, I think. I send serious cases to the mainland."

"So I'm not a serious case."

The doctor smiled. "No. I just wanted to keep an

eye on you overnight." As she said this, she put the ear-pieces of her stethoscope in her ears and placed the cold metal disk on Theodora's chest. "And your dad wanted to make sure you were all right before the constable talked to you. Deep breath, please."

Theodora inhaled and exhaled and then asked, "Constable? Isn't that some kind of police officer?"

"Yes. You knew about the fire, you see, before it happened. She has a few questions for her report."

For the next few moments the doctor was busy poking and prodding, tapping Theodora's knees with a rubber hammer and shining a small flashlight in her eyes. She seemed satisfied with what she found.

"Well, I don't see any reason to keep you. I'd like you to eat something, then around noon I think you can go home."

Home. Suddenly the longing for their house in Cambridge was an ache.

The doctor smiled and said, "Rest a little. I have to see to my other patient." She disappeared behind the other side of the curtain.

"Now, Mr. MacRae," Theodora heard her saying. "How are you feeling this morning? I heard you gave the staff at the center no end of trouble."

A gruff voice muttered a curse.

"Now, none of that, please," said the doctor.

There was the sound of glass breaking and a spoon

clattering to the floor, as though Mr. MacRae had knocked away a dose of medicine.

The gruff voice was raving in a thick Scots brogue Theodora couldn't make sense of, but certain words leaped out at her.

"Demons . . . fire . . ."

Demons . . . fire . . . MacRae . . . Theodora felt all the hairs on her arms rise in goose pimples. *It couldn't be,* she thought. *He'd have to be a hundred.*

"The girl," said the gravelly voice. "The girl from across the sea."

"Who do you mean, Mr. MacRae?" said the doctor. "What girl from across the sea?"

"I must see her," and then he was just muttering again about demons and fire.

There was the crinkle of a candy wrapper, and the doctor said, "Time for your Nutto bar, Mr. MacRae."

The muttering was silenced by the smacking of lips.

The doctor reappeared on Theodora's side of the curtain. She was holding the fragments of a brown glass medicine bottle in her hand.

"He does love his Nutto bar. He'll sleep now. I think I got all the glass, but if you get up to go to the loo, mind you don't cut your feet. I don't want to have to stitch you up."

Theodora nodded. "Who is he?"

"Hamish MacRae. He caused quite a scene at the

old folks' center last night, going on about demons and a girl from across the sea."

She left the room, and Theodora lay in bed with her thoughts in a crazy whirl. As soon as she made sense of one small thing, she'd think of something else and it all fell apart again. Then she noticed her clothes, neatly folded and lying on a chair. Her mother's brooch was lying on her cargo pants, the red stone winking.

Theodora got up and picked up the stone, looking at it. Then she turned, took a deep breath, and pulled aside the curtain that divided the room in two.

Hamish MacRae was the oldest person Theodora had ever seen. He was wrinkled and burned brown by the sun. His pale eyes were startling in his deeply tanned face, and what hair he had left clung to his skull like lichen on a rock. His sunken cheeks were covered with a stubble of white beard. In his prime he must have been a strong man, but now the cotton pajamas he wore hung loosely over his withered arms and sunken chest. His hands were all knuckles and sinew, callused and scarred as though he had once worked with tools and often cut himself.

But you could tell there was life in him, and cunning, and wit. On the bedside table lay a pill, sticky with caramel from the Nutto-Caro-Crema-Latté bar where the doctor had hidden it. Hamish saw Theodora looking at it and began to cackle softly under his breath.

Theodora sat down on the edge of the bed. "Hello, Mr. MacRae. I'm Theodora." Now that she had started she felt ridiculous, but there was no stopping. Theodora licked her dry lips and went on. "I'm the girl from across the sea. I have something I want to show you. I think you might be able to tell me what it is."

She opened her hand to show him the dragon brooch. Hamish MacRae's eyes looked at it and then at Theodora.

"It's the Mote," he said. "The Mote in the Dragon's Eye."

She had been afraid it would take powers of persuasion she didn't possess to get the story out of old Hamish MacRae, or at least a box of Nutto-Caro-Crema-Latté bars. But he seemed glad enough to tell his story, once he got started. At first she had a hard time making out his Scots accent, but after a while, as the *dinnae*s and *summat*s washed over her, she stopped trying to make sense of each word. As Theodora listened to the music of his speech, not trying to understand it, the meaning came floating up from the middle of it, like a thread of harmony.

"That morning my father said I could go with him to cut peat. I was nine years old. I had been begging him to take me with him because the year before, the cutters had found a body in the bog near Pitlochry, and the great men from the museum in Edinburgh had paid them well for it. I was certain I was going to find my own bog-man, and had already planned how I would spend the money, on chocolate and a tin airplane with a propeller you wound with a key.

"Cutting peat was man's work, and I was soon weary. But I had asked to cut peat instead of doing other chores I did not like so well, so I kept at it. My father was cutting peat a short ways from me, and I heard his knife strike against stone. He called me over to see.

"It was a four-sided pillar, the height of a wee lad, and covered in strange marks—men with wings, strange beasties. I knew the museum men would offer a fine price, but my father spat on it and covered it back up with a block of peat and told me to leave it alone—he would mark the spot and tell the minister about it. A wizard stone, best left where it was, and a prayer said over the ground.

"But when the minister came out to the field to see it, he became very excited and told my father the stone needed to be dug out and put somewhere for safe-keeping until the important men in Edinburgh could come and take it away.

"It took six draft horses to pull it out, and the brutes gave us no end of trouble, as though they knew what the stone was holding in. At last they pulled it out—it made a sound as though the bog did not want to let it go—and then it was free and we could see what lay beneath."

Hamish paused to lick his dry lips, and Theodora got up and poured him a glass of water. She held it to his mouth while he drank, the water dribbling down his chin onto his cotton top. His pale eyes looked at her while he drank.

"What was under the stone?" Theodora asked, when he seemed ready to go on.

"A well of nothing. Nothing*ness*. The horses kicked and screamed as though the barn was afire, and the men cut the harness lines so the animals could run away before they harmed themselves.

"The minister was there when the stone came out of the ground, and he cried out in a language I had never heard—not the pope's Latin, but something else, older and eerie. The nothingness quivered, but then it yawned wide"—here Hamish spread his arms as wide as they would go—"as though it would swallow us all. And the minister shouted strange words again and stepped forward into the middle of the gaping hole, and it swallowed him. It closed over him and then they were gone, man and void both."

Hamish lay back against his pillows, breathing hard. But telling his story had brought a flush to his cheeks.

"The pillar was taken to the hill where the Stane Folk are. It was of Faerie, they said, and back to Faerie it should go. But the Faeries did not want it, so there it stayed. And in time the young people forgot the old ways, and laughed at the old folks' superstitions. Then the men who had been there grew old and died, and I was the only one who remembered."

"But what is the Mote?" Theodora asked.

"Do you know the mark on the pillar? A man holding a stone with rays coming from it?"

"Yes." The mark Jamie thought was a lodestone. "It's some kind of magnet."

"It is the Mote, the Mote in the Dragon's Eye. That is what the minister called it. He had many old books, all about faerie markings on the stones."

Pictish carvings, Theodora thought.

"And what did he think it was for? The Mote, I mean."

"It's a thing of power. There was a book that told of a girl who would come across the waves and use the Mote to defeat a great evil."

Theodora stared at the brooch in her hand, sure now that this was what Mad John was looking for. Before she could ask Hamish anything else, they heard footsteps approaching. Hamish hid the pill under his pillow, and Theodora barely made it back to her own bed before the doctor came into the room carrying a tray with toast, a boiled egg, and tea.

"The constable just arrived. I told her you needed to

have a little something to eat before you could answer questions."

Theodora was just getting dressed when she heard someone come in and greet Mr. MacRae. Then the curtain was drawn aside and a woman peeked in.

"Hullo, Theodora. I'm Charlie. Why don't you and I go to the doctor's consulting room? We can talk there and Mr. MacRae here can watch his *Baywatch.*"

They went into the room where Dr. Moody talked to her patients after she had examined them. There was another, larger fish tank. In among the serious-looking medical books were framed photos of what Theodora thought must be nieces and nephews all dressed up for church, and Dr. Moody in academic robes, getting her MD. Charlie sat in an armchair, and Theodora sank into the doctor's padded desk chair, her hands clasped in her lap.

But it wasn't bad at all. She told Charlie the same thing she had told her dad: that she'd had a foreboding, a sudden splitting headache, a vague but certain feeling something was wrong. She hadn't noticed anything funny around the museum. She hadn't heard anyone say anything suspicious. She hadn't seen any kids playing with fire. Charlie wrote it all down and shut her notebook.

"That's all I need for now," she said. "Your father

tells me you'll be on Scornsay for another week yet. Be sure to phone me if your plans change or if you think of anything you forgot to tell me."

When the constable had gone, Dr. Moody came in to take Theodora's temperature one last time. She looked at the young girl thoughtfully. "You know, my gran was a little like you. She could read the weather, read animals—read people, too. She knew once that a brother of hers had had a heart attack down in Kingston, half an hour before her sister-in-law rang her to tell her. Some people think it's a gift." The doctor smiled. "And I've seen all kinds of things on this island none of my medical training can explain. So try not to worry. Your dad's come to fetch you . . . he's in the waiting room."

Her father greeted her with a kiss and a hug, and when they got outside, Theodora saw Mrs. Fletcher waiting to drive them back to the cottage. On the way, Theodora looked out the car window.

Was that what she was? Gifted? If that was the case, it was feeling more and more like a gift she wanted to return. Back last summer, when she had Delved with Merlin, she'd been aware for the first time of that part of herself that was different. Right now, in the car, driving back to the cottage, she wished she was 100 percent ordinary, boring, unmagical Theodora. But she suspected it wasn't going to be up to her. She suspected that was why she kept dreaming about her twelve-year-old mother in cutoff jeans and a camp T-shirt. What had happened to her mother the year she was twelve? Had she made some kind of choice? Or failed some kind of test?

She was remembering more about the night before. Dancing toward Colin and away from him, the pattern of the music flowing through her. The brief moment he seemed to forget *ceilidh*s weren't cool, how he had laughed as she flubbed a step. What did Colin think of her now, after her outburst about the fire? She closed her eyes, leaned against her father's shoulder, and pushed the thought away.

"Tzz-*schtff!*"

With the sound of the dragon's sneeze came a smell of burnt sugar, and Merlin set down his crossword to go see what had happened.

He found the dragon in the kitchen, standing over the upturned sugar bowl, wearing a sticky mask and hood of hardening caramel.

"So that's what happens when you sneeze on the sugar bowl," Merlin said, laughing. "Dragon brulée. Come here, let me see you."

He tapped the hardened caramel with the back of a spoon and managed to pry most of it off. During the procedure Vyrna didn't so much as whimper, though she did tremble. A chastened wyvern slunk off behind the sofa to nurse her wounded pride and lick the remaining caramel from her wings. Merlin was just about to return to his crossword when he heard the chime on his spell-casting desk, indicating that some mail had arrived.

There was an odd flat package postmarked from Spain, with the return address of C. Crumplewing. Merlin dropped the rest of the mail and tore the package open. A curious object slid out onto the floor, something like an oily puddle that shimmered slightly with magic. There was also a letter in the funny handwriting Merlin remembered now from his student days in Alchemy II.

Dear Iain:

Margery has asked me to tell you what I know about seeps. I'm enclosing a device of my own invention. It will bring you directly to my house. Do remove your shoes before stepping on it.

Cordelia Crumplewing

When he smoothed out the object, he found it was a circle, shiny as a waterproof raincoat and curiously slippery. Merlin spread it out on the floor. The middle of it shimmered faintly, and it hummed with its own magic.

Merlin whistled for Vyrna. As far as he remembered, Cordelia was odd but not devious, but in case this was some kind of trick he felt better having a dragon along.

Vyrna appeared from behind the sofa, looking a little sticky. She peered at the circle and hissed her disapproval.

"Now, now, none of that," said Merlin, slipping off his shoes. "Heel, and claws in."

Vyrna did heel, and, holding his shoes, Merlin stepped into the shining circle with the dragon. Instantly they were whisked from their own Where and deposited on a flowered sofa in a cottage on the edge of an almond grove in Spain. Vyrna was off like a shot, in pursuit of one of Cordelia Crumplewing's many cats.

"Hello, Iain."

Cordelia was seated opposite him in a velvet wing chair. She looked just the same as she had at G.A.W.A. Academy, Merlin thought to himself: Shapeless dress with a shapeless cardigan over it. Ladylike owl and moon cameo pinned to her meager bosom. Elephantine stockings that bagged around her ankles and knees. Sturdy brown Featherweathers. Half glasses that kept falling down her nose, despite the spell she continually muttered under her breath to prevent them from slipping.

The cottage itself was wildly untidy. The self-washing tea set seemed to have abandoned all hope, and the broom leaned sullenly in the corner. On the table beside the wing chair was a pile of Whither-When journals and yellowed copies of *The Proceedings of the Society for the Advancement of Seep Science*. And, God bless her! If that wasn't the very carpetbag she was always toting around during alchemy class, and the same unfinished man's cable-knit vest from 1905–1906.

Merlin did notice one change. The cuffs of her cardigan weren't singed. Cordelia caught him looking.

"No, no, I'm afraid I'm not old Crumpet-Cuffs any-more," she said, smiling. "I've set out a small lunch for us under the trees. You'll find I make a better cook than I ever did an alchemist."

The table beneath the arbor was spread with a cloth and set with brightly painted dishes. There was a potato omelet and paper-thin shavings of ham and crusty bread and garlicky olives and a nice Spanish wine. Merlin tucked in happily while Cordelia Crumplewing launched into a long explanation of seep theory. From inside the cottage came the sound of Vyrna chasing cats and dishes breaking. When Merlin started to get up, Cordelia waved an unconcerned hand in the direction of the mayhem.

"I switched to self-mending dishes ages ago," Cordelia said, pouring the wine, "and a breed of cat with ninety-nine lives. Let her chase them. She can't hurt them, and they'll all nap later."

She had pushed her own plate aside and spread out some papers closely covered with complex mathematical calculations, a kind of theoretical Wizard's Calculus

Merlin had never mastered: Whither divided by When to the Never power.

"You can see I've performed the calculation over and over, and I'm pretty certain of my result."

"If I understand you properly," said Merlin, "no one on Scornsay is safe."

"No, they aren't really. It's a shame they have that festival . . . the summer thingummy—Midsummer Fling, is it? All those people headed to Scornsay on ferries. Much better if they were headed in quite the other direction. I keep writing to the O.I.G. to tell them, but the mucky-mucks there keep advising me to get psychotherapy from the Wizards' Assistance League. But I don't need my head examined."

"No," said Merlin. "I don't think you do. But it's very interesting that the O.I.G. wants everyone to think so." Merlin was thinking of Margery, Theodora's only protector on Scornsay, and the fact that she worked for the O.I.G. He thought of the tapestry hanging in his study, the boy in blue armor with Theodora's face. He thought of what Theodora's life would be like if the O.I.G. decided she needed a Demotion.

He got to his feet, brushing crumbs from his lap. "Vyrna and I shall go to Scornsay at once."

"Oh," said Cordelia, clasping her hands together. "I was so hoping you would! Now, don't go just yet—there are a few items I would like you to take with you."

16

The Whirligig's Secret

WHEN THEY GOT BACK to the cottage, Theodora noticed that something was different, and after a minute she realized what it was: Her father had cleared away all signs of the scale mystery. His field equipment and laptop and science journals were out of sight. The only things on the kitchen table were some tourist brochures and a schedule of sunset cruises around the seabird colonies offshore.

"I thought we could make the most of the time we have left on Scornsay by seeing some of the sights," he said.

She started to ask her dad about the scale, but then she remembered the fire. Of course there was no way Jamie could continue the investigation now, with a fire to clean up after, and a museum to rebuild.

Theodora thought her dad was right: The best way to salvage the trip was to use the few days they had left on the island to relax and just be tourists.

Andy Oglethorpe looked at Theodora. "Do you feel up to a bike ride?"

"Sure."

"I thought we could bike to the artists' colony and see if we can find some souvenirs to bring home."

"Okay."

On the way through the village they spotted Jamie in front of the boarded-up museum. He looked exhausted, and one of his hands was bandaged. He was picking through a stack of wet and blackened items that had been piled outside the door.

"Jamie, we're so sorry. Are you all right?" Andy asked.

Theodora stood there uncomfortably, wondering if Jamie was going to be weird about her outburst in the pub. But he had other things on his mind.

"I'm fine," Jamie said, waving his bandaged hand. "Just some blisters and a wee cut. I wish I could say the same for the museum," he added grimly.

With its two broken windows and their soot-stained

sills, the museum seemed to be looking at them forlornly through blackened eyes. The storefront had been scorched by the intense heat; the paint on the sign that said SCORNSAY HERITAGE MUSEUM had blistered and buckled, and the banner about the Old and New Religion exhibit trailed on the ground, wet and bedraggled.

Jamie was holding what remained of the rowan cross that had hung on the museum's door. He turned it ruefully, scattering ash and getting soot on his hands. "It was an extraordinary fire, they tell me. It didn't start small and smolder, and then reach a flash point. It was one huge flash, a great eruption of flame all at once—almost as though there was an explosion, only nothing blew up. It's a real mystery. A giant whoosh of flame, out of nowhere."

Theodora kneeled by the pile of waterlogged papers and objects that had been thrown out of the building by the fire brigade. Her heart skipped a beat. There it was, the familiar face of Hamish MacRae, the photo half singed away. All you could see was the boy's face and the marks on the pillar.

"May I have this?" she asked.

"Aye," said Jamie. "Take it."

"Can we help you clean up?" Andy asked.

Jamie shook his head. "No, this is all rubbish now. Everything that could be saved has already been taken to the kirk and locked up. I'm just making sure nothing was overlooked."

As they rode away, Theodora asked her father, "What will Jamie do without the museum?"

Mr. Oglethorpe said, "Well, I guess he has to hope Mr. Murdoch is willing to replace the building and help him rebuild. Otherwise he'll have to move on and find another job."

"Oh." Theodora felt a curious mixture of shame and guilt, as though just knowing about the fire made it all her fault, and she herself was somehow to blame for the fact that Jamie now had to find another job.

Halfway to the artists' colony they were caught in a downpour—the wind suddenly shifted, the sun went behind some clouds, and out of nowhere the rain sluiced down in an unbroken curtain. They arrived at the Curlew's Nest with their clothes clinging to their skin and dashed into the nearest workshop. It was a potter's studio, with a wheel in the middle and various items waiting to be glazed and fired filling the tables and shelves. A potter was working at a nearby table. Theodora recognized him as one of the men who had been at another table the first time she paid a visit to the Veil—the man who had been kneading the air with his hands as he spoke.

As they stood making puddles on the floor, the

potter got up and greeted them, then went into a back room. He immediately reappeared with an armload of towels and some spare men's and boys' clothes, many of them paint-spattered.

"We're all used to soggy tourists showing up," he said, handing them each a pile of clothes. "It's easy to misread the weather if you don't know it. You can change in the storeroom." Then he stepped into the studio's tiny kitchenette, and they heard the clink of china mugs and the rattle of spoons and the sound of a kettle being filled. By the time Theodora emerged from the storeroom wearing oversize jeans and a wool pullover, her dad was putting on a pair of heavy socks. The potter reappeared carrying mugs of tea.

While they waited for their clothes to dry, the potter sat back down at the table, where Theodora saw he was working not on a new piece of pottery, but on a piece of brightly painted wood, something like—

"The whirligig!" she said in dismay, starting up and sloshing tea from her mug.

"Yes, we had some vandals last night," the potter said. "The whirligig garden was smashed."

Looking out the window, they could see the broken and scattered folk carvings. The big scarecrow whirligig with the china saucer teeth was gone, the large bird had been toppled, and the monkey was lying in pieces. Theodora scanned the ruined garden looking in vain for another whirligig she remembered—a mermaid or a sea serpent. It was gone too.

She turned away from the window, feeling sick to her stomach. "Who would do such a thing?" she murmured.

Andy looked thoughtful. "Strange that vandals would ruin your whirligigs the same night as the fire was set at the museum."

"You have to wonder, don't you?" said the potter. "I'm afraid our constable is too busy with the fire to worry about our little problem here."

"Hallo, hallo," said a voice from the doorway. "Look what I've found."

It was the woman with spiky hair, the one she'd seen on the street and met again in the ladies' room of the Veil. She was holding the head of the large whirligig. He was looking rather the worse for wear after his night of adventure. One of his mirrored eyes was gone, and quite a few of his china teeth, too. He looked more rakish than ever, even without his body. Somehow the sight of him made Theodora more cheerful.

"Well, hello," said the woman, recognizing Theodora. "How are you feeling? I heard you were taken to the clinic overnight." Her eyes were dark and sparkling. "I'm Margery—Margery MacVanish."

At the sound of the word "MacVanish," Theodora felt something—the same something she'd felt when she was around Gideon. Someone sympathetic and wise, a strong, calm presence. Was Margery a wizard too?

The potter had taken the whirligig's head from Margery and carried it to a table, where he'd been mending the other parts of the broken sculpture. Theodora could see he had been running a hospital for whirligigs: There were spools of wire and scraps of wood, pots of paint and glue, sheets of tin and tin cutters, and a box full of bits of china and mirrored glass for eyes and teeth.

The latest patient was looking well already, except for his missing head. Tenderly the potter set the whirligig's head back on top of the neck that protruded from the tattered jacket and tapped a wooden peg into place to hold it. Then he tacked on a new beard of nylon rope and stepped back to judge the effect. With scissors he trimmed the beard to a goatee, and satisfied with that, gave the whirligig a spin. They all held their breath, afraid it would fall apart, but it spun rapidly with a reassuring wooden clatter.

"Good as new," said the potter.

Theodora stood rooted to the floor, staring at the whirligig. "Do that again," she said in an odd, thick voice that made her dad turn around and look at her.

Margery and the potter stood looking at her too. At last Margery said, "Yes, Jacob. Do that again, please."

Jacob the potter spun the whirligig again. The figure's

arms and legs pumped wildly, making the sound of a bicycle with something caught in its spokes. The checked green jacket fluttered.

Theodora stared at it as if in a trance. She was remembering something she'd seen with her dad at a museum in Boston: a spinning disk that looked like nothing until you turned a knob the right way on a strobe light. Then a pattern emerged. At one speed the pattern had been dancing girls with flower baskets, but when she'd turned the knob a little in the other direction, they had changed to leering hobgoblins, kicking their skinny legs and sticking out their tongues.

Suddenly she realized why she thought there had been a whirligig missing from the garden and why she thought it had been a mermaid or a sea serpent.

"Can he spin faster?" she asked.

The potter looked at her in a puzzled way, then rummaged in a drawer of odds and ends and produced a crank handle. He attached it to the whirligig and began to turn the crank, faster and faster, until the room was filled with a high-pitched zithery sound of mechanical speed and the frantic clatter of wooden limbs pushed to their limit.

The whirligig was now spinning as fast as it would have during a gale, with the wind howling in from the sea. As it spun, it seemed to change before their eyes: The tattered green overcoat became wings, the furiously pumping legs with their strange checked trousers now a pair of scaled legs. It even seemed that the long nose stretched into a snout.

Before Theodora's eyes the whirligig became a dragon. In her mind's eye she could see it, smashing the whirligigs with a single blow of its tail.

The others saw it too.

"Well, well," said Margery.

Theodora turned to the potter. "Who made this whirligig?"

"One of the residents at the old folks' home. Old Hamish . . . Hamish MacRae."

Theodora thought about her talk with Hamish. She remembered how she'd noticed his hands: ancient knotted hands, scarred as though he'd worked with tools. And his wit—the whirligig had been a kind of warning, but also a joke. A man transforming into a dragon. Theodora thought about the carving on the pillar in the middle of the Stane Folk, and all the legends on Scornsay about dragons.

She turned to her dad. Andy Oglethorpe was standing at the window, looking at the garden. He had that excited gleam in his eyes.

"I'd like to go and look at the garden. Do you think the constable would mind?"

The potter shrugged. "There isn't much to see."

But Andy Oglethorpe was already out the door.

The rain had stopped, and the trampled garden was now a sea of mud, splinters, and broken glass. But after some searching, he found what he was looking for. He squatted by a ruined wooden sculpture and gently peeled away some splintered wood that had been trod into the ground.

There: It was beginning to lose its shape and it was full of water. But to a trained eye it was a perfect half footprint of some reptile. A dragon footprint. Theodora felt the Mote in her pants pocket grow cold and she sensed something—something Other brushed against her mind, and Theodora felt the Other's regret and sorrow—regret for the museum fire and smashed whirligigs. But who or what was the Other?

Theodora looked at the two artists. Jacob didn't seem to have realized the significance of what Mr. Oglethorpe had found, and if Margery had she wasn't saying anything.

Andy Oglethorpe stood and looked around at the hill where the Stane Folk stood, and across the road where the cliff fell away to the sea.

"What's the shoreline like?" he asked the potter.

"Rocks at high tide, a narrow strip of shingle at low tide. And there's a sea cave that goes far into the cliff."

Theodora looked at her father. If he were a cartoon, she thought, there'd be a big lightbulb over his head. He always bit his lower lip slightly and squinted, as though he were taking an eye exam, when he was having one of his "Eureka" moments.

He turned to the potter. "Do the caves connect to the sea lochs?"

"Yes. No one's quite sure how. You can't rappel down—the rocks are too sharp."

"Is there access from the sea?"

The potter frowned. "I suppose when the tide was right you might be able to bring a dinghy over. But it would be risky."

Theodora knew what her dad was thinking. The creature whose scale Colin had found, who had wrecked the whirligigs, whose footprints her dad had found, was using the sea cave and the lochs to move around the island.

Andy Oglethorpe looked down at Theodora, and the lightbulb over his head dimmed and went out. He smiled a little sadly. "Well, we'll have to leave it for someone else to explore. Won't we, Dodo?"

Theodora's thoughts were spinning madly like the whirligig.

If a dragon had smashed the whirligigs, could it have started the fire at Jamie's museum?

Why had Colin found the first scale near the Stane Folk?

Why did William's collar go cold around Mad John?

Why had the Mote glowed red at the *ceilidh*?

What did the man-dragon whirligig mean?

Theodora thought she knew the answers, but she pushed the thought away. *I can't,* she thought desperately. *I'm not ready. I'm not that strong.*

When she looked up, the woman with the spiky hair was looking at her. Her eyes seemed to say, *You can. You will be. You are.* Theodora remembered her walking down the street with the magical umbrella. A wizard's umbrella.

Andy Oglethorpe and Jacob were walking back to the pottery studio. Margery MacVanish hung back a moment with Theodora.

"I saw you in the street with that magical umbrella," Theodora blurted out. "You're a wizard, aren't you?"

"I'm a friend of Merlin's, and a friend of yours, if you'll trust me."

"How can I?" Tears were sliding down Theodora's face, and she swiped them away impatiently with the back of her hand. "You and Gideon and Merlin and the rest of you—you're all wrong about me."

Margery looked over her shoulder at Andy Oglethorpe and the potter, who were out of earshot, deep in conversation. Suddenly Andy noticed Theodora wasn't there and turned around.

"Are you coming?" he called out.

"Tell him you want to see how the loom works," said Margery in a low voice.

"We'll catch up," Theodora called back to her dad. "I want to see how the loom works."

Andy cupped a hand to his ear. "What?"

"The *loom*," she hollered. "I want to see how the *loom works*."

Andy nodded and turned back to the potter, who seemed to be in the middle of a good story, to judge from the way he was shaping the air with his hands. Margery and Theodora watched them go.

"For now," Margery said in her regular voice, "will it be enough to know that Merlin trusts me and I am on your side?"

"No!" said Theodora, with a short, disbelieving laugh. "It won't. But I guess it will have to do."

At that, it was Margery's turn to laugh. But she quickly grew serious again.

"All right, I'll tell you what I can, but not here," she said. The rain clouds had gone, but now a fitful breeze was tossing the branches of the trees. "The wind has ears."

Margery's studio was set a little apart from the rest of the Curlew's Nest. Like the other artists, she occupied her own low concrete building, brightened with paint and window boxes of flowers. Unlike the others, her studio had a collection of wildlife: ravens and a jackdaw and some kind of owl were lined up on the roof, and milling near the door were some cats and a few toads. The cats had brought résumés in the form of mice laid out at their feet, and from the beak of the owl dangled an unlucky vole.

"Get lost, you lot!" Margery muttered, shooing them away. "Honestly! What part of 'No familiars' don't you understand? Word gets out there's a wizard in the neighborhood and they come out of the woodwork, looking for a job. You heard me—scoot along, then!"

None of them budged, and Margery opened the studio door with a sigh.

She led Theodora past the loom and the tables piled with blankets and weavings and pulled aside the curtain that closed off the private room where she lived. Theodora didn't see anything magical, but then she wasn't sure what she expected to see. Gideon and Merlin worked magic with words, not wands. No magical apparatus, no spellbooks, no crystal ball. All she could see was a silk bathrobe patterned with cranes, a toothbrush in a glass on the edge of a sink, a damp washcloth draped over the chair back to dry. Then she noticed the printing on the tube of toothpaste. EVERBRITE, THE WIZARD'S TOOTHPASTE. WHEN ALL YOUR TEETH ARE WISDOM TEETH.

Margery sat on the edge of the bed, Theodora took the chair.

"So, Theodora, you think we're all wrong about you, we wizards."

Theodora nodded.

"I think you're wrong about that," said Margery quietly. "But first I'd like to talk about your mother. Tell me what was special about her. Besides the fact that she was a beautiful, funny, loving person."

"How do you know that?"

"She had you, didn't she?"

Theodora looked at Margery for a long fifteen seconds, and then seemed to make up her mind. She let out a long breath, and the words came out in a great rush.

"It's a dream I keep having—there's a maze, and my mom's there, and there are footprints and a cold, white fire. She's in the dream. . . . she's my age, and she's wearing this camp shirt, but when I follow her I lose her, and suddenly I *am* her, I'm running through the maze in the YMCA T-shirt, and the white fire gets me. It's like she's trying to tell me something, but she can't get through."

"Did she ever talk about the year she was twelve? The summer she was at that camp?"

Theodora shook her head. "I don't think so. If she did, I don't remember it. I was still little when she died."

Margery's face didn't give anything away. She was looking out the window. Just visible at the top of the hill were the rounded shapes of the dwarf stones.

"I don't know much about your mother, Theodora, but I know quite a lot about the Greenwoods. In fact, I think you have something special in you, a kind of sleeping magic, a kind of Greenwoodness that's very rare. I think your mother had it too, but something happened to her that summer. It started to bloom and then died, like frost on a flower. But she passed her Greenwoodness on to you." The wizard's dark eyes were gleaming.

"And now I'm twelve, and it's waking up."

"Something like that."

Theodora clutched her arms, thinking about her veins full of green sap, her fingers growing into twigs.

"I want to go home," she said. *I'm scared and confused and I'm so, so tired.* "Please, won't you all just let me go home?" Theodora's voice rose and broke on the word "home."

"No, not yet," said Margery gently, putting her hand on Theodora's arm.

With the touch, the wizard Delved, and while their minds were joined Theodora learned what Margery knew: about the O.I.G., the vanishing of Ellic Lailoken, the jolt of magical energy that had registered on Scornsay, Merlin's visit to Thaqib.

Theodora broke the connection and leaped up, knocking over the chair. She twisted angrily away from the wizard's reassuring hand. "Who are you to tell me I can't go? Why should I trust any of you? You're probably some G.A.W.A. spy, or working for Kobold."

Margery was looking at her with sympathy.

"Poor Theodora. You must wish you were back at the beginning of last summer, feeding ducks with Mikko. When your only problem was how to keep from dying of boredom through a long, hot summer."

Theodora blushed. "That's what you wizards do, isn't it? Just help yourself to my memories."

"I'm sorry," said Margery. She leaned back against the wall and closed her eyes, holding her palms outward and open. "Help yourself to mine."

Again their minds were joined, and Theodora saw through Margery's eyes. A wartime girlhood of poverty and cruelty and hopelessness. Picking a wizard's pocket, discovering her own gifts, being recruited to the O.I.G.

Theodora let go of Margery's mind and sat back on the chair. For something to do, she picked up the tube of Everbrite and saw that it read, in tiny lettering, CHEMISTS TO THE FAERIE QUEEN SINCE 1702.

"So you and the O.I.G. think that Mad John, or Lailoken, or whoever he really is, came out of this hole to Never-Was and has brought a dragon with him? You think that's what started the fire in the museum and wrecked the whirligigs? Then why hasn't anyone seen it?"

"I wasn't sure until just now, when we were watching the whirligig," said Margery. "But I think I know now." The wizard shot Theodora a piercing glance. "And I think you do too."

Theodora thought of the carving on the pillar, of

the winged man emerging from the pit. She thought of Hamish's frightened face in the old photograph. She thought of the scales with their flashes of opal fire and the rain-filled footprint. The smell of fish behind the waterfall and running into Mad John. And she thought of the whiligig, spinning faster and faster until a tramp in checked trousers turned into a dragon.

The young girl looked up at the wizard, and Margery felt sorry for the child. In her face you could see the battle raging inside her between relief and bravery on the one hand, and misery and fear on the other. As Margery watched, the relief seemed to win.

"Mad John *is* the dragon," Theodora said at last.

17

Ham's Pipes

"AT LEAST, HE IS sometimes—at night."

Margery nodded. "The Wingless Opalfire needs a human host to complete its metamorphosis. It attaches itself to a human, and the venom it injects begins to change its host. Every cycle of the moon there is more and more of the dragon, and less and less of the host, until finally a dawn comes when the possession is complete and irreversible."

Theodora stood up and started walking around the room, the way her dad did when he had to think out loud. "He wants the Mote, the stone in my mother's brooch. It's what he's been looking for." She looked up at Margery. "It's a carbuncle, isn't it? The Mote in the Dragon's Eye from the legend." Theodora was remembering the Otherness she had sensed, standing among the ruined whirligigs: the sorrow and regret. "He didn't mean to wreck the whirligigs or burn the museum. He did it by accident. He doesn't want to hurt anyone."

"I think the Mote must have belonged to your ancestor Gwynlyn. It was a powerful stone that magnified and focused its wearer's own magic. But the Mote in the Dragon's Eye is also the name of a hero in an old wizard's legend. The Mote is a wizard who comes to end a reign of darkness. Lailoken was looking for the wrong Mote . . . he was looking for the stone. But the dragon was looking for the right Mote. It was looking for you."

That stopped Theodora in her tracks. She sank slowly back down into the chair. "For me? I'm the Mote?"

Margery nodded. She reached forward and looped a strand of Theodora's hair back behind her ear in a gesture that was almost motherly.

"If you choose to be. I think there is a wizard, someone powerful and ambitious, who does not want you to succeed and develop your powers."

Theodora remembered the dark shadow that had slid across her mind when she was sitting alone outside the Veil. "Are they here—on the island—now?"

"They might be. Long ago someone started a campaign to convince the Guild that *The Book of the New Adept* was dangerous. But our wizard unknown guessed it was something else—that it held a secret the Guild didn't want revealed. They made a bunch of decoys, books full of banned spells, so that the real book, the original book, and what it had to say would be suppressed and forgotten." Margery looked out of the room's one window across the moor. "I find it suspicious that the O.I.G. files have nothing to say about your mother. It makes me think that someone got there before me. Perhaps the O.I.G. had something to do with the thing that happened the summer she was twelve. We may never know. But I think perhaps when she was about your age, Theodora, your mother somehow found the stone Mote. Or it found her—that would be more likely. But for whatever reason, she did not develop her ability to Delve and her other gifts. She grew up and married Andy Oglethorpe and passed along her talents to her daughter . . . to you."

Theodora tried hard to remember anything her mother had said about the brooch, but the only image that came to her mind was the photo of her mother on the refrigerator, the one she used to kiss hello when she came home.

"I've had the brooch in my jewelry box all this time. How come it never—I dunno—spoke to me?"

Margery shook her head. "Perhaps your Greenwoodness hadn't yet awakened. You're at the age we wizards call the Age of Awakening. It's the age when promise most often manifests itself, when it's going to. Magic hatches. Or it doesn't."

Theodora was going to say, *What promise?* when she remembered the broken bat skeleton in Dr. Naga's studio, and the sound of it reassembling itself. "And if I have these talents, just what am I supposed to do with them?"

"Stop pushing them away. Turn off the part of your brain that keeps saying no. Go toward the thing you're most afraid of."

Theodora clutched the Mote tightly in her hand and thought of what she was afraid of.

"I *can't*," she said. "Whoever this guy is, he almost got me at the *ceilidh*. What if he wins next time? Or what if I help you and G.A.W.A. and the O.I.G. to fight him and I fail and I'm lost or trapped or dead, even, and can't get back to my dad, and he never knows what happened to me? I can't do that to him." The tears that had been brimming in her eyes now spilled over and fell in large, wet drops onto her shirt.

If Margery was disappointed, her face didn't show it. If she was thinking of the day she and Theodora had locked gazes through the museum window, she gave no sign. She simply nodded in a businesslike way and held out her hand.

"Well, that's it, then. Fine. It is a heavy responsibility for a child. But I will have to ask you for the Mote, and Electra, and William, too. When you've returned to Boston, the O.I.G. will contact you to let you know where you can report for your Demotion."

"A Demotion?" Theodora didn't like the sound of that. "What's that?"

"A short, painless procedure to remove any trace of your powers and any memory of magic. You'll be the same Theodora, but you won't remember Gideon or Wycca or Merlin. Or me."

"You just wipe it out without a trace?"

"Not without a trace. The technique is not perfect. But whatever you remember will be dim and dreamlike, especially when it comes to faces."

In fact, Margery thought sadly to herself, it was a terrible procedure. Theodora would not be herself afterward, because whether she liked it or not, magic was part of her now. Whether she chose to go forward or backward, there would be loss and pain.

Theodora was hesitating, standing there with the Mote in her hand, when Mrs. Fletcher burst into the studio. Instantly Theodora could tell something was terribly wrong. Mrs. Fletcher's face had the look of frantic, desperate worry.

"Theodora—thank God. Have you seen Colin? He

went off on his motorbike and it was found in the bushes by the path to the sea—"

"No," said Theodora, "I haven't."

Mrs. Fletcher lost the last shreds of her courage and sank to the floor, shaking with silent sobs.

For a few long seconds Theodora and Margery stared at her, then Margery crisply said, "Stay with her," and dashed outside where Catriona was sitting in the Fletchers' car with Bridie.

Theodora found a blanket for Mrs. Fletcher and started the water for tea.

"I'm sorry," said Mrs. Fletcher. "I'll be all right in a minute."

Theodora suddenly realized that the Mote, which she had shoved into her pocket, was ice-cold. When she went to get Mrs. Fletcher's tea, she dug the brooch out and looked at it, nearly dropping it.

The Mote was glowing. It was so cold it stung her skin painfully. At its cold heart, a flame seemed to dance.

When she brought the tea, Margery was back with Bridie and they were talking to Mrs. Fletcher in low voices.

"Theodora," said Bridie, "would you go to Catriona? Just keep her company."

Theodora slipped into the car beside Catriona. She was sitting in the rear seat of the car, clutching a fistful of dry Kleenex. There was no sign that she'd been crying or was about to, though she looked pale and distracted. Catriona seemed to be holding it together, or at least holding it in, better than her mother. Which didn't make sense, not unless—

The realization hit her, and Theodora's jaw dropped. "You know where he is!"

Catriona looked at Theodora and gave a tiny nod. "Yes. He went to Ham's Pipes—the sea caves."

Of course, thought Theodora. She remembered their walk to the Veil, how eager Colin had been to be accepted onto an expedition . . . the way he'd been saving up for an underwater camera. Maybe in his own way he'd been even more eager than his sister to get off Scornsay.

"He'll be all right," Catriona said. "He took his diving kit, he's been cave diving with our dad since he was eight. Mum's a worrywort, she'd never have let him go." Now Catriona's lower lip was trembling, and when she thrust her chin out stubbornly she could only whisper, in a kind of weak fury, "He's going to be okay!"

Theodora dragged the rest of the story out of Catriona.

While Theodora had been recuperating at Dr. Moody's and talking to Hamish MacRae, Colin had gone to help Jamie sort through the soggy papers outside the museum.

"He found an old picture in a book, a picture of the Stane Folk without the pillar, and on the back was a sketch of the pillar and some writing. And there was a strange kind of map, like an anthill. Tunnels and chambers underground."

Sea caves, Theodora thought. *Hic Sunt Dracones.*

"Did he show it to Jamie?" she asked. Before Catriona answered, Theodora knew the answer.

"No, he lifted it when Jamie wasn't looking and took it back to our house. Then he told me he was going to the sea caves, and not to worry. He was going to find something marvelous."

"Did he take it with him?"

"He took a copy. He gave the original to me and said to hide it until he came back."

Theodora looked out the car window to where a small knot of worried grown-ups had formed. She saw her dad and Jacob, and now Jamie and Mr. Perley, too. Dr. Moody was just pulling up in her car, and the constable was arriving on her bike.

She had to get back to the cottage to get Electra and William. But how?

Then Margery approached the car and got in on the driver's side. She turned around and smiled at the girls.

"I'm to take you both back to the Lodge. Catriona, your dad's on his way back on the fast train. Someone will stay with you until he arrives."

"What about my mother?" said Catriona.

"She'll be waiting at the cliff path in case Colin comes back. They've set up a caravan there with first aid." The wizard gave Catriona a meaningful look. "Apparently Colin's diving gear's gone missing, and there was a folded-up tarp near where the motorbike was found, as if he'd hidden supplies there. Everything suggests he's gone to Ham's Pipes. Mr. Oglethorpe and Mr. Perley are going after him."

The full extent of her brother's folly was now dawning on Catriona. As Margery MacVanish turned the car around and headed for the Lodge, Catriona slipped her hand into Theodora's and squeezed it tightly.

Theodora squeezed back.

There was the problem of what to do with Vyrna. There was no convenient Wizards' Club with a rooftop landing pad on Scornsay, and he could not arrive with a dragon in tow. And he had not brought Vyrna's dogcoat disguise with him.

Cordelia had an idea. She dug down to the bottom of an old workbag ("I never like to throw away a shadow—never know when they will come in handy") and produced some dark scraps and something that looked like a phaser from the old *Star Trek*.

"Is that some new gadget of yours, Cordelia?" Merlin asked.

"Oh, no. It's an ordinary glue gun. Of course, I've made a few modifications to the glue." Out of the slippery dark scraps from the workbag, she had glued together a sleek, snug-fitting garment for the hatchling, but when it was on Vyrna she was still unmistakably a wyvern.

"I don't see——" Merlin started to say.

"Tsk, so impatient! Just a moment and you'll see." Cordelia fastened a collar around Vyrna's neck. "Now watch." She produced a small metal charm in the shape of a dog and clipped it to the collar. Instantly the dark coat shimmered, stretched, and there stood before them a sleek greyhound. The illusion wasn't perfect—if you knew what to look for, you could see something not quite convincing about the shape of the head, and a faint suggestion of wings folded close to the body—but most people would not know what to look for.

"Don't linger to chat with any dog show judges," said Cordelia. She handed Merlin a small pouch. "There are a few more charms. And here is the bolt-hole. It should put you in the middle of Scornsay, if my calculations are correct."

Her calculations placed Merlin and Vyrna on Scornsay, square in the middle of a sheep pen. It was hard to say who was more surprised: the wizard or the sheep. After staring at the newcomers in silence, the eldest ewe bleated a long, nasal protest, and the rest joined in, and amid the cacophony Merlin hastily cast a spell. The first spell that came into his head was one to induce a profound slumber. The sheep were instantly unconscious on their feet. By twos and threes, they toppled over in midbleat, legs stiff.

Vyrna wasn't paying any attention to the sheep. She was standing still, looking away from the sheep pen to a cottage just visible across the fields. She let out a keening dragon call that didn't sound even slightly like a greyhound.

"What have you found? Magic or malice?"

Again, the keening. Like the eager whine of a dog whose master's car has turned into the street and is a block away.

"Theodora!" said Merlin. "Quietly, then. And no fire."

It was a wet slog, and Merlin was glad more than once that he was wearing his trusty Bogtreaders, which were more than equal to the task of keeping his feet dry. He did have to say a little spell to erect an invisible half bubble immediately in front of him, like a windshield, to deflect the shower of mud Vyrna threw up in her wake.

She paused only briefly, to sniff the wall of the ruined castle, and didn't stop again until she'd reached the cottage and plunged through its front door, dragging Merlin behind her.

Vyrna stood expectantly in the middle of the kitchen with her neck craned upward and her head tilted to one side. If she had been a dog, her tongue would have been lolling out. Merlin produced a dragon treat from his pocket, and Vyrna retreated underneath the kitchen table to gnaw at it.

Merlin was just sitting down to catch his breath when a bottle of blue fire came floating into the room. As Merlin watched, the bottle stopped about level with Merlin's pants cuff, and around it began to materialize a little terrier, wearing the most comical expression, which seemed to say, *At last! I thought help would never come!*

Merlin felt his mind noisily sniffed, and he gently pushed the damp presence away. He patted his knee invitingly. "Hop up. I'm fluent in Terrier, if you forgive my accent."

Just inside the entrance to Ham's Pipes, Colin stood up in the shallows and stowed his tank, mask, and regulator on a stone outcropping, the same ledge his father always used when they went diving here; the tide never rose high enough to reach it. Still wearing his wet suit and carrying a light, Colin made his way farther into the network of caves. The wind in the tunnels started up the whistling that gave the caves their name, a curious bassoon sound like the one you can produce by blowing just right across the top of an empty bottle. It was eerie, but Colin wasn't bothered by it. At least, not much.

Farther on, the tunnel rose a little, and the floor of the cave was dry enough to allow Colin to examine it. He shone his flashlight along the tunnel floor, looking for evidence, and soon he was following a trail. A scale here, a scale there, then a pile of spoor and fish bones, and jackpot! There they were. Footprints.

Colin shivered with excitement. He imagined what he might find at the end of the tunnel. A nest with eggshells. A nest with live babies. Maybe even the creature itself. For a brief moment he allowed himself to imagine how everyone would react—his dad proud, his classmates jealous, famous scientists saying he showed real promise—but he reminded himself sharply that the tide wouldn't wait while he was daydreaming. He pocketed a scale and pressed on.

The tunnel he was following widened into one of the larger chambers marked on the map, its walls covered with Pictish carvings: circles, spirals, strange beasts, and winged men. Some time in the past, the sea level had been low enough for shamans to come here, or else they'd braved the sea and made that dive without gear, as some kind of test. There was a low shelf or altar, black with soot, as though a fire had burned there.

Colin spread his map out on his knee to study it, glad he'd thought to seal it in a plastic zip bag from the supply in his mother's kitchen.

Then he noticed it by his foot . . . a luminous scale, larger than any of the others, flashing with white fire. He took out a flashlight to examine it better, but behind him there was a sudden strange sound, a rapid slithering and scraping, and then without warning a violent rush of heat and air and light. Colin was thrown to the floor of the cave by the blast, superheated air that stank of sulfur and something else.

Fish.

18

The Color of Night

Margery had sent Catriona to bed with a hot
drink, cocoa charmed just enough to ensure she
would sink quickly into a deep, untroubled sleep.
Theodora's cocoa was not charmed, but Margery had
sternly ordered her to curl up on the sofa under a blanket and drink it.

"Then try to catnap if you can," she said.

Theodora looked up the stairs where Catriona had
just disappeared. All she could think of was her dad
going down into the cave to rescue Colin, down where
It was.

"But shouldn't we be——"

Margery shook her head. "We need to know what we're going up against. And I need to think. Please." She pointed a finger toward the Fletchers' living room, and Theodora picked up her cocoa and went.

Into her own cup of cocoa, Margery sprinkled cinnamon and cayenne—a recipe an old Mayan priest had taught her long ago. It was supposed to quicken the brain, and right now her brain needed all the help it could get.

She had not gotten stellar marks in the course popularly known to G.A.W.A. Academy students as Snakes and Adders. Professor Sylvan Smoot had somehow managed to make dragons boring, slogging his way through those endless volumes of *Walker's Dragons of the Old World.* There had been all those details to memorize: wingspan and number of toes; tail prehensile or not; what color the eggs were; whether it ate knights roasted in armor or liked to dig miners out of mines, like termites. Most dragons were extinct anyway, hunted to oblivion centuries ago. So what was the point?

Some smaller dragons were rumored to survive. The smaller species, and ones that could live deep underground, or in boiling mudpits, or in the calderas of volcanoes. Some of these small ones had been domesticated long ago, a class of dragons called Seekers.

As she sipped her chocolate, Margery tried to

remember everything she could about Seekers, small dragons originally bred to follow faint trails through Time. She remembered Smoot's scrawl in the margin of her exam where she'd listed the Wingless Opalfire as a form used for Seeking. *Never . . . too dangerous. Reread your* Walker*!!!*

Margery hadn't—she'd sold her *Walker,* all eleven volumes, spent the money on some new Italian levitation gloves, and enrolled in a seminar in Japanese shape-shifting with a visiting professor.

Had Ellic Lailoken read up on his Wingless Forms? Or had he chosen the wrong kind of dragon for his Seeker?

All of a sudden, the pocket of her coat where she kept her spell-casting desk started to flap up and down as though the desk were trying to escape. She took it out, pressed the catch, and set the desk down on the floor. When it had finished unfolding, she found a package wrapped in heavy yellow paper, bearing the return address of the Librarian, Owl and Moon Club, Edinburgh.

Thaqib, she thought.

"Unwrap," she told the parcel, and obediently the string and paper fell away to reveal a book.

It was a copy of Volume Nine of *Walker's Dragons of the Old World,* the volume that dealt with Wingless Forms. There was a note from Thaqib.

I DID LOCATE A COPY OF THE ACADEMY YEARBOOK
FROM 1906. YOU MAY BE INTERESTED TO KNOW
THERE WAS AN ACTING HEADMASTER THAT YEAR, FOR
ONE TERM, WHILE THE HEADMASTER RECOVERED FROM
A SUDDEN ATTACK OF LARYNINVISIBILITY. HIS NAME
WAS—

"Septimus Silvertongue," Margery said, letting the note fall from her hand. She had forgotten about that chapter in Septimus's checkered career. He had gone on to join the O.I.G., rising high in its ranks before leaving in a scandal. Then he had dropped from view. He was likely to have changed his name—and his appearance. Was Silvertongue responsible for the disappearance of Ellic Lailoken? Could he even have been behind the business with Kobold back in Boston? It was a thought.

She murmured her thanks to Thaqib, picked up the note from the floor, and hid it in one of the desk's pigeonholes. Then she pressed the catch on the desk that made it fold back up and carried the book in to where Theodora was half-asleep on the sofa. Margery shook her shoulder gently. When Theodora opened her eyes, Margery placed the book in her lap.

"I'm going to the cottage to get William and Electra," she said. "While I'm gone, read Chapter Eleven."

Still a little groggy, Theodora sat with the book unopened in her lap, looking around the Fletchers' living room, remembering everything that had happened that day.

How much could your life change before it wasn't your life anymore? How much could *you* change before you were someone else? Was she still Theodora Lenore Oglethorpe, known as Dodo, or had she been transformed by everything that had happened, by knowing about wyverns and wizards and demons and Delving and all the rest of it? Was she always going to feel this way, like there was a giant part of herself she couldn't share with anyone? Was this what Mom had felt? Was this what had made her turn her back on it, once and for all?

She sat lost in thought for some minutes, then slowly realized that there was something peculiar about the book that lay in her lap. For one thing, it hardly seemed to weigh anything for such a bulky tome. It had fallen open in her lap to page 721, and the page seemed to glow faintly, as though it were lit from within by fireflies.

Of all the Wingless Forms, the least well-known exemplar is the Wingless Opalfire. The two specimens, known only from museum collections and badly preserved trophies, are so different that they have, for some centuries, been recognized

*by draconologists as two separate species. Looking at the
blind, wingless juvenile morph, so well suited for a subterranean mode of life, it is easy to see why earlier scholars
failed to associate it with the large, active winged adult form
shown in Plate 176.*

*Because of its long subterranean juvenile phase, it is
one of the dragons believed to have survived widespread
extirpation, and it is believed to use a host in its final
transformation to its mature, reproductive morph. As of
this writing, no live specimens have been recovered to con-
firm this supposition, and its complete mode of life, if the
species is indeed extant, remains a subject of conjecture.*

Theodora was just turning to look at the picture of
the Wingless Opalfire when the door opened and she
heard the skittering of talons on tile. She looked up just
as a sleek black form hurtled into her lap, sending the
book flying.

"Vyrna!" Theodora tried to put her arms around the
wriggling creature's strange, slippery coat, but it is hard
to hug a shadow. "Is that you?"

"It is indeed," said a familiar voice. Merlin stepped
forward and unclipped the dog charm from Vyrna's
collar. The dragon gave herself a violent shake and
immediately looked more like a wyvern, though her
wings were still pinned to her sides by the sleek
shadow coat.

Theodora turned to Merlin and hugged him fiercely. "I'm *so* glad to see you."

Merlin went bright pink and cleared his throat. He removed his glasses and made a big show of polishing the lenses, which were already clean. "Likewise, my dear. Likewise."

"Ahem." Margery was standing in the doorway to the kitchen, William in her arms, Cordelia Crumplewing's carpetbag slung over her shoulder.

"I hate to break this up, but we really must get a move on. William and I will remain here and keep an eye on Catriona. Theodora, Merlin will take you, Vyrna, and Electra to the caves."

She set the carpetbag down on the floor and opened it to display Electra, in her traveling bottle, and a number of items that had been packed by Cordelia.

"What's all this?" Theodora asked, wonderingly.

There was a curious pair of enormous shears, the metal dark with age, and a tag hanging from the handle that said in spidery handwriting

Cuts All

There was a narrow, corked bottle of brown glass, labeled in the same handwriting

Cures All

And there was something white and soft that had been folded into a square, like a pillow covered in feathers. Embroidered along its edge were the words

Consoles All

Theodora stroked the feathery surface and, as she did, a faint music sprang up under her fingers, as though she had run her hand over the strings of a harp.

"It's so soft," she whispered. "What is it?"

"An angel's wing," said Margery.

Merlin peered into the bottom of the carpetbag. "A pamphlet about seep theory. Cat-food coupons. I think those must be left over. Some dragon treats. And enough ham sandwiches to feed a small army."

"Won't I need a flashlight?" Theodora said.

"You'll have Electra, and she is quite bright," said Merlin. "Now, I think we had better go find your friend."

Theodora hugged William and told him to be good and said good-bye to Margery. Their conversation in Margery's workshop seemed a million years ago. All that talk about her mother's legacy and the Demotion. *Well,* Theodora thought, *I'm definitely a Greenwood now.*

"I guess I get to keep William after all," she said shyly.

Margery smiled, started to say something, then

pulled Theodora close and abruptly kissed the top of her head. Then she gave her a little shove toward Merlin.

"You'd better go."

Merlin was a terrible driver. After taking one tight turn on two wheels, he muttered a spell through clenched teeth, something that sounded like "Calamity, calamine, calabash!" and the ride was suddenly smoother. Theodora looked out the window and saw that the Fletchers' car was rolling along six inches off the road on a cushion of fog.

"Are we flying?" she asked Merlin accusingly.

"Technically, no. Now, I must insist you leave the driving to me. You need to figure out a way for us to get to the cave without interference."

Theodora had forgotten about the first-aid station that had been set up at the spot where Colin had gone down the cliff path. How *would* they get past it? She couldn't exactly float down—

"Merlin, I have an idea."

They parked the Fletchers' car beside the road and made their way through wet sheep pastures. Vyrna was all business, ignoring the odd fox and rabbit and keeping close to Merlin's side. At last they came to a point just above the roadway. Below they could see a small camping trailer lit with floodlights, and various islanders standing around talking. Theodora couldn't see her dad or Mr. Perley. Had they already started into the cave after Colin? Theodora's knees went all wobbly, and she felt sick with worry. She missed William's comforting nose in the palm of her hand, but she was glad to have Vyrna. The dragon now smelled the sea, and something else, and she quivered with excitement, eager to rid herself of the confining coat of shadows.

"Can you get me across the road without being seen?" Theodora asked.

"I thought you had an idea."

"I do, but first I have to be on the other side of the road. They've lost one kid—no one's going to let me go down the cliff on my own."

Merlin considered this. "There are any number of invisibility spells I might use. But it's far more draining to make someone else invisible, and making both of you invisible might drain my powers. I have a feeling I might be needed later, if your father runs into trouble on the water. But I have an idea."

Even after the idea was explained to her, Electra needed some coaching. If it hadn't been so desperate, it would have been funny: a portly gentleman and a young girl madly pantomiming pulling something over their heads, stepping into pants, and holding their hands up like spectacles to their faces.

At last the Fire understood. She rose in the air above

Theodora's head and started to flow down over her head and shoulders like a bucket of glow-in-the-dark paint, carefully leaving eyeholes for Theodora to see through. Then the Fire carefully dimmed her light until she was exactly the color of twilight. Theodora was now all but invisible.

Merlin fished in his pocket and found a little charm shaped like a cloud, and when he had clipped it onto Vyrna's collar she took on the color of fog and was not quite invisible, but not really visible, either.

"Oh—the bag!"

Merlin made a face. "The bag!"

They had forgotten about the carpetbag containing Cordelia's gifts. At last Merlin decided that a small spell to make the bag invisible wouldn't sap his powers too much.

Theodora, Vyrna, and the Fire started across the road. When they had made it across, Theodora gave Electra a new command.

"Bubble."

In a large bubble the color of twilight, Theodora and the wyvern floated off the edge of the cliff, hung in the air for a moment, and slowly began their descent to the mouth of Ham's Pipes. None of the islanders gathered by the caravan noticed. Only the wizard on the small rise overlooking the scene saw a telltale glimmer of something against the Highland twilight.

The bubble descended toward the waves. The tide was high, and the narrow strip of pebbles that allowed access to the cave was gone. Theodora told Electra to hover at the cave entrance, and she slipped out into the cave, Vyrna at her heels.

Theodora unclipped the cloud charm and helped Vyrna squirm out of the shadow coat, and the dragon beat her wings a few times to get the kinks out of them before folding them close against her back once more. She thrust her sleek head forward, her beak agape, seeming to taste the air.

Theodora could smell it too: an acrid odor of burning asphalt and rotten fish.

Electra had resumed her regular form, and now she glowed with a bright white light.

Theodora looked down at Vyrna. Did wyverns Delve too? The dragon looked at her new mistress with glowing eyes, but there was no sniffing of her mind.

"Come on, girl," she said. "You, too, Electra."

They went forward into the dark tunnel, following the ball of white light into the dragon's lair.

The entrance to the cave was fed by the tide, and the sea anemones and sponges clinging to the wet cave floor made the going treacherous, even by the light Electra gave off. Theodora could see that the walls of the tunnel were covered in Pictish symbols: the spirals; the funny, flippered letter *S* that her guidebook said meant shape-changer; and the one of the winged dragon-man. The tunnel dipped, and she had to wade through icy water. Vyrna slipped under the water happily, a sleek torpedo.

Farther along, the tunnel began to climb, and soon the path was dry again. The stink of spoiled fish was getting stronger and the air in the cave hotter. Vyrna suddenly seemed to lose her confidence, and she slunk back behind Theodora's legs with a whimper. Theodora paused. She thought she could see an orange glow up ahead, around the next bend. She was hesitating, wondering whether to douse Electra's light or use the twilight camouflage trick again, when she felt her mind roughly grasped and held by another consciousness.

It was not like Delving at all. The creature was too strange, too Other—a "we," not an "I," part dragon and part human, inseparable.

As if she felt it too, Electra separated into two blobs of light, covering Theodora first in a suit of glowing blue armor, and then doing the same for the wyvern.

From the tunnel up ahead, someone groaned in pain and fear. Theodora wanted to rush forward, but the dragon's mind was still holding hers, whuffling and snorting inside her head, searching. As it rooted around, it pressed on memories: Theodora finding Vyrna in a tree and hiding the hatchling to keep her safe. The dragon seemed satisfied and released its hold.

Theodora turned the corner and saw what was making the glow. A large white dragon was curled up, resting its chin on a rock, and its breath had heated the cave walls red-hot. Pinned under the dragon's talons lay Colin.

19

Dragon's Bower

H E WAS ALIVE.
Colin opened his eyes and looked at Theodora, his eyes glazed with shock and fear. Even in the heat of the chamber, he was shivering.

The dragon turned its head to Theodora. It was blind and whiskered all along its muzzle with catfish like barbs. It opened its jaws to reveal rows of slender, sharp teeth. It snorted, its nostrils flaring as it sampled the air around Theodora. Again Theodora had the impression that it wasn't a single being, but two.

"Colin, are you all right?" Theodora said under her breath.

"I think I broke my ankle, and my ribs hurt." A look of panic flashed across his features as his glance darted sideways to the dragon's toothy maw. "Is it—is it going to—"

Theodora shook her head. "It eats fish, and by the look of that pouch, a lot of them. That's why all the fish have been disappearing."

"Then why'd it grab me? What's it going to do with me?"

"I think in a funny way it's been waiting for me," Theodora said, looking at the dragon.

It was beautiful, its scales fiery-white opals. The webbing between its toes and the backs of its ears and a patch on its throat were all a deep, iridescent blue-green. Its unseeing eyes had extra eyelids, and it seemed to have a throat pouch for holding fish, like a pelican. Its wings—small vestigial frills at its shoulder blades—were so small she almost overlooked them.

The Opalfire started to make a rumbling sound deep in its chest, so loud that tiny stalactites broke off the roof of the cave and fell around them in a tinkling rain. The rumbling turned into music, a strange buzzing sound like a cicada. Then the dragon threw back its head and sent a white plume of flame up to the roof of the cave, so that sparks showered down.

"It's singing," Theodora said, wonderingly. The Mote in her pocket began to flash in time to the dragon's song and then gave off its own humming.

The dragon bobbed its head and sang, then raised its head and spouted fire again. Then it nosed Colin and pushed an object toward Theodora's feet. She bent down and picked it up.

It was a broken whirligig from the artists' colony. Now Theodora noticed that the dragon's lair was filled with other items: a road sign, the side mirror from a truck, a fisherman's float—and a jacket she recognized as Mad John's.

Suddenly she remembered a nature program she'd seen on TV while doing her homework, an African bird strutting and bowing under an archway, in an arena decorated with fruits and feathers and flowers.

"A *bower*! It's made a *bower*!" She turned to Colin. "You—you and all these other things—you're, you're *offerings*."

But Colin didn't answer—his eyes were barely open now, and when she called his name he didn't stir.

Theodora grabbed the carpetbag and took out the shears. She willed her hands to stop trembling as she approached the dragon and slipped the blades around one of its massive claws. As promised, the shears did cut all, even dragon talons. She trimmed three of them, just enough so she could roll Colin free.

He was cut and bruised, and his wet suit had been shredded and singed by the dragon's fire. Theodora took out the angel's wing and wrapped it around Colin's shoulders. But he mumbled a protest when she held the brown Cures All bottle to his lips.

Theodora squinted at the label. Beneath the words "Cures All" she could make out a list of active ingredients: chameleon's tears, sugared almonds, spiderweb dew. She took a tiny sip. It tasted pleasantly of caramel and cherries, and she felt a slight tingling in her veins and a pleasant warmth in her muscles.

She lifted Colin's head and held the bottle to his lips, and this time, despite his protests, she got a good slug of the stuff into him. Immediately some color returned to his face, and when he opened his eyes some of the glassiness was gone.

"Can you walk?" Theodora asked.

Colin felt his ankle. "Yes," he said, puzzled. "I thought it was broken, but I guess I just sprained it."

"You have to make it back to the front of the cave on your own. Vyrna will go with you."

Colin hesitated. She could see him wondering about Vyrna's sharp beak and about leaving her here with the white dragon. "Will you be okay?"

"Yes," she said, and meant it. She looked up at the large white dragon. "It won't harm me." She was sure of that, somehow.

Colin looked at her in an odd way. "Catriona was right about you," he said. "She said you were into magic and stuff."

"No," said Theodora. "She's got it backward. The magic is into me."

She sent Electra with them, and as the white light disappeared around the corner she could see Colin's shoulders covered in the angel's wing. Then they were gone and she was alone with the dragon.

But not in the dark: the red-hot walls of the chamber gave off some light, and the dragon itself reflected what light there was.

Theodora stepped forward and shyly placed a hand on the side of the dragon's head. It was singing again, and now the Mote was amplifying the song, flashing when the dragon spouted fire. The dragon's mind closed with hers, and this time it was a single entity, all dragon, with no trace of its human host—the man who had been Mad John.

When the dragon joined its mind with Theodora's, she understood many things. Man by day, dragon by night, Mad John had roamed the island searching for the Mote. As time went on, the dawn transformation from dragon back to man had become less and less complete. The flash Theodora had noticed on Mad John's forearm had been dragon scales. Little by little, the dragon had taken over until, one morning, Mad John had failed to resume his human form.

Had there been other man-dragons? Was that what the carving on the pillar and the HCSVNT in the cave and Scornsay's many dragon legends all meant? Theodora sensed, as her mind and the dragon's remained intertwined, that this dragon had not been the first on Scornsay, that the island had known others. It was the latest in a chain that stretched back centuries.

The dragon broke the connection and uttered a plaintive call.

Theodora knew now what it wanted. She placed her hand on its scaled head, on the wide brow between its eyes. She could feel the low tremor of its purr.

"I choose you," she said.

It was really a job for an Intercessor First Class, but Merlin did not think it wise to wait for the O.I.G. to arrive. On the way from the cottage to the Fletchers', Margery had shared with him her suspicions about Septimus Silvertongue, the former acting headmaster of the G.A.W.A. Academy, and what she thought had become of Ellic Lailoken. If Margery was right, Theodora was safer with the Wingless Opalfire than her father was in that dinghy.

Fortunately, one of Merlin's languages was Merlandish, though to judge by the local sirens' reaction, his accent needed a lot of work.

He stood with his trousers rolled up, ankle-deep in

the cold water of a cove, trying to convince a couple of Highland merrows to carry out a mission for him. The mermaids bobbed in the water a few yards offshore, their dark heads sleek as seals, but nothing so friendly.

"I need to find a boat and stop it," Merlin explained. "An inflatable dinghy with two men on board—mortals."

One of the mermaids lifted her head out of the water and smiled, showing her neat, sharp teeth.

"And then what?" she said. "Sing them pretty songs, songs to make them forget?"

Merlin waved both hands in alarm. Many a sailor had come to grief, listening to mermaids' pretty songs. "No, no singing! Sleep will do, and dreams. And keep the dinghy away from Ham's Pipes."

"The other man wanted us to drown them," said the second mermaid. "Wrap their ankles in kelp so they'd never be found."

"But his speech was not as bonny as yours," said the other, tossing back her wet hair. "We did not like the look of him."

Thank God for that, thought Merlin. As calmly as he could, he cleared his throat and said, "What other man? Can you describe him?"

They described a man of wealth and station, dressed in common farmer's clothes. No one Merlin knew. Could it have been Margery's mystery man?

Lots of dinghies went missing off Scornsay, and there

was a notorious whirlpool. Magical mischief could easily be disguised as an accident of nature.

Merlin didn't have much to barter with: The mermaids didn't want his watch, which was useless in water. Likewise his glasses. In desperation he turned out his pockets and discovered the tin of Nevergone Peppermints Cordelia had pressed into his hand as he departed. At the time he'd wondered why. Hardly daring to hope, Merlin opened the box.

Inside were a dozen plastic hair barrettes in bright colors, studded with fake gems, the kind little girls put in their pigtails. These were in the form of flowers and butterflies and dragonflies, and they sparkled in the sun enticingly. To the mermaids they might as well have been gem-encrusted hair combs from Shangri-la.

Bless you, Cordelia, Merlin thought to himself. *You are a genius.*

The mermaids gave the barrettes looks of envy and whispered to each other in the hissing that was their private language. Then the taller one spoke.

"We will do as you bid, in exchange for the hair jewels."

As the mermaids swam away, Merlin breathed a sigh of relief. Then he had a sudden awful thought.

Margery and Catriona were alone in the Fletchers' lodge, and the man who had tried to hire mermaids to overturn the dinghy might still be on Scornsay.

—〰—

Margery had gone upstairs to check on Catriona and was coming back down when she was met by an anxious William.

"What's wrong, boy?" Margery squatted beside the little dog and patted his head clumsily. She was not a dog person, but even she could tell the little terrier was unsettled. For some reason, he wasn't Delving—he wasn't even whining. It was as though he were wearing an invisible muzzle.

An invisible—

Margery spun around and saw a man seated at her spell-casting desk, leafing through the copy of *Walker*.

It took her a moment to realize it was the man who called himself MacKenzie Murdoch. He seemed completely transformed. He still wore the same clothes, but in his manner and expression he was someone else entirely. Gone was the country gentleman demeanor. If his masquerade as Murdoch had been achieved through spellcraft, then that spellcraft had left the wizard's face deeply lined and haggard. Margery had heard about such spells. . . . You could disappear so deeply into the new persona you might not find your way out in one piece.

William's body trembled with a silent growl, and he looked at Margery pleadingly, as if to beg her forgiveness for not barking a warning.

"Murdoch. Or should I call you by your real name, Septimus?"

The other wizard smiled.

"Don't feel bad that I deceived you, Margery. I've made a career of keeping one step ahead of the O.I.G. Though I have to admit, you kept me on my toes." He glanced at the ceiling. "Who's upstairs?"

"The Fletcher girl."

"And Theodora?"

"She's not here."

"No, I didn't think so. A pity."

The moment she had seen Septimus, Margery had cloaked herself in a protective spell, to prevent the kind of mischief he had worked on William. But she could feel the spell eroding under the tide of the other wizard's malice. She tried not to panic. In the time she had left, she meant to find out all she could so she could somehow help Theodora.

"I have been wondering," said Margery, "where you came from when you showed up at the Academy in 1906. Were you visiting from some other When . . . perhaps this one?"

Septimus smiled indulgently. "Let's just say I do rack up frequent flier miles, as Time goes."

"You were searching for a copy of *The Book of the New Adept.*"

"Yes. I was convinced that all the G.A.W.A. propaganda about it was bunk. There was something else in the book, something the Guild wanted hushed up."

"But Lailoken got to the book first."

"I had spent so much time searching for it, at great cost. I'd narrowed the search to the Academy and had managed to install myself as temporary headmaster in order to conduct my search more freely. And still it eluded me." Septimus laughed. "And where did it turn up, in the end? Wrapped in waterproof cloth and chained to the bottom of a cistern."

Margery looked at the wizard. He was doing a good job of incriminating himself. He would have to silence her so she could not relay his confession to anyone at the Guild. But at the moment Septimus Silvertongue appeared to be enjoying his chance to get the whole story off his chest.

"Sparkstriker insisted on locking it up overnight. What could I do? When I went back for it, I found Lailoken reading it. *Holding* it! *My* book! The one I'd—" The wizard's face briefly contorted into a mask of anger. Then just as quickly Septimus got control again.

"Well, I realized I could take the book from him and make it look as though he'd vanished with it to Never-Was."

Septimus's spell was like a slow drip of acid. Holding out against it was agony, and Margery could feel herself growing weaker.

"But that backfired, didn't it?" she said softly. "Most of the book went to Never-Was with him, leaving you with only fragments. And they put you on the wrong track. They made you think the New Adept was Gideon. But it wasn't Gideon, after all. It was Theodora."

"You seem to have it all figured out," said Septimus.

"No," said Margery. "Not all of it. I don't know how you ended up on Scornsay."

"I'd sent Ellic to Never-Was, but I knew that the Opalfire would emerge eventually. That was my specialty, you see. The Wingless Forms. I knew there were a few spots around the world where Opalfires had been known to reemerge. Scornsay was one of them. When Ellic emerged I planned to be there."

"Yes," said Margery. "He could have exposed your treachery. But he was already too far gone, wasn't he?"

"Never-Was had driven him mad. The Opalfire was taking over. And when the Fletcher boy found the scale, I realized I could use the dragon as a lure to bring Theodora here."

"You took rather a chance with that, didn't you? Andy might have left her at home, despite Murdoch Single-Malt's generous offer of plane tickets. And you needed Theodora. She was the last piece in the puzzle, wasn't she? She was the New Adept . . . the Mote in the Dragon's Eye. And you needed the other Mote, Gwynlyn's carbuncle. What was it? A key to Never-Was? A way there and back?"

Septimus scoffed at that. "It wasn't *Never-Was* I

wanted! The portal was old—Opalfires had been coming out of it for centuries—and it was due to go bad, to turn into a seep. But I also knew what the prophecy said: that the New Adept might get there before me and claim the prize."

"A new kind of magic from the cauldron of the seep?"

"The most powerful magic the world has yet seen!" The words escaped in a low hiss, and as Margery looked at Septimus, his eyes blazing cold fire, she wondered if he, and not the hermit, were the real madman.

"If *The Book of the New Adept* was right, the seep would release a magic more powerful than any the Guild has ever seen. But I only had a handful of pages from the real book. I couldn't be sure."

Margery felt the spell that stood between herself and Septimus growing thinner and thinner. How long would it last? She pushed the thought aside.

"It's puzzled me," said Margery, "why you didn't simply destroy her, once you knew about Theodora, once you knew of her magical pedigree and the talent that was waiting to be awakened. You could have used any number of spells." Margery narrowed her eyes suspiciously. "What stopped you?"

Septimus grew thoughtful. "I thought she might be turned. A pity for all that talent to go to waste. But it was clear that wouldn't do. You and that interfering old windbag O'Shea have poisoned her mind. And taught her a few tricks about Delving."

"The strength is all Theodora. We just had to show her it was there." Now the spell was paper-thin. Margery steeled herself for the full force of the other wizard's spell.

But Septimus almost seemed to have forgotten she was there. He seemed to be taking some comfort or enjoyment in confessing to Margery—probably because he knew Margery wouldn't be in a position to tell the O.I.G. or anyone else.

"So you see, I have no choice but to let nature take its course. Cordelia Crumplewing is quite right about seeps. And this one is scheduled to take out the whole island in about forty-five minutes. Every man, woman, child, sheep—and wizard. Except me. I have made other plans."

"How convenient for you." Her protective spell failed, and Margery felt the full force of Septimus's hatred, his cold evil.

"As for you, Margery, I need you where I can keep an eye on you."

There was a brilliant flash, and Margery was gone. Her kimono coat lay on the floor in a puddle of silk, but of the wizard herself there was no trace.

There on the spell-casting desk, amid its lacquered scenes of an imaginary Japan, there was a new figure, a woman crossing a footbridge into a garden. Unlike the kimonoed women around her, this woman wore a long coat and trousers and little high-heeled boots. Her hair was still spiky, but now the spikes were gold instead of silver. It was Margery MacVanish, rendered one and a half inches high in gold lacquer paint.

Septimus put the copy of *Walker's* into the desk, then pressed the catch that made it fold up. When it was all folded, he put the tiny black and gold object in his pocket, picked up his wizard's staff, and started for the door.

When he had gone, William materialized. He sniffed at the kimono coat and pawed it, as though looking for Margery. He lay down beside the coat and whimpered. Then he suddenly seemed to make a decision. He tore a piece of the kimono off with his teeth and left the Fletchers' house through the window. He could not smell Theodora anywhere, and it took him a minute to distinguish Merlin's scent trail from the evil wizard's. But once he had found it, he was off, the scrap of kimono clutched in his ghostly teeth.

The Opalfire made its way through the maze of tunnels that were Ham's Pipes, squeezing through tight passages that left scales behind, diving through passages completely filled with water until Theodora felt she could not hold her breath any longer. More than once she thought she would be scraped off and left behind, but she held on for dear life to the spike just between the dragon's shoulders that provided a place to hold on to, like the pommel on a saddle.

It was all one song now. The high keening of the dragon and the sympathetic tone of the Mote, forming a perfect chord that rang in Theodora's head, in her very bones, so that her body became a tuning fork, a third voice joining theirs. The song flowed around Theodora, and with it, the certainty that *this* was what it had all been about: Gideon's wyvern had come through a rabbit hole in time to lay an egg so Theodora could find the hatchling and start on the journey that would bring her here, to this cave on this island, on this dragon's back. The Pictish symbols of the shape-changer and the dragon-headed man told the story of the dragon and its transformation. But what part was she supposed to play? Theodora heard Hamish's voice in her head, describing the yawning well of Nothing, and she was afraid. But she could see shadowy faces, Gideon and the young Hamish and her mom, their faces full of love and encouragement, and she knew it was going to be all right somehow, in a way she couldn't yet understand.

She was meant to find the Mote and bring it to the dragon, and bring the dragon to Hamish's spot in the peat bog. Or perhaps the Mote had been meant to find her—it didn't matter. It was all the same. She pressed her face to the dragon's cool scales and closed her eyes, letting the notes of its song flow through her.

The dragon went down again, but this time the water above was dappled with moonlight, and at last they surfaced in one of the island's sea lochs, startling some ducks into noisy flight.

On land the dragon seemed uncertain, and outside of the caves the song faded. The dragon stretched its head along the ground, its jaws agape, sniffing. It made a mournful sound.

Theodora clutched the Mote tightly. In her mind's eye she could see clearly the face of young Hamish, white with cold and fear, and the minister, speaking the terrible words in an eerie, ancient tongue. She leaned forward and patted the dragon's neck, whispering into one of its translucent ears.

"It's all right," she said. "I think it's this way."

It moved forward uncertainly at first and then seemed to catch some scent, or recognize some signs it had been looking for. It was off and running again, and Theodora clung to the shoulder spike.

Most of the island had turned out to search for Colin, so there was no one to see the dragon with a girl on its back speeding through the peat bog.

How will we find it? Theodora wondered. Half the pillar was on the hill with the Stane Folk, but how would they find the other half, in the place where Hamish had been cutting peat as a boy? It seemed hopeless.

All of a sudden the dragon came to a stop, and Theodora was nearly thrown from her perch.

The dragon snorted and let out a deep lowing sound.

The Opalfire had stopped on a small rise, and below them, Theodora could see a well of nothingness, a patch of blackness in the peat the size of a bathtub. As she watched it seemed to spread, swallowing up peat and rocks and gorse bushes. Small animals and insects were fleeing from its edge, sending up a rustling sound that crackled like fire. It was starting to lick at the base of their little hillock.

The nothingness was eating the earth, eating up light and life. It was dreadful to watch.

Theodora lay her head on the dragon's neck and began to sob, from fear and fatigue and because she was tired of this new Theodora, the Theodora she didn't know how to be. Tears slid down onto the dragon's neck and down its massive scaled body.

"There, there," said a voice. "Is it as bad as all that?"

Theodora looked up and recognized MacKenzie Murdoch.

20

The Wizard of Never-Was

MURDOCH WAS WEARING a cape and carrying a staff. All of his smooth, easy manner was gone, and his expression was hard and cold.

"You," Theodora said. "It was you outside the pub. You're the one Margery warned me about."

"True, true. I suppose the time has come to drop my pretense. I'm a wizard, like Gideon and Margery and Merlin. My name is Septimus."

The hole of nothingness was spreading. Small creatures, little brown mice and helpless toads, were drawn struggling into the hole and vanished.

Theodora turned her head from the dreadful sight. "We have to stop it," she said frantically. "If we don't, it will destroy everything!"

"Well, almost. It will destroy most of this island and everything on it, but I am going to ride the final gasp out of here, into another When. And I am willing to take you with me."

And the awful dark shadow gripped her mind, and this wasn't Delving, it was something somehow beautiful and dark. She caught fleeting glimpses of a faraway place, a lake of silver ringed with trees whose brassy leaves rattled like wind chimes. Above the lake hovered a craft, a weightless barge borne on the air, and on its deck, wearing ornate robes that seemed to be made out of light, was Theodora.

"G.A.W.A. doesn't know what to do with you. They just see you as a freak, a threat. Do you think Margery is your friend? She's been sent by the O.I.G. to eliminate you! Why do you think Merlin hasn't sent Vyrna to you? Because he knows what Margery has in mind. He helped her plan the whole thing."

"I don't believe you." But inside, some tiny part of her did, and tears slipped down her cheek and fell on the ground, the ground that was being swallowed by the terrible cold magical fire.

The shadow gripped her mind more tightly, and Theodora could feel the silk of the robes, feel something running through her veins that made her all-wise, all-powerful, invincible—

The Opalfire writhed beneath Theodora and shot a burst of flame at the wizard. Immediately the shadow let go, and the image was gone, and Theodora shuddered and seemed to escape its spell.

"No," she said. "I'll stay here, thanks. I'll take my chances with Merlin and Margery and the good side."

Septimus was nursing a burn on his wrist. He looked as though he would like to do something to the dragon but didn't dare.

"You've made your choice," he said bitterly. "Now you can live with it." He swept his cape around himself, struck his staff on the ground, and was gone.

The hole yawned, and Theodora and the dragon toppled on the edge and almost went over.

Theodora screamed. Then she seemed to see a face in the middle of the darkness. Now the darkness seemed to reflect light, like a mirror. And reflected in the mirror, very faintly, was the face of Joan Elizabeth Greenwood, aged twelve.

Now the dragon lifted its white, whiskered muzzle and made that lonely, keening call again. Theodora took a deep breath and made sure the Mote was safe in her pocket. She gripped the dragon's pommel spike with one hand and patted its scaled neck with the other.

"Now," she said, and the dragon dove into the circle. It closed around them, and they were gone.

They were falling—not along a tidy Wonderland rabbit hole past jars of marmalade on shelves, but not along a science-fictional wormhole of starlight, either.

It was a tunnel, but instead of rock or earth its walls were covered in waving fingers of light, like sea anemones. Whenever the dragon brushed against them, Theodora felt a dull sting, and an image flashed vividly in her mind. An archaeopteryx preening. An Egyptian queen putting on eyeliner. Sweaty men, stripped to the waist, struggling to reload a cannon. Theodora hugged the dragon's neck more tightly and tried not to brush against any more of the light anemones.

They fell and fell. Now the fingers of light were gone, and they were passing through a cloud of something like sparks or fireflies but not either one. The lights brushed against Theodora's face and hands, and this time there was no sting, just a feeling of intense peace and contentment. As one of the sparks passed by her face, she saw it was nothing like a firefly, nothing like a Faerie—at least not in a Tinker Bell way. Instead it was something winged and wonderful, transparent with a tiny, fluttering heart.

Then the cloud of living light was gone, and there

was nothing but darkness. It was very cold, and frost formed on the dragon's scales. Then they seemed to pass through something like a waterfall, a black curtain of darkness swirling on darkness. Somehow Theodora knew they had arrived at the end of the journey. She slid from the Opalfire's back and stepped cautiously onto the ground.

It was like some of the weird modern paintings in the Museum of Fine Arts: impossible staircases ascending to nowhere, buildings turned inside out, strange-looking people who had angles in all the wrong places. Everyone seemed like a triple hologram: you could see the child they were, the person they were now, and the person they would be, all at once. Theodora passed a silver fountain with a mirrored surface and caught sight of her own reflection. She, too, was like a triple hologram: She could see her younger self in an octopus-mermaid Halloween costume, and her twelve-year-old self, and an older self, like a younger version of her mother.

Looking behind her at the dragon, she could see the faint outline of a dark-haired man and in his arms a small, white, wingless dragon. Then with a flicker it was the Opalfire again.

All around them rose a babble of voices, many languages spoken at once, forward and backward and inside out. The denizens of this strange place began to close in around them, triple holograms of men and women, flickering shadows.

Theodora scanned their faces, looking for her mother, for Gideon, for any face she knew. No one was familiar. So this wasn't a place like heaven or limbo. But then what was it?

Her mind was grasped by that double-consciousness, that other We. She could sense a presence that had once been the mind of Ellic Lailoken. Grateful. At peace. And something else, almost like reverence. Reverence for *her*, for Theodora. She turned around.

It was Mad John, or a hologram-shadow of him. He was holding the dragon that had taken him as its host and eventually transformed his body into the Opalfire.

It was an awkward Delving, not like Delving with a person or with a dragon, but something in-between. Like using scissors with your other hand, awkward but not impossible.

You were the one making the Mote light up.

Yes.

You were trying to warn me, weren't you?

Yes.

And you needed me, you needed a human to show you the way here, the way home. You were only trying to get home.

Yesyesyes.

Theodora took the Mote from her pocket and held it out to Mad John, wondering if the stone could break the spell and release the man from the prison of the dragon's body. But it was too late for Mad John. He was beyond words, beyond even Delving. She sensed that the creature was content . . . it was all dragon now and sniffing the air, eager to be off into the shadows, following a dragon scent-trail only it could smell. The Opalfire sniffed the Mote that Theodora held out to it without real interest, and then nudged her head with its massive muzzle, leaving dragon drool in her hair. It rumbled a low dragon purr, an unmistakable farewell.

It struck out into the shadows, leaving this place for a den only it knew, searching for others of its kind.

But the Mote had begun to attract attention. Suddenly the flickering shadows began to gather around, triple-hologram shadows of wizards—men and women banished to Never-Was. The babble of voices rose and fell, forward and backward. Hands reached out to pluck at her.

Their collective minds pressed against hers like a tide. *She has come! She has come! She will release us! Release us!*

Theodora took a deep breath and let the shadow wizards close in around her.

How could she release them? In her hand the stone that had been Gwynlyn's, the magical Mote, was glowing faintly, but when she held it up to the nearest wizard, to see if its magic could release them, nothing happened.

Then Theodora thought, *Margery said I was the Mote.* Maybe she had to become part of the stone, the way she had become part of the dragon as they raced through the sea caves, its song ringing in her bones. She pressed the Mote to her forehead, and immediately she felt it begin to amplify her own thoughts, the sleeping magic Margery had called Greenwoodness. It wasn't some superhero aura or anything like that—light didn't begin to shoot out of the stone, and Theodora didn't fall back in a trance the way the heroines always did in those Japanese cartoons while they were being magically transformed from prim schoolgirls into righteous babe warriors. Theodora pictured the wizards in front of her, whole again and free, imagined their fear and pain and loneliness draining away, replaced by hope and joy, and her thoughts seemed to flow into the stone. Now the Mote began to glow more brightly, pulsing with energy.

She reached out to touch the closest wizard with the Mote, and as she did he turned into one of the firefly-Faerie beings with a transparent fluttering heart. Then Theodora understood what she was supposed to do. She touched another wizard, and another, and they began to form a cloud of light. When the last captive wizard had been transformed, they rose together and passed through the black waterfall.

Now that all the triple holograms were gone, Theodora could see the other denizens of Never-Was emerging from the shadows: leering imps and hobgoblins and things she couldn't name. A reptilian fellow with a forked tongue stepped forward and held out a small, white, wingless dragon.

"Seeker? Seeker? I'll give you a Seeker for that red stone," he hissed.

"No, thanks!" said Theodora hastily, stepping back. "I was just leaving."

She made her way back to the black waterfall, not knowing what she would do when she got there. But on the other side of the dark curtain all the light-creatures were waiting. They surrounded Theodora in a cloud and carried her up through the tunnel, past the light anemones to the black surface of nothingness. Theodora broke through into the sweet, peaty air and crawled out onto the damp ground. She felt the wet, springy ground making the knees of her pants damp, and she heard the chirp of crickets, and she was so glad to find the island still there she almost wept.

She turned around to look at the well of nothing. In her absence it had eaten away a hole the size of a meadow. But now it was retreating on itself, closing like a lens. Theodora watched as it grew smaller and smaller. It continued to shrink and then it was gone, leaving an unbroken expanse of peat and gorse and heather, with only a slight depression to show it had ever existed.

Something told her that the passageway was closed for good and that no one could be banished there again.

She was glad her mother wasn't there, with the imps

and the creepy Seeker guy. But something told her that her mother wasn't one of the light-beings, either. She was somewhere else. Ever-Was, maybe. Some kind of heaven, anyway, with a pair of those soft, white musical wings.

All of a sudden, a familiar black, wet nose pressed itself into her hand.

"Oh, William." Theodora pressed her face into his misty fur and then saw the scrap of kimono fabric he held between his teeth.

The Highland night was beginning to lighten. Every bone in Theodora's body ached, but she followed William to the road and began the long walk.

At last she turned a corner and saw the caravan. The floodlights were off, and the sun was coming up over the hill. It looked as though the whole populace of Scornsay was gathered there. Dr. Moody was at a hot plate, making coffee. There was a shout, and someone came running out of the caravan toward her.

It was her father.

"Theodora! Where have you been?"

"I thought I knew where Colin was. I went to look for him, and I got lost."

Mr. Oglethorpe was too relieved to be angry. "We found Colin hours ago. He's safe at home. They got a helicopter from the mainland and lowered a crew into the cave. He's fine . . . got caught in the Pipes and got pretty well cut and bruised. He doesn't remember anything that happened."

Theodora wondered about the ingredients in the bottle of Cures All. If she had had more than a sip, would she have forgotten everything too? Or was Colin just pretending not to remember?

"But Dad—I thought you and Mr. Perley were going out in the dinghy. What happened?"

Mr. Oglethorpe looked a little confused and a little embarrassed. "Well, Theodora, you weren't the only one to get lost last night. It was the weirdest thing. It was as though the sea just didn't want us to get there." He laughed and raked a hand through his sandy hair. "Those Highland mermaids, I guess, up to no good."

Theodora tried to answer him but only yawned. And that was all she remembered.

21

The Beginning of Thereafter

BEFORE THEY'D RETURNED their rented bikes, Theodora had ridden one last time around the island with her camera. She had taken pictures of the castle, the pub, the waterfall, and the Curlew's Nest, with its partly rebuilt whirligig garden. She had a picture of old Hamish MacRae in a lawn chair outside the old folks' home. She had a picture of the Stane Folk. And she had a picture of herself posing with Colin and Catriona, taken at the good-bye party at the pub.

"Here," Colin had said. "This is for you."

It was a long, waterproof tube for carrying architect's

drawings. Theodora remembered it from their hike to the Veil.

"Go on," he said. "Open it."

"I know what it is," she said. "It's the rubbing you made in the cave."

He fought back a smile. "Really? Check and see."

It was a big cartoon of the island, drawn in a funny scale, with the squat little islanders half as tall as the funny cartoon houses. There were sheep reading newspapers and sheep riding motorbikes and a long-haired Highland steer with dreadlocks. Theodora could recognize all the villagers: Bridie, Jamie, the doctor, the Sardinian cook from the pub, the fishermen, Mr. Perley. There was Catriona, striking a *Vogue* pose, and there was Colin, scuba diving off the coast, with a shark sneaking up on him.

"Oh! There I am," said Theodora, pointing.

Colin had drawn her high on the hill with the Stane Folk. She was sitting alone, hugging her knees, her hair blown back on the wind. She was smiling.

She couldn't think of what to say. The Cures All had done its trick. Colin didn't remember anything about the Wingless Opalfire. One more person to keep her magic secret from. She sighed.

Colin seemed crushed.

"Sorry," he said, blushing. "I know it's not a good picture of you—"

"Oh, no! It's great. I love it." She looked up. "Really." She smiled. "Thanks."

It was only later that she found the tiny writing in one corner of the cartoon that said, in all lowercase letters, without punctuation,

remember 2 rite ok ta colin

Catriona had made her a friendship bracelet. It was twined out of pretty blue-green threads the color of the sea, and she'd tied little pieces of sea glass and shells to it.

"I made it in art class," Catriona said.

"Thanks," said Theodora. She was embarrassed, but apparently not half as embarrassed as Catriona.

"Well," said Catriona hurriedly, "I just wanted to say good-bye, be cool, and all that."

"Have fun on that trip to London," Theodora said.

To her surprise, Catriona said, "I'm not going after all. The class voted to use the trip money to help Jamie out. But it's okay, really. After what happened with Col, my mum's not so keen to have me away from home."

Home. Theodora closed her eyes and tried to picture their kitchen, the bowl of oranges inside the front door, her mom's photo in the frame on the fridge.

It was time to go home.

—⁂—

Theodora was packing when her father called.

"Theodora? Someone to see you."

Theodora started downstairs, wondering if it could be Merlin, or Colin, or maybe even Margery. But it was the potter from the artists' colony, Jacob.

"I was cleaning out Margery's studio. She seems to have cut and run on us for some reason. But I found this."

It was a brown-paper parcel labeled THEODORA OGLETHORPE. Theodora recognized Merlin's handwriting.

"Thanks."

She took the parcel upstairs to her room and unwrapped it. Inside were Electra in her bottle and the angel's wing. And a note.

> Theodora,
>
> With our friend Margery missing, it seems best to return Vyrna to the security of my home up north, so she can't fall into the wrong hands.
>
> There wasn't enough of the Cures All to be worth saving, and Cordelia wanted her shears back, but she said you were to have the wing. And of course Electra is your Biddable.
>
> I will personally tell every wizard in G.A.W.A. about what you've done,

*and at least for now your enemy, who-
ever he might be, dares not show his
face. But you will need to be careful
back in Boston. Keep William close to
you. And hold on to that Mote.*

*I'm sure Margery will resurface
when she's ready. Please don't worry.*

Merlin

Theodora stroked the angel's wing. This time the harp music was fainter. Maybe the wing had lost some of its power to console. She closed her eyes and imagined her mother, in the green and distant heaven. She could see her only in a kind of misty way, but she knew her mother was smiling.

Well, okay, she couldn't tell, not really. The most she could manage was a really fuzzy, vague outline of her mom, without detail.

But she was going to let herself think it, anyway.

The mystery would be the talk of the whiskey world for years—what had happened to the whiskey magnate MacKenzie Murdoch, who had walked into his office at his Glasgow distillery and never emerged? The locked door had been broken down and revealed the office to be empty, the head of Murdoch Single-Malt vanished.

—⁂—

Septimus had made his escape to a little property he kept for exactly that purpose: a country house outside St. Petersburg, around 1899. He was sitting now out on the veranda, enjoying the evening air and working on his dollhouse.

It was a model of the Owl and Moon Club, faithful in every detail, right down to the spiral staircase in Thaqib's library and the tiny chess sets and wizard newspapers in the reading room, down to the bottles of Twelve Elves Ale in the bar. There was even a lonely umbrella in the club's Lost and Found. A nice touch, that.

He was having trouble finding the right location for the little black-and-white spell-casting desk. He held it up to the light and turned it this way and that, admiring the gilding, running his finger over the figure of Margery MacVanish, halfway across the bridge, perpetually on her way to the pagoda, wearing the grimace she'd worn when the spell hit her.

He'd meant to leave her in a shed back at the distillery, to be eaten by termites, but he'd relented. Margery MacVanish might still come in handy, and it would be a pity to destroy something as lovely as the spell-casting desk.

The whole seep business had been a washout. He'd waited for the eruption and it had never arrived.

Scornsay had survived, with its sheep and its islanders and a stock of fish that was beginning to recover nicely. He supposed he had Theodora Oglethorpe to thank for that.

Well, he wasn't done with G.A.W.A. and the O.I.G. and Margery MacVanish. And he most certainly wasn't done with Theodora Oglethorpe.

"Theodora, the cab's going to be here any minute."

"I KNOW, Dad! I KNOW."

Where was William? Theodora was searching their hotel room frantically, casting her Delving mind here and there, desperately looking for any sign of the ghost dog. But he was nowhere to be found, and it was time to go.

She had Electra. The Biddable Fire was at the foot of the bed, a clear blue jelly handbag with Theodora's passport, wallet, camera, and a book for the plane. But she couldn't find William, or his collar, anywhere.

She'd had him on the ferry ride from Scornsay, and in the rental car all the way to Glasgow, where she'd kept him quiet in the backseat with a steady stream of prawn crisps. She'd smuggled him into the hotel and let him chase pigeons in the park for exercise while she and her dad went to a Pakistani restaurant for curry. She'd seen him safely tucked in last night, in the shoebox that she'd told her dad was full of faerie tears from the rock shop.

But in the morning the box had been empty, and William was nowhere to be found.

She fought back tears in the cab to the airport and in the ladies' room at the airport and cried quietly into a Kleenex hidden in her fist as they waited by their gate. By the time the flight attendant called their row and they were stowing their carry-ons, she was okay. *Maybe ghosts can't cross international time zones,* she thought. *Maybe William needs to be on the island, near the castle where his master was. Or maybe he's just not meant to be my familiar,* she thought.

"Are you okay?" her dad asked.

She nodded. "Just tired."

He gave her such a pitying, fatherly look that Theodora realized with total embarrassment that her dad thought she was crying about Colin. He thought it was puppy love, but he had the wrong puppy. She turned a laugh into a cough and buried her face in a magazine.

They taxied and took off, and soon they were over water, and then in a cloud. Theodora sipped a ginger ale and thought about the time she'd walked in on Mikko kissing the visiting Russian professor and the smile on her dad's face whenever he talked to Brenda on the phone. She wondered if Val still had a crush on Jake Woo from the pool party and whether Milo was really into agility trials or more into his new friend, Sylvie. Then she thought about Colin. She remembered the day they'd made the rubbings in the cave, and the way he had looked in profile, intent on what he was doing. She remembered dancing with him at the *ceilidh*. She remembered him wrapped in the angel's wing, headed away out of the cave.

Well, just maybe her dad wasn't completely wrong about the puppy love.

Then she noticed something sticking out of the overhead compartment. Something a little misty, that grew darker through all the shades of gray before it started wagging. In Theodora's mind, there was the faintest of whimpers.

"Hey, Dad," said Theodora. "Are there any more of those prawn crisps left?"

Mr. Oglethorpe handed her the bag. "For someone who doesn't like prawn crisps, you've eaten a lot of them."

"They've grown on me." Theodora forced herself to eat a shrimp-flavored potato chip, gagging slightly, and let a second chip fall at her feet.

C'mon, boy!

The tail faded back through gray to mist and vanished. A few seconds later Theodora saw the crisp at her feet shatter into fragments and disappear. Then something heavy and warm settled itself for a nap on top of her shoes.

You'll like Boston, she told William. *I'll take you to the Public Garden. There's a swan I want you to meet.*

—⁓—

The magic continues
with more fantasies
from Aladdin Paperbacks

The Dragon Chronicles
by Susan Fletcher

Flight of the Dragon Kyn
0-689-81515-8

Dragon's Milk
0-689-71623-0

Sign of the Dove
0-689-82449-1

Silverwing
Kenneth Oppel
1-4169-4998-4

Mrs. Frisby and the
Rats of NIMH
Robert C. O'Brien
A Newbery Medal Winner
0-689-71068-2

The Chronus Chronicles
The Shadow Thieves
Anne Ursu
1-4169-0588-X

May Bird and the Ever After
Jodi Lynn Anderson
1-4169-0607-X

May Bird Among the Stars
Jodi Lynn Anderson
1-4169-0608-8

The Gideon Trilogy
The Time Travelers
Linda Buckley-Archer
1-4169-1526-5

Aladdin Paperbacks
Simon & Schuster Children's Publishing
www.SimonSaysKids.com